Music to Die For

ISBN 9781783751549

This book is dedicated to my number one American fan, Teresa Kahl, with thanks for her loyalty

DRAMATIS PERSONAE

<u>The members of the band 'The Dalziels'</u>
Edmund Alexander – keyboard accompanist
Grace Alexander – associate member and librarian. Edmund's mother
Fern Bailey – viola
Wendy Burnett – oboe
Campbell Dashwood – musical director and conductor
Harold Grimes – trumpet
Cameron McKnight – first violin
Myles Midwynter – clarinet
Myrtle Midwynter – cello
Vanessa Palfreyman – double bass
Gayle Potten – flute
Gwendolyn Radcliffe – second violin
Geraldine Warwick – piccolo and miscellaneous percussion
Lester Westlake – saxophone

<u>Others</u>
Rev. Christian Church – vicar of the parish
Olivia Church – his wife
Oscar Littlechild – a professional opera singer
A host of cats and dogs

<u>Market Darley Police Personnel</u>
Detective Inspector Harry Falconer – Market Darley CID
Detective Sergeant Davey Carmichael – Market Darley CID
Desk Sergeant Bob Bryant – Market Darley CID
PC Merv Green – uniformed branch, Market Darley Police
PC 'Twinkle' Starr – uniformed branch, Market Darley Police
PC John Proudfoot – uniformed branch, Market Darley CID
Dr Philip Christmas – police surgeon

PROLOGUE

Swinbury Abbot is a village divided by its small commercial centre, the High Street. This throughway lies at a diagonal, from south-west to north-east, and comprises a hairdresser's, a stationer's (with sundry toys, novelties, and souvenirs), a mini-market, a post office, a junk shop, a take-away food establishment, and a pharmacy which also sells beauty products.

There are two public houses, which are situated like bookends one at each end of the small parade of shops. At the north-east end is The Clocky Hen, and at the south-west, The Leathern Bottle, and both have their own, very distinct clientele. The Clocky Hen, due to its proximity to the Wild Flowers Estate (more of which later), draws its clientele from these crowded dwellings and maze-like roads. The Leathern Bottle, being at the other end of the High Street, and more convenient to the residents of the older houses, draws its custom from this source.

In The Clocky Hen there is a snooker table, a dartboard, and a jukebox; occasionally a live band on a Saturday night. In The Leathern Bottle, Vivaldi and his little friends play a genteel background music that deafens no one, and allows for civilised conversation without the need to bellow across the table at one another; and occasionally there is a jazz night, for aficionados of that style of music, which has proved unexpectedly popular.

To the north-west of the High Street, the village green and pond are to be found, but now find themselves facing, across Chopping Knife Lane, an estate built in the eighties and named the Wild Flowers Estate. By those who do not live there, it is referred to as The Starfish, having five roads that radiate out in

1

the shape of the aforementioned creature.

There had been terrific opposition to the building of this maze of modern, cramped housing. The Parish Council was up in arms, letters were written, signatures sought on petitions as far away as Market Darley, and even the storming of a meeting of the Planning Committee, by some people who felt strongly enough about what they considered would become an eyesore so close to their village centre, and were willing to risk being arrested and, maybe, charged with causing a breach of the peace. But all their efforts had been in vain. The pressure for new housing was so great that, eventually, building went ahead, but it brought with it benefits that had not been expected.

Down in the south-west corner of the village, where only The Grange, the old meeting hall, and the row of terraced houses known as Columbine Cottages previously existed, now sat new buildings that housed a playgroup, an infants' school, a doctor's surgery, and a dental practice.

Due to the density of the new housing, at about the same time, the Church sold off over half the garden previously enjoyed by the incumbent resident at The Parsonage, and the New Village Meeting Rooms had been created, much to the disgust and fury of the incumbent reverend gentleman, who requested to be moved to another parish shortly after its erection.

Once the new estate had 'settled in', however, it began to prove its usefulness to the old village, for it was an excellent source of cleaning ladies, ladies who could sew, gardeners, and general handymen, even if the hourly rate they asked did seem a little high at first. After a few years, it became a relationship of convenience, the old village families never looking anywhere else when they needed a little help with something, the residents of the estate, glad to get the income, paid in cash and with no records kept. The two diverse communities may not have thought well of each other, but they had found a way to co-exist in fairly close quarters, without a war breaking out.

To the south-east of the High Street, there are a few fine old residences, and more are to be found to the south, below where the High Street makes a T-junction with the Stoney Cross Road, and these are variously addressed as being in Beggar Bush Lane, Back House Alley, and Groat Lane.

The only building of architectural interest in the whole place is its church, St Luke's. By some error, now lost in the mists of time, it was built with its spire facing east instead of west and, through a great many years, petitions to the Church had failed to rectify this catastrophic error. The result had been, that it was impossible for a peal of bells to be installed in the steeple, due to the fact that the east window had to be situated below it, and there were fears that it could not withstand the weight.

The problem had been solved, again, back in the mists of time, and, it was then hoped, only temporarily, by the construction of a small stone structure atop the roof at the west end of the church, to contain a single bell. And from that time on, that single ball had been the only voice to ever call the faithful to service. Officially called St Luke's, everyone from thereabouts referred to it as 'St Back-to-Front's', and if it were decided now to rectify its architecture, there would be an enormous outcry. The locals were used to their church, and would not have it any other way.

There are quite a few hobby groups that meet regularly in Swinbury Abbot at regular intervals, but the most controversial is the local band. It is an enthusiastic little ensemble of diverse instruments, and it has performed for many local functions, doing a sterling job every Christmas, when its wandering performances collect a great deal of money for the local air ambulance, but whether donations are so generous because their playing is enjoyed, or because those listening would prefer it if they just packed up and left the audience in peace, will never be known.

They are now referred to, and actually bill themselves, as 'The Dalziels', because when anyone new to their playing hears them, the usual reaction is 'b***dy 'ell', and the name has been adopted without any resentment or rancour. The members only play for fun, never pretending to be professionals, or even any good, and if their playing amuses people *and* raises money for

3

charity, then each and every inept musician is happy and fulfilled. As with the estate and the village, the band and its residents have found a way to co-exist, if not in completely accurate harmony, at least with an acceptance of the disharmony their playing provides.

Chapter One

Let us open this story at the beginning of the events that led to the violent upheaval in the normally smooth timetable of the band's rehearsals, and the way in which these upheavals occurred.

At the moment, the band was without a musical director, and therefore without someone of sufficient training and experience to arrange and write parts out for new pieces they wanted to play. Its members, however, didn't want to spend any money on purchasing them, as they were a diverse mix of instruments, no two the same. Two out of the three previous musical directors were able to write for all tunings of instrument, whether in C, B flat, or E flat, could read and write for treble, bass, and alto clefs, and were, in consequence, sad losses.

A further complication meant that this also meant that they had no conductor, and to allow them to play without someone waving a baton, or their arms around, was akin to letting a lion perform un-caged and without its keeper.

The first of these previous MDs had suddenly had a whim to move to the Lot in France, and was gone within a few weeks. The next MD did exactly the same thing when her husband accepted early retirement, and they moved to the Dordogne. The third MD was also a woman, but she could not read either bass or alto clef, and could not cope with writing parts for transposing instruments, so for the best part of a year they had to make do with what music they already had and had had nothing new to tackle.

Two months short of the anniversary of this particular lady taking over the position, she announced that she and her husband had purchased a property in Normandy, and that they would be moving there in the very near future. 'What the hell did France have that England didn't?' many members were heard to mutter between themselves, but no open resentment was shown, and she went off on her adventure with the goodwill of all.

This left them all in the aforementioned dilemma, and when the vicar turned up at The Grange at their next rehearsal, and announced that he knew someone who had just moved to the village who had spent his whole life working with bands, it seemed like a miracle – although they'd have to ask him how he felt about France, before getting used to him and settling down again. To lose three musical directors to that country was catastrophic enough: to lose four would simply be calamitous and beyond belief.

Everyone knew, of course, that Wheel Cottage had recently been bought, but no one seemed to have any information about who now lived there. Granted, there had been a large removals van that had turned up one morning about a week ago, and unloaded a lot of rather fine furniture, but the new owner himself (or even herself) didn't seem to be present.

A few days later, there were suddenly curtains at the windows, and lights on in the evening, but still no visits to the village shops from whoever had moved in. Curiosity had nearly reached fever pitch, when the vicar announced that he might have someone to fill the void, and he would bring him – *him* – along to their next rehearsal, so that he could hear them play, and they could get to know one another a little bit.

Friday 25th June

It was the fourth Friday of the month and, therefore, it was rehearsal night for the village band in Swinbury Abbot. The members had gathered, as usual, in the home of Myles and Myrtle Midwynter. The Grange was a large residence situated on Beggar Bush Lane, to the south of the village centre, and backing on to the terrace of dwellings known as Columbine Cottages. It had no near neighbours, and there was, therefore, no need to worry about complaints about the noise – either its volume, or its quality.

The players had assembled, as was normal, at seven o'clock, to commence with a glass (or two, or more) of wine and a bit of a chat. They knew that Rev. Church would be bringing round his mysterious stranger, as a candidate for the role of musical director, but did not expect the visitation until rather later in the evening.

When Myrtle Midwynter called them to the dining room at a quarter to eight, they settled themselves round the large table to an excellent meal of poached salmon, salad, and new potatoes, followed by a delicious strawberry trifle, still chatting with enthusiasm, and it wasn't until nearly a quarter-past-nine that Myles announced that he rather thought they ought to play a little something.

There had been a whole month of news and gossip to catch up on, and as only a few of the musicians had been nominated as the designated drivers, the other players had continued to imbibe, with scant attention to exactly how much they had drunk, Myles topping up their glasses whenever they showed any signs of having room for more.

The Midwynters made a good team, despite the disparity in their ages, with Myrtle being only thirty-six years old to Myles's fifty-eight, and anything they hosted, usually ran on oiled wheels. Every guest's needs were immediately noticed and catered for, and nothing was too much trouble; this was one of the main reasons why the band met there. Myrtle didn't mind either the time or the expense of feeding them all, and they all felt at home and welcome.

As Myrtle cleared away the dirty dishes, everyone assembled in the large drawing room, and began to get their instruments out of their cases, search for sheet music, and take on the monthly battle with the music stands – one which the music stands usually won, leaving at least two or three pinched fingers and, on one memorable occasion, a badly squashed nose, but that was more due to alcohol, than ineptitude on the part of the victim, and fortunately, didn't require any medical attention.

There was a sharp knock at the front door, as Myrtle was coming through the hall, still drying her hands on a tea towel, and she answered it before going into the drawing room to unpack her cello. Standing on the step, she found Rev. Church, and the person she presumed was the candidate for the position of Musical Director.

As Rev. Church introduced her, she took note of the small man with whom she was shaking hands. He was only about five foot seven, with white hair cut fairly short, probably in his late sixties – but it was his eyes that captured her attention, for he seemed to be looking in two directions at once. One of them stared her squarely in the face as they greeted each other, the other had an alarming habit of wandering around, as if in search of something just out of view, and she longed to turn round to see what it could be looking for.

Remembering her manners, she invited them in, and preceded them to the drawing room, opening the door and calling over the loud buzz of chatter and the sound of instruments being both tuned and warmed-up.

'Quiet everybody! Your attention, please!' She clapped her hands loudly, in the hope that this would penetrate the hubbub, then called again, a little louder this time, 'Silence! Be quiet! We have visitors. If I could have your full attention, please, I would like to introduce you to … Oh, I'm terribly sorry, but I never asked your name. Rev. Church, perhaps you would do the honours?'

'Of course, my dear,' replied the vicar, smiling fondly around at all those present. 'May I present to you Mr Campbell Dashwood, who has recently moved into Wheel Cottage. He has been involved in music all his life, both as an enthusiastic amateur performer and, later, as a professional.

'He has a great deal of experience as a conductor, and is sufficiently multi-talented,' (here, the vicar made a small bow in Mr Dashwood's direction), 'to produce arrangements for all of those – oh, what do you call them, now? – transferring instruments.'

'That's 'transposing', Vicar,' interjected the newcomer, with a small, superior smile.

'Precisely, Mr Dashwood; just what I meant to say. Anyway, here is the man himself, and perhaps I could hand over to you now, Mr Midwynter, so that you can introduce him to all your players, and then, perhaps, you could find us somewhere to sit, so that we can listen in on your rehearsal, and just give Mr Dashwood here, a flavour of your playing.'

As Myles Midwynter put down his clarinet, Campbell Dashwood extracted a small notebook from the breast pocket of his jacket along with a minute pencil, licked the end of the latter, and stood, ready to take notes. Before Myles could speak, however, Campbell Dashwood was moved to verify some information.

'I understand that your performance later this summer is to celebrate the tenth anniversary of the forming of the band, and that it will take place in the church, with half the proceeds going to the church restoration fund, and the other half to a charity to which you regularly contribute.'

'Absolutely correct, Mr Dashwood.'

'Please, call me Campbell,' suggested the little man, but his smile never reached his eyes – either of them – and was somehow chilly.

'Right, Campbell,' continued Myles, 'may I begin by introducing you to the strings section of the band. Perhaps when I call out your name, you could stand, so that Mr Dashwood – sorry, Campbell – can identify you,' he requested, moving to the front of the assembled musicians.

'Let's start with first violin. May I present to you Mr Cameron McKnight.'

Cameron stood, still clutching his violin and bow, and made a small bow to Campbell. 'Very pleased to meet you,' he said, smiling, but as Campbell made no answer, he sat down again, feeling a little flustered.

Myles cleared his throat in embarrassment about the lack of response, but put this down to, perhaps, a bit of initial shyness on Mr Dashwood's part. Dammit, it didn't feel right calling him

Campbell. He'd have to do something about that later; and he put his mind to finding a suitable ruse to address this enigmatic little man in a more formal manner; one that felt comfortable.

'Next,' he continued, 'we have second violin, Mrs Gwendolyn Radcliffe.' A short, dumpy lady with an iron-grey perm and more than a hint of a moustache rose to her feet, blushing, then sat straight down again, without even waiting to see if any response was forthcoming. Dashwood considered her to be in her early sixties.

'On viola, we have Miss Fern Bailey,' intoned Myles, and a slightly plump woman shot up off her seat and beamed round at all assembled. She wore a hairband and had a 'jolly hockey sticks' air about her that proclaimed her to be just an overgrown boarding school girl, even though she was in her mid-thirties.

Myles continued gamely, 'Now we have my own lovely wife, Myrtle, on cello.' Myrtle didn't stand, but as they had already met on the doorstep, waved her tea towel in the air instead, before folding it into a small square on which to place the spike of her cello so that there would be no damage to the carpet.

'I say, old girl,' called Myles. 'All this announcing is thirsty work, do you think you could do the honours, and top up all the glasses. There are a couple more bottles of white in the fridge if you need them, and a couple more red, breathing, on the dining room sideboard. May I get you a glass of wine, Mr Dashwood?'

This time, Campbell didn't correct Myles's form of address, and said, with a certain amount of smug pride, 'I never touch anything alcoholic. Not only does it damage the liver, but I am convinced that it rots the brain as well. I don't suppose I could have a glass of water, could I, if it's not too much trouble?'

'Got that!' called Myrtle, and disappeared in the direction of the kitchen.

'Moving on, we have Miss Vanessa Palfreyman on double bass. Stand up and show yourself, Vanessa. Don't be shy.' A tall, somewhat stout middle-aged woman with short-cropped dark hair, just beginning to show signs of grey, slid out from behind the camouflage of her large instrument, then ducked back out of sight as quickly as possible.

'Right, that's the strings dealt with. Now we move on to woodwind, starting with Gayle Potten on flute.'

'Overweight mutton dressed as lamb,' thought Dashwood, disparagingly. 'She could do with losing at least three stone, if not more, and if her T-shirt were any tighter there would probably be a very nasty explosion of flesh to be dealt with.'

'Geraldine Warwick, on piccolo and miscellaneous percussion.' Myles had dropped the use of titles; it was all too wearing to remember which of the women were Miss, Mrs, or Ms, when he'd already sunk a few sherbets.

'Mouse,' was Dashwood's only thought about the apologetic pixie, who had bobbed briefly to her feet in response to her name.

'Wendy Burnett, on oboe,' Myles droned on, stifling a yawn. Surely it wasn't that late.

'Methuselah's mother,' thought Dashwood, unkindly, as Wendy was a very spritely eighty-nine, and looked years younger than her actual age.

'And last in this section, but certainly not least, we have Lester Westlake, on saxophone.'

Dashwood observed a tall, slim man rise from the back of the room, bowing to all present, and grinning a smile that seemed to contain a great number of large and very white teeth. 'Lounge lizard!' His thoughts allowed him the luxury of a minuscule smile. He knew the type, all right. All looks, and nothing much of anything else. Well, he'd better play well, or he'd have his guts for garters.

'Oh, not quite last. I'm afraid,' Myles apologised. 'I've forgotten myself. I'm on clarinet. The brass section has only one player, I'm afraid, but it is the unforgettable Harold Grimes, on trumpet.'

A fairly short, elderly man rose to his feet and, extraordinarily, to one who hadn't seen how much wine he had imbibed, did a little dance on the spot.

'The fool of the group,' was Dashwood's silent verdict.

'And our last member to be introduced is Edmund

Alexander, who plays keyboard for us, and generally keeps us in line.'

'We'll see about that!' thought Dashwood. 'He'd better be good, or he's out.'

'Come on, woman; where's that glass of water? We've got a man dying of thirst here,' shouted Myles, with such volume that Geraldine Warwick was observed to physically jump in her seat.

'I've put it on the little table between the two red leather armchairs. Oh, and I've put a glass of red wine there for you, Vicar. I know how you like a little tipple.'

'You get yourselves sat down, and we'll just have a little discussion on what we're going to play for you this evening.' Moving back to his place in the band, Myles exhorted the others to wrack their brains, and come up with something interesting.

'Come along, you lot! Mr Dashwood and the vicar don't want to be sitting here all evening, while you bicker and squabble about what we ought to play,' he said, cutting across the babble of talk. 'I know; let's do 'The Teddy Bears' Picnic'. That's always a good laugh – at least it is for me. You know what my timing's like!' he finished, with a rich chuckle, drawing smiles from all the other band members, who did, indeed, know how erratic his timing was, and how many hilarious moments it had produced in the past.

After an enthusiastic, but wildly inaccurate fifteen minutes of fighting the chosen piece, Dashwood whispered something in the vicar's ear, then rose from his seat and left the room, dragging an embarrassed clergyman in his wake.

Once out in the hall, Dashwood turned to Rev. Church and asked, in a furious whisper, 'Have they really been together for ten years?' His rogue eye seemed to rake the ceiling, as if he were looking towards the heavens for an answer.

'Yes. The odd person has left, and another one joined, but they're basically the same people here now, who started it all.'

'And how often do they rehearse?'

'Once a month,' replied the vicar, now mortified after what he had just listened to in the drawing room.

'Well, that's going to have to change, if I'm taking over. It's got to be once a week. And tell me something else. Do they always start that late, and drink so much?'

'They have a meal first, and there's wine with that, and more during the rehearsal if anyone wants it.'

'Well, that's got to stop as well. And that drawing room's no use for rehearsing in – people sitting in low armchairs, and on drooping sofas. Would it be possible for us to use the old meeting hall on a Friday night?'

'I have no problem with that, Mr Dashwood, but who's going to tell them about the changes?'

'Oh, I will. They don't frighten me. If they want to be a decent band, then they'll have to learn discipline – and I'm the man for the job. I'll drop a note through Midwynter's door first thing in the morning, then I'll telephone him later, if you would be so kind as to supply me with his number.

'We can thrash it out between us over the phone. If we can get the rehearsals started earlier, there will be plenty of time for them to go for a drink afterwards, but, in my opinion, one mouthful of alcohol in the system completely befuddles the fingers, whatever instrument one plays.'

'Rather you than me, old chap,' retorted the vicar, his face a mask of dismay at the outcome of such straight talking, to a man of such entrenched habits as Myles Midwynter.

'Oh, it's not luck I need, Vicar, just determination and structure, tempered with an iron discipline. I'll soon have them playing like professionals. You just wait and see. They just need the alcohol-induced scales to fall from their eyes, and they'll realise what an appalling racket they actually make. I'll soon have them eating out of the palm of my hand.'

It had been one of those frustrating days for Detective Inspector Harry Falconer, with a very awkward moment with Detective Sergeant Davey Carmichael. The moment had occurred when they were both in the office, up to their eyes in paperwork, and Carmichael had suddenly said, 'John Proudfoot' [PC] 'said something very odd to me today, sir. He patted me on the arm and said, 'You're a very brave lad, carrying on working like this, and we're all very proud of you. You keep on eating those lollipops – they'll help to build you up. Now, I'll say no more.' What do you think he meant by that?

'And then, when I went to the canteen, the woman behind the counter gave me an extra doughnut, and then wouldn't charge me for it. She said I needed to keep up my strength and just carry on taking my medicine. I'm fair flummoxed. And I've had some odd, sad looks from some of the others working here – you know, the civilian staff? What the hell's going on?'

'That does sound odd,' Falconer replied. 'I've got to go down to the desk, so I'll see what Bob Bryant has to say. He's usually got his ear to the ground and knows just about everything that goes on around here.'

Ten minutes later, the inspector stormed back into the room, a look of fury on his face. 'You and your stupid Kojak look!' he exclaimed [see: Murder at The Manse].

'What about it, sir?' asked Carmichael, puzzled at the out-of-the-blue reference to his recently shaven head.

'Proudfoot's only put two and two together, and made eighty-seven. He's been going around telling everyone how tragic it is that you've got *cancer*! They think you're having chemotherapy and still coming into work, despite the way you obviously must be feeling.

'Well, I bearded him in his den – asleep behind a newspaper in the canteen – and I told him that there was nothing wrong with you, and that he'd better get round to spreading *that* good news. There never had been anything wrong with you, and now everyone thought you were ill. I said he also needed to apologise to you, personally, as you had no idea what people were thinking, and couldn't understand why you were being treated so differently.'

'You didn't tell him about Kojak, did you, sir?' asked Carmichael, nervously. He didn't want anyone extracting the Michael about his little fantasies.

'Oh course I didn't, you twerp. I told them you'd forgotten to put the spacer into your hair clippers, and after the first run

14

across your head, you realised you'd made a mistake, and had to shave the rest of it off, to make it look acceptable, otherwise you'd have had a great bald stripe right across the top of your head.'

'Phew! Thanks, sir. I didn't want anyone to think I was a fantasising twit.'

'Even if you are – although not the fantasising bit,' Falconer muttered under his breath, so that Carmichael wouldn't hear. How things can be twisted all out of shape, if someone gets the wrong end of the stick, and just happens to be the station's biggest gossip and rumour-monger.

Harry Falconer was late finishing work that day, and it wasn't until seven o'clock that he packed up the paperwork he needed to take home, and prepared to leave the Station, but he wasn't to escape the building that easily.

At the foot of the staircase, he was hailed by the desk sergeant, Bob Bryant. 'Hey, sunshine, not so fast! There's been something left here that I don't think will keep overnight, so I'd be grateful if you'd collect it now and take it with you.'

With a puzzled expression, Falconer crossed to the desk, only to have his gaze directed to the floor just behind it, where a small grey-spotted cat nestled on part of an old blanket, in a wire cat basket. 'Oh, no,' he thought. 'I'd forgotten all about that.'[1]

'I seem to recall,' Bob Bryant went on, 'that you promised to take this tiny, helpless creature into the care and comfort of your own home. That fella from the hotel phoned the RSPCA to take her away, but fortunately, word had got around about your very kind offer, so one of their lads went and collected it, and here it is. I don't know whether it's a he or a she, but it seems very placid.'

'So did they say why it's taken so long to get her here?' asked Falconer, still slightly puzzled.

'Had to catch it first, apparently. It can run like the very devil, when it wants to. Anyway, sunshine, it's all yours now. I

---

[1] See *Murder at the Manse*

can't be having animals behind my desk. Gives completely the wrong impression to visiting members of the public, and the next thing you know, we'll be inundated with all sorts of waifs and strays. Here it is,' he said, handing over the cage. 'And good luck. You're going to need it with that snooty Mycroft of yours, not to mention the other two you took in after that affair at Stoney Cross.'[2]

Falconer took the cat basket with a sinking feeling in his stomach. After the first day or two, he thought everyone had forgotten his rash offer to give Perfect Cadence a home, then he had conveniently forgotten it too, making sure he didn't mention it to anyone, in case his spontaneity came back to haunt him; and yet here it was, much more substantial than a ghost, and liable to cause chaos with Mycroft (his seal-point Siamese), Ruby (a red-point Siamese) and Tar Baby (a huge, black, furry monster of a cat). Still, such is life! He'd just have to learn to keep his mouth firmly shut in the future, and not let his sentimental side get the better of him.

Placing the basket on the passenger seat of his Boxster, he carefully fastened the seatbelt round it, and headed for home, full of trepidation. The cat had woken up as soon as he started the engine, and managed to howl mournfully for the entire journey, which did nothing for his spirits.

Entering the house, three furry figures skittered out of the sitting room to meet him, skidding abruptly to a halt when they saw what he held in his left hand. They couldn't quite see what was in the cage, but they could smell 'cat', and it wasn't one of them. What was going on here? Why had he brought another cat home? Weren't they enough for him?

Before Falconer had even had the chance to close the front door, the three furry bodies had turned their backs on him in disgust, and gone about their business, feigning total disinterest in what he had brought home for them, for if it was a present, he could just take it away with him again, because they didn't want anything to do with it.

---

[2] See *Choked Off*

16

Fortunately, they had all stalked out of the cat-flap in a huff, to see if anything interesting was going on in the back garden, and he was able to set the flap to 'in only', and release Perfect Cadence from her prison. Setting the cat box, door still open, in case she felt she needed somewhere to retreat to, he filled a fresh bowl with food, and another with water, and put both down on the floor, on the plastic mat he used for the other feeding bowls, so that his kitchen floor did not get too dirty, for his pets had absolutely no table manners at all.

Reaching to the top of one of the kitchen cupboards, he retrieved a litter tray, removed the emergency bag of litter from the cupboard under the stairs, poured the latter into the former, and put it down near the back door for the new cat's use, until he felt she was at home, and ready to go outside, and still know where to come back to.

Perfect Cadence performed like a natural. She slunk over to the food bowl, eyes going from side to side, in case there were any of those other cats that she had smelled around, then lowered her head, and ate, making unnerving growling noises, as she made the food disappear. When the bowl had been licked clean, she took a dainty drink of water, then approached the litter tray with an intent look in her eye.

Falconer finally found the poop scoop about ten minutes later, under a pile of old newspapers that he had placed under the stairs to take for re-cycling, and then completely forgotten about. Armed with this, and trying not to breathe through his nose, he set about cleaning the foul little present that his new house guest had deposited in the litter tray, tied the carrier bag in which he had placed it, and then stood thinking.

He couldn't take it outside to the dustbin, because she might get out, so he'd have to distract her, and shut her in another room, before he could discard his noisome little bundle. Oh, boy; was life going to be more interesting from now on, and he could only hope that his three other cats would accept her as easily as Mycroft had accepted Ruby and Tar Baby, last year.

Once free of his stinking little bundle, he went into the sitting room, and sat down in his favourite chair with his newspaper, only to find the little cat sliding gently on to his lap, purring like a little engine, and rubbing her face against his left hand as it held the pages of the paper up. 'You little darling, Cadence,' he crooned, already having shortened her name for the sake of simplicity, and, dropping his paper to the floor, started to stroke her silky soft fur. 'You're going to be no trouble whatsoever, are you, you little poppet?' he predicted.

Saturday 26th June

When Myles Midwynter came downstairs, a little later than usual as it was a Saturday, he espied an envelope sitting on the doormat which definitely had not been there the night before, and could not have come by post, as the postie never came before eleven on Saturdays.

He picked it up with some interest, slit it open with his thumb, and unfolded the single sheet of paper contained therein. As he read, his face grew redder and redder, and he began to shake with rage. 'Myrtle!' he shouted, loud enough to wake the dead, then charged back up the stairs again, holding the letter at arm's length, as if it were alive. 'Myrtle!' he bellowed again, and found his wife sitting up in bed, rubbing the sleep out of her eyes.

'What on earth is wrong? And why are you making all that noise?' she asked, in a husky, just-woken-up voice.

'This – this letter! This bloody letter!' he exclaimed, thrusting it under her nose, before she had even had the chance to reach for her reading glasses.

'That bloody man!' he exclaimed, his voice rising to a shout again.

'What the hell has he – whoever he is – written, to get you into such a fine old state?'

'It's that Dashwood, the bounder! He's suggesting that we completely reorganise how we run our rehearsals, if we're to be under his baton. I'll give him 'under his baton'! He wants us to rehearse in the old meeting hall, so that we can sit on *suitable* chairs in our *proper* musical groups ...'

18

'Well, the old meeting hall's just a few yards down the road for us, so that's not a real problem, but as far as musical groups go, that'll leave Harold rather lonely, won't it?' cut in Myrtle.

'Harold be damned! He's always sat with the sax. But – get this – he doesn't think it *appropriate* that we should be under the influence of alcohol when we play, as this obviously leads to inaccurate note-reading and an under-par performance. My arse! That's the way we've always done things! Who does he think he is, telling us what to do, when he's not even been in the village for more than five minutes?'

'Calm down, Myles. You know you need to be careful of your blood pressure.'

'And,' he went on, 'he thinks that a heavy meal before playing is also a bad thing. Dammit, we've been having a meal together before we've played, for the last decade.'

Myrtle had now located her reading glasses behind her nightly glass of water, and held the letter up to the light, the better to read it. When she had finished, she dropped the sheet of paper on to the bedclothes, and pierced her husband with a gimlet eye.

'We have been getting rather lax of late, you know,' she stated baldly. 'Why, on at least two practices out of the last half dozen, we haven't even bothered to play more than one or two pieces. And I can see his point in rehearsing weekly. The concert's only a couple of months away, and there's no way we can be ready if we carry on as we are, you've got to admit.'

'What are you suggesting then? That we give in and do exactly what he says, like naughty schoolgirls and boys being told off by the headmaster? Dammit! I won't be written to like that! I won't be bullied!'

'No, but you will be swayed by simple common sense. If we really want to do this concert for charity, then we're going to need to practise a lot more, not just at home, which I don't think anybody bothers to do at the moment, but together, and on a much more regular basis.'

'Traitor!'

'Don't be so childish! This is a perfectly polite and

reasonable letter, and I think we should give his suggestions serious consideration. And, as for the food and wine, there's no reason why I can't leave out a finger buffet here, if I put cling film over the plates. He says here that he'd like us to start at seven. If we do that, and he runs it competently, we can be back here by nine, stuffing our faces and having a few glasses of the old vino. And if he doesn't run it well, we can tell him to sling his hook.'

'I vote we tell him to sling his hook now, and just go on as we are.'

'Now, you know that's not really an option. The vicar bringing him along, has at least opened my eyes to how much work we actually need to do, to be ready to perform in front of an audience, and I think we should give him a chance. If he can get us through this concert, you can do whatever you like after that, but it's been much more of a social club than a band practice lately, and you can't deny that.'

Myles sighed, ran his hand over his suspiciously dark hair, then used both hands to twirl the ends of his magnificent (and also suspiciously dark) handle-bar moustache, actions that indicated that he was thinking. 'You're right, of course, but I don't like admitting it. I'll do an e-mail for those who've got computers, and phone those who haven't, but they won't like it.'

'Then they'll just have to lump it, won't they. It's either practise like the very devil, or cancel, and we simply can't let the vicar down – or the church restoration fund.'

Chapter Two

Friday 2nd July

Campbell Dashwood was extremely dismayed to find that he was not the first to arrive at the old meeting hall that evening, even though he was half an hour before time. He was also furious to discover that the two persons present hadn't just put up their music stands, and tuned their instruments, ready for his instruction.

Instead, he found Vanessa Palfreyman, bow discarded, plucking away at her double bass with a very competent jazz rhythm, Gayle Potten accompanying her on the flute with a high, teasing melody that flew here and there, but never faltered or sounded wrong. There wasn't a music stand or a chair in sight, and there was no music that he could see from which they were playing.

'What do you think you're doing?' he asked, with acid in his voice.

'Just jamming, squire,' answered Vanessa, not missing a syncopated beat. The band was the only place she felt she could let herself go a bit, being painfully shy in the presence of strangers, and not able to make friends easily. 'We got here early so that we could throw around some ideas. It's just a bit of improvisation. Do you have a problem with that?' she asked, still plucking away at the deeply pitched strings of her bulky instrument, her self-confidence at its highest, in familiar company.

'I do, in fact,' answered Dashwood. 'I have called this rehearsal, and I would have expected anyone who arrived early would have set out chairs for the others, put up their music

21

stand, and had their music ready for my arrival.'

'But we don't know how you want the chairs set out, do we? So we couldn't do that, and it hardly takes more than a minute to put up a stand. As for the music, we don't know what you want us to play yet, so we just thought we'd warm up with a bit of a session. Is warming up all right?' she finished, uncharacteristically insolent.

At that exact moment, the mood was broken with the arrival of Myles and Myrtle Midwynter, and an uneasy truce reigned, as they gave Dashwood a hand setting out chairs in sections near the piano, but sideways on to it, as it was an upright, and Edmund Alexander needed to be able to see the conductor, as well as his music.

When they had finished, Myles looked at the arrangement, and asked, 'Why have you got one chair sitting all on its own?' already knowing the answer, but wanting to get this particular matter settled before anyone else arrived.

'It's for the trumpet. It's the only instrument in the brass section, or had you forgotten the make-up of your own band?' Oooh, that was throwing down the gauntlet, and no mistake! Dashwood's good eye stared at Myles in mute confrontation, his wild eye roving from side to side restlessly.

'Harold always sits with the saxophone! The instruments are the same colour and material, and it's more sociable than making someone sit alone, as if they've got chicken pox or some other infectious disease.'

'The saxophone is a woodwind instrument, and should not be placed next to one from the brass section.' Dashwood was determined to have his way. This was *his* band now, and its members would do as they were told.

'I know damned well it's a woodwind instrument, although God knows why: the wretched thing makes enough noise to waken the dead. But in our band, Harold sits next to Lester.'

'And in my band, Harold sits separately, as the sole representative of the brass section,' Dashwood countered.

Other members had been filtering in as this discussion was underway, and the matter was solved, in the end, by Harold

Grimes himself, who walked over to the lone chair, and moved it next to the one where Lester Westlake was unpacking his saxophone. 'Evening, Lester,' he greeted his fellow player, and sat down in the recently moved chair and opened the carrying case of his trumpet.

'What are you doing sitting there, Mr Grimes?'

'Well, I saw as how you'd put my seat too far away from my old mate Lester, so I moved it to where it should be. Me and Lester always sits together, don't we?' he asked the band at large.

There was a chorus of yeses, and Campbell Dashwood had to admit defeat, although only on this one, small matter. If he let them get their own way on this one, maybe they'd be more cooperative with some of the other things he had in mind to introduce, like a dress code for performances.

Everyone having arrived now, Dashwood erected his own stand and removed his baton from his music case, tapping it on the music stand to attract attention, but this ploy went unheard, drowned in the babble of conversation that filled and echoed round the large hall. 'Quiet, please, ladies and gentlemen! It is nearly five-past-seven, and we aren't even ready to start playing. Oboe … oboe.' Here, he consulted a list he had placed on his stand, and continued, 'Ms Burnett, can we have an A please, so that we can get tuned up?'

'I'm sorry, Mr Dashwood, but my reed isn't spitty enough yet. Another minute or so, and I should be able to blow it. Sorry to keep you waiting.'

Dashwood sighed, as he surveyed the shambles before him. There were piles of music on the floor, instrument cases strewn round like discarded rubbish, and light jackets and cardigans slung over the backs of chairs 'Never mind, my dear. I've just realised that there are other things to be attended to first.'

'Now, listen up everybody. We can't possibly have a rehearsal, when you look like you're sitting in the middle of a corporation tip. I should be grateful if you would hang any garments not presently being worn on the coat-hooks in the entrance foyer. Please take your cases to the right hand side of the room – my right, not yours,' he added, as Geraldine Warwick, with only a piccolo case to carry, was already out of her seat, and heading in the wrong direction.

'And when you've settled in your seats once more, please gather together any music that you have, with the exception of the Cornelius March, and put it all in a neat pile under your chairs. Place the piece I have named, on your music stands, and when we are all in tune we will start with that.'

At a quarter-past-seven, he had to raise his voice again to restore order, as various people had stopped to have a chat before going back to their seats. 'Please, please, ladies and gentlemen, will you settle down and pay attention! That A, if you'd be so kind, Ms Burnett.'

'Please call me Wendy,' she requested, as she raised the instrument to her mouth.

'We are meeting on a semi-professional basis here, and I think it would be more appropriate if we used a more formal mode of address. I shall continue to call you Ms Burnett, and you may call me Mr Dashwood. Do I make myself understood?'

'Perfectly,' replied Wendy in a small voice and, blushing furiously, played an A for all the other instruments to tune to.

Myles Midwynter had also turned the colour of a turkey cock, something he usually only did when he was playing his clarinet or, in this case, seething with anger. This man was a mountebank of the worst order and, if he had any say in the matter, would be dispensed with as soon as was humanly possible.

Finally, as settled as they would ever be, and purporting to be in tune, Dashwood raised his baton, declared, 'I shall give you four beats in,' and proceeded to start the piece.

By the end of the first line, he had stopped it again. 'I should be very grateful,' he said in a sarcastic tone, 'if you wouldn't mind observing the beat I am giving, and not all play at different speeds. It would sound so much better if we played at the same rate, don't you think? Now, one more time. After four.'

24

It didn't! – sound any better, that is. It was still awful, and the conductor stopped it at the same place, a look of despair creeping across his features. 'How long have you been playing this piece, may I ask?'

'About a year,' responded Myles, now slightly subdued, as he had produced more than a couple of very high-pitched screeches with his instrument in the last two attempts at the piece.

'And when, exactly, did you last play it?'

'About a couple of months ago, I think. Not sure, really.'

'Thank you, Mr Midwynter, and would you like to explain to me exactly what the problem is?'

'You're going too fast for us. We usually take this at a rather more sedate pace.'

A few voices murmured in agreement with this statement.

'Well, you clap your hands for me to show me how fast you usually play it, and I'll match my conducting to that, for now.'

Myles clapped a slow rhythm, Dashwood raised his baton to beat them in, and the band launched on its third attempt at the piece. This time the conductor allowed it to continue through to the end, before sighing and laying down his baton on the little shelf of his music stand.

'I don't know if there are any funerals booked for the near future, but that's all that is fit for at the moment. It's a march, not a funeral dirge. We've got to get it more lively, and observe at least some of the dynamics. May I request that you work on that at home, for us to have another look at, at next week's rehearsal?'

With a quick glance down at his crib sheet of names again, he asked, 'Ms Warwick, you didn't play in that piece. Would you be so good as to explain to me why that was?'

'Because I don't have a part for it,' she explained in a quiet voice.

'Have you lost it?'

'No, I never had one.'

'Why not?'

'Because the last Musical Director said she couldn't write

25

parts.'

'And which instrument did this dear lady play?'

'The clarinet, Mr Dashwood. It's not my fault. It really isn't.'

'I know it isn't, dear Ms Warwick. I shall write one when I go home tonight, and put it through your letter box first thing in the morning, and then we can have the pleasure of you playing with us next week.'

'Thank you, Mr Dashwood.'

'Now, what about that Teddy Bear thing you did last week? Let's find out how that sounds without the aid of alcohol.'

There was a deal of movement, as all the band members searched for somewhere to put down their instruments, before scrabbling under their chairs to look for the appropriate piece of music, and Dashwood, looking at his watch, realised that it was already going on for eight o'clock. This would never do. He'd have to get a stronger grip on them than this, it they weren't to be there until midnight.

'The Teddy Bears' Picnic' was even worse than it had been when they had last played it. Not only was it slow and funereal, like the other piece, but was full of wrong notes, with several people losing the beat, and either playing a bar or two behind, or several bars ahead, which was the case in point with Myles Midwynter.

'Stop, oh, stop that dreadful racket,' shouted Dashwood, wringing his hands in despair. 'Mr Midwynter, you were several bars ahead of everyone at letter B.'

'Oh, I always am,' explained Myles guiltily. 'I've never quite been able to sort out the timing in that section.'

'Sort it out? You doubled it!'

'Oh, is that what I was doing wrong? Couldn't work it out, myself,' Myles thanked him, a mystery solved at last.

'Let's try it again, but just the first section, and very, very slowly. And you *must* watch my beat.'

'But we can't,' called Myrtle from her seat in the strings. 'We need to look at the music.'

'And just how long have you been fighting this nursery

26

masterpiece?'

'About two years now,' she answered meekly.

'And you don't know your parts yet? How often do you practise between rehearsals?'

There was an ominous silence.

'And you really expected to be ready for a concert that is just a couple of months away?'

A second silence filled the room to bursting point.

'I can see that things are more serious than I thought. I'm going to have a word with the vicar, to see if it's possible for us to use the new village meeting rooms. If we can secure that for our rehearsals, then we can have sectional rehearsals in different rooms, at seven, then all meet together at eight o'clock, to put together the progress we've all made in the previous hour. Would that be agreeable?'

'Yes,' was chorused meekly by all the members of the band but one. Myrtle Midwynter had her hand over her husband's mouth, to stifle the protest that she knew he was about to make. She didn't want him rocking the boat this early on and, basically, Dashwood was right. They had used the band as a social club, and now they were going to have to pay the price of laziness and lack of practice, whatever Myles or anyone else thought. It was time to take their medicine like good children.

Harry Falconer had learnt, over the past week, not to leave around anything paper, for Cadence had a passion for shredding anything made of this fascinating stuff. Her formal introduction to the others had not been as bad as he had feared, but there had been a good deal of hissing and spitting over the week, and if one of the others walked within paw's reach of the newcomer, she never missed the opportunity to biff them one.

It was the paper that was the biggest problem, however. He'd only suffered that once before, with the other three, and it had been an isolated incident, as far as he was concerned. With Cadence, it was a passion, and since she had arrived, he had lost every newspaper he had carelessly discarded, his copy of the Radio Times, and three paperback novels.

Realising that the little treasure wasn't going to suddenly cease her beloved game, he now kept his current newspaper and television guide in a drawer of his desk, and made sure he confined his other reading matter either to the bedroom or behind the glass doors of a wall unit.

Today, he came home with a spring in his step, believing that everything had gone reasonably smoothly, and his last problem seemed to be under control. It was, therefore, with a light heart, that he inserted his key in the door and let himself in, hoping that there would be, perhaps, four happy felines rushing to welcome him home.

Instead, there was a complete absence of a welcoming party, but still he was not suspicious. Perhaps they were out in the garden soaking up the sun, or chasing insects with the determined absorption in their mission that they always displayed when a bug or a butterfly attracted their attention.

They weren't! He opened the living room door on to a positively Alpine scene. The whole room was covered in a layer of paper snow that was so realistic it almost made him shiver.

What the hell had happened? He'd hidden all the paper items that he could think of. Where on earth had all this paper confetti appeared from? The only thing that it could possibly be – and here he bent to pick up a small handful to confirm his fears – was the twenty-four pack of his favourite toilet rolls, which had been on special offer when he had done a little shopping, after leaving the office the previous evening.

But he's put them upstairs, safely in the bathroom, hadn't he? And he'd shut the bathroom door; he remembered doing it as part of his 'save the paper' fund, knowing that toilet paper would prove a superb challenge, even if it was just the one roll that hung from its holder on the wall. How could that cat – and he knew it was *that* cat – get into the bathroom? It was a 'mission impossible' situation.

Taking several deep breaths, he curbed his rising temper, and walked briskly up the stairs. He had noticed Mycroft, Ruby, and Tar Baby peering out of the kitchen doorway, but had ignored them, as part of their punishment. At the top of the stairs, the main culprit was caught bang to rights, still with a half-unravelled roll of paper in her mouth, and shaking it too and fro, as she growled it into submission.

'You little beast!' he exclaimed. 'How on earth did you get into the bathroom to get that lot out?' But Cadence ignored him, still intent on killing her prey.

With only the very slightest suspicion that he had not closed the bathroom door firmly enough, Falconer leaned over and pulled it tight shut. That got Cadence's attention, and she turned to the door, leapt up, caught the handle with her front paws, and hung from it until it unlatched, then gave it a little push with her head, and returned to what she had been doing before she was so rudely interrupted.

So engrossed was she, that she had not even noticed Falconer, nor heard his voice when he had spoken. She did this time, though, for he raised it to a shout of disbelief. 'You can open doors! Nobody told me you were a cat thief. Get down from here and give me the chance to clean up, you little home-wrecker.'

By the time he had finished speaking, the cat had ceased her play, realised that she had been rumbled, and shot off down the stairs with all the hairs on her tail fluffed out in trepidation.

Downstairs, in the living room, the wall that housed the fireplace had been faced with stone, and when Falconer looked over the banisters at her, she made a jump of panic for this wall, and effortlessly climbed her way to the ceiling.

'S-H-I-T!' he ejaculated, but rather more quietly than he had spoken before. How, in the name of all that's holy, was he going to get her down from there? And did he have enough black bags to collect up the shredded remains of twenty-four triple-thick quilted toilet rolls?

Saturday 3rd July

Several members of the band met in The Leathern Bottle on Saturday evening, some by accident, others by arrangement, but the result was, nevertheless, the same. Most of them were gathered round two tables pulled together for that purpose, and were giving their candid opinions of Dashwood's new regime.

'This'll only be the beginning; mark my words. He'll have us in military-style uniforms, and marching to the beat of his drum in no time at all. I can't believe the way he exploded when he found me and Gayle having a bit of a 'jam' when he arrived at the hall.

'You'd think he'd be glad to see anyone playing their instrument outside official rehearsal hours, wouldn't you?' complained Vanessa Palfreyman.

'He's already banned our lovely chatty pre-rehearsal meals, and the wine, and now he's going to split us up into little groups for the first hour, for intensive practice.' Myrtle Midwynter was just as furious as Vanessa.

'But you did us proud with that buffet afterwards,' piped up Geraldine Warwick.

'That's not the point,' continued Myrtle. 'Last night wasn't fun. He's taken all the joy out of it. Myles and I always used to look forward to band practice, and now we're dreading the next one.'

'Well, at least you didn't get singled out like I did,' Geraldine Warwick chipped in again. When he asked me why I didn't have a part for 'Cornelius', I nearly died with embarrassment. I couldn't even pretend that I'd mislaid it, because he'd expect it to turn up sometime.'

'There was no way I could get out of telling him that Mrs Farr couldn't write parts. I know she was very good with her own stuff, but she played the clarinet, and I'd have needed a part in C. She just didn't have the self-confidence to have a look at the flute part, and see if she could do something to harmonise with that. I really, really couldn't help but tell the truth. I hope you understand.'

'Don't let it worry you, Geraldine,' comforted Myles Midwynter. 'It won't reflect on you badly. I've been the one responsible for this band, in the main, as I – well, Myrtle and I – started it. Dashwood will probably just put another cross by my name, deeming it incompetence on my part, that I put a Musical

Director in charge who couldn't deal with writing parts, or arranging music. You wait and see – it'll all be my fault in the end. I know how the mind of someone like him works.'

'And I thought we were getting rather good at the old 'Teddy Bears',' commented Fern Bailey, who had played her little heart out on her viola the previous evening.

'Not with that old fart, Cameron McKnight, on first violin,' opined Harold Grimes, who had arrived, uninvited, on the arm of Gayle Potten.

'Don't be such a bastard, Harold. When he finds out that you still have to write in the notes, he's going to throw a hairy fit,' retorted Gayle.

Harold chuckled, envisaging the moment in the future when this would come out, rubbed his hands together with glee, and replied, 'Oh, I can hardly wait to see his face. What a picture that'll be. And he can stick his rehearsing in our 'musical groups' where the sun don't shine. I'm damned if I'm sitting in a little room all on my own for the first hour.'

'I'll be there. Don't forget, we told him to get lost about splitting us up, last night,' Lester Westlake, the saxophonist, reminded him.

'That's true,' Harold replied, his aggression suddenly evaporating.

'You don't normally come in here, do you Harold?' asked Wendy Burnett, the oboist, a petite, precise and pernickety woman, fast approaching the age at which life is said to begin. If anything out of the usual happened, she could not resist the temptation to find out why.

'Harold came with me,' answered Gayle Potten, Harold's current squeeze, though no one could understand what she saw in him. 'We usually go to The Clocky Hen – there's a bit more life up there. They've got a jukebox, and live music some weekends, but it would seem that things are much more interesting in here tonight, and when Myrtle rang up and asked me to come along, I decided to bring Harold with me. After all, I've got to have someone to buy my drinks for me, haven't I?'

This got a laugh, and when the table had settled down again,

Myles had an expression on his face that suggested that a light bulb had just been switched on over his head – one of the old fashioned ones that suddenly bursts forth with light, not one of the new energy-saving bulbs that seem to take forever to produce more than ten watts. How on earth was one to surprise a burglar or, more probably, ones teenaged children up to mischief, if one could not surprise them with sudden and immediate light?

'I've had an idea, guys. The gang's nearly all here. Why don't we go back to our place and have a proper session. The outhouse is stacked with wine, and we could have a real old bitch about that dipstick, Dashwood,' suggested Myles, twirling the ends of his fine moustache, mischief glinting in his eyes.

Myrtle was in full agreement. Come on everybody,' she encouraged them. 'We can phone the others from our place, then we can have a good old moan, like Myles said, about our pocket Hitler. If we can get it out of our systems on a weekly basis, we should be able to put up with that old tosser until this concert's over, then we can give him the old heave-ho, and get back to the way things were.'

This was greeted with such an enthusiastic cheer, that everyone else in the pub looked round to see what on earth was going on, only to see the occupants of the two joined tables rise and exit without a word of farewell, obviously on a mission.

It was a good session, and by the end of it, one action of defiance and protest was planned for the following Friday evening – nothing drastic; just a little demonstration of their resentment at Dashwood's 'control freak' changes to the normal rhythm [!] of proceedings.

It had taken Harry Falconer some considerable time to coax Cadence down from her precarious perch on his wall, just below the level of the ceiling. That done, he set to in clearing up the papery mess she had made. On reflection, he decided that she couldn't have done it all on her own. There had been one occasion, in the recent past, when the other three cats had decided to shred a translation from Greek that he had worked like the very devil over one evening, and then forgotten to put away when he went to bed.

That had seemed like a lot of work for just that, but compared to the sheer volume of shredded (triple-thick and quilted, as it was) paper he faced tonight, it had been a drop in the ocean. By the time he had gathered up every piece to his satisfaction, then vacuumed most thoroughly, it was past ten o'clock, and he hadn't had even a bite to eat.

Well, that was all to the good. If he had to throw together something quickly, it would be baked beans on toast, with lashings of brown sauce slathered all over the top of it. He hadn't worked out what wine went best with this, his guilty secret of a meal, so he decided, in the end, that a big mug (he usually used china cups and saucers) of strong tea would be the perfect accompaniment to such a feast as this.

At ten-thirty, he was rummaging around in a box in his garage, searching for a number of little anti-Cadence devices that he was determined to fit before going to bed. At last! There they were! He extracted from the box, a packet containing little hooks on the end of a short arm, and little horseshoe nails. He would fit one of each of these pairs to the doors of the rooms he didn't want the cat to gain access to, and then he could hook them up, so that no amount of jumping up at the handle could open them. That was the only way he would get a good night's sleep, and not be kept awake for most of the night listening for furtive little forays to raid the upstairs rooms for more deliciously fun paper.

It was midnight, when he finally retired to bed, having fitted a hook on the inside of his bedroom door as well as the outside. He didn't want Cadence wandering in here in the wee small hours, and having a go at all his books. Thus reassured, he slept like a log until about half-past five, when the most distressing chorus of howls and near-human screams rent the depths of his sleep asunder.

He sat bolt upright in bed and listened, trying to identify what the hell was making all the noise. He could hear that there were cats involved, but what was that dreadful other noise.

33

What the hell had they got downstairs? Had they caught something and brought it in for a little play before they killed it?

He could stand it no longer, and leapt out of bed, without donning either his dressing gown or his slippers, and faltered at the first obstacle. His door wouldn't open! Realisation dawned within a second or two, that he had locked the door from the inside with one of his little hook and eye affairs and, feeling a right nelly, he exited the room and raced down the stairs, to break up whatever was going on in his living room at such an hour of the morning.

As anyone with a number of cats will have already realised, the 'screaming' was, in reality, only two very angry cats shouting into each other's faces, each with tails all fluffed up, trying to look fiercer than the other. As he descended, the spectators – in this case, Tar Baby and Ruby, suddenly joined the fray, and the fight turned into one with four combatants.

'Stop this nonsense at once!' Falconer commanded, in his best army voice. As this order echoed round the room, the four feline figures became absolutely frozen then, as if at a signal, turned as a pack and ran into the kitchen, from whence he could hear the cat flap flapping backwards and forwards, as all the miscreants made their exit to safety, in the garden.

There was fluff everywhere! He'd have to get up a bit earlier – that is, if he ever got back to sleep again – and vacuum again in the morning. If life was this difficult with cats, what on earth must it be like with children? he wondered, and he determined to ask Carmichael about this when he next saw him.

Chapter Three

At six o'clock, all the members of the band were assembled in The Leathern Bottle, instruments and all, although this didn't matter too much, as they were about the only customers at such an early hour. At a busier time of day, this would have been impossible.

'So, what'll you all have? The first round is on me,' offered Myles Midwynter, generously. He was really looking forward to band rehearsal, for the first time since Dashwood had taken over. 'No, Gwendolyn, you cannot have an orange juice, unless you let me put a vodka in it. We need a united front here, and I wouldn't put it past the bastard to smell everyone's breath when we get there. We don't want any scabs in this band. We must present a united front, mustn't we?'

'OK, Myles,' agreed Gwendolyn meekly, clutching her violin case close to her chest, as if it could confer the comfort of a childhood teddy bear.

Spread around the bar, some leaning on it, others just resting their drinks on it, there was the shared feeling of a bunch of children doing something naughty, knowing they were going to be found out, but simply not caring. It was the camaraderie of the prison camp – us against them, or him, in this case; their combined wits against his.

'My round!' called Lester Westlake, and called for the barman to replicate what Myles had ordered.

By the time that the hands of the pub clock reached five to seven, they had had four drinks apiece – even Gwendolyn – and were ready to face anything that Dashwood could throw at them.

'Come on, you lot! Let's go and make that old bugger's life a misery,' bellowed Harold, well-mellowed by now, with the four drinks he had had at the pub, and the three he had managed to throw down his throat before he left home.

'Not so unsubtle, old chap,' advised Myles. 'Softly, softly, catchy monkey. We'll not be too rebellious tonight – just show him, quietly but firmly, whose band this really is. Agreed, everybody?'

'Agreed!' said everyone, and they marched out of the pub in a body, and headed down the road to the new village meeting rooms, determination writ large on their faces.

It was an impertinent four minutes past seven when they reached the new village meeting rooms, and Dashwood was standing in the main entrance, hands on hips, a confrontational expression on his face.

'What time do you call this, then?' he called across to them as they approached, pointedly holding his watch in front of his face and tapping it with one stubby finger. 'Seven o'clock on the dot, I said, and here it is, already – five past now. That is sloppy in the extreme. In fact, you should be here fifteen minutes early to set everything out, and be ready to start playing at seven.'

'Give it a rest, will you? We're here now, and if you stop gassing at us, we'll be ready to start a lot quicker than if we stand out here being lectured by you.' Myles was feeling in a particularly rebellious mood, and vented his feelings, inhibitions shed, in the rosy glow of alcohol that surrounded not just him but all of them.

'If you would be kind enough to go inside, you will notice that I have labelled the rooms for the different sections of the instruments, and put the appropriate number of chairs in them. I should be grateful' (here, Dashwood really was holding his temper at bay with difficulty) 'if you would find which room you are in. Inside, you will find your part for a new piece of music, which I would like you to perform during the concert.

'Spend the first hour practising this, and running through that 'Cornelius' March you played last time, as at least you managed to start together, even if you all wandered off individually in the bits in between. I shall visit each room to check on your progress and playing, then we will all gather in the largest room, to play through those two pieces ensemble. In you go. Edmund, you go straight into the hall. I've left the music out for the new piece for you, to give you a chance to run through it a few times before we all come together.'

As they filed past him into the building, his voice sounded again, in an angry squeak. 'I can smell alcohol. I expressly forbade the consumption of alcohol before rehearsals. Which one of you has been drinking?'

His face turned to thunder as all present raised a hand. 'How dare you! How bloody dare you, after I made such a point of how alcohol dulls the senses and inhibits accurate playing. Get inside, before I really lose my temper.'

'Right you are, guv,' said Lester Westlake, loud enough for the man to hear, and Harold Grimes and Myles Midwynter both saluted him as they marched past him.

'And don't call me 'guv'!'

Dashwood started his tour of inspection in the room he had designated 'strings'. Inside, he found Cameron McKnight and Gwendolyn Radcliffe both tuning their violins. Fern Bailey was running up and down a scale on her viola, and Myrtle and Vanessa Palfreyman were still tightening and anointing their bows, lost in conversation.

'But I'm really not keen on going this year. Couldn't we just give it a miss for once?' he heard Myrtle say to Vanessa.

'But we always go. We've gone for years, now. Why should this year be any different?'

Myrtle Midwynter and Vanessa Palfreyman were considered to be very close friends, and always went on a hiking holiday together at the end of the summer, when the crowds had disappeared back off to work or to school.

'Please excuse me butting in, ladies, but this is supposed to be a band rehearsal, not a ladies' knitting circle. Chop chop! or we'll never get started.' Dashwood was poised for action, his small notebook and pencil at the ready to take notes.

There was a general sigh, expressing the joint thought 'oh, God', and the five stringed instrument players placed the music for the familiar march on their music stands, Cameron McKnight, as first violin and, therefore, 'leader of the orchestra', counted them in, and off they went, all of them fighting to keep, not only in time, but in tune, their nervous fingers betraying them as they endeavoured to make as good an impression as they could on Dashwood.

When they had finished that piece, he asked them to place the parts for the new piece of music he had brought with him on their stands so that he could hear them sight-read. They were only four bars in when he said, 'Thank you,' in a voice loud enough to halt playing, and stalked out of the room, in search of other prey.

'Oh my God! That was awful,' exclaimed Myrtle, echoing the feelings of everyone in the room. 'I forgot, as usual, to look at the key signature, so I didn't play a single flat in it.'

'And I read it in cut time, so I was playing at twice the speed of everyone else,' offered Fern Bailey, gloomily.

'I shouldn't worry about that. I had, what I now realise to be page two, on my stand, and outdid you all, by playing completely the wrong music, added Vanessa Palfreyman, with a heartfelt sigh.

Myrtle started it. It was just a wheezy little chuckle, but it was infectious, running round the room until everyone had caught the silliness, and within ten seconds, they were all howling with laughter at the complete shambles they had presented to their new Musical Director.

'That'll teach him!' said Gwendolyn Radcliffe who had, until then, remained silent.

'Maybe he was right about the alcohol,' suggested Fern Bailey, laying her viola on the floor, in case she dropped it, in her mirth.

'Absolute rot!' exclaimed Myrtle, leaning over her cello for support, as she continued to chuckle. 'We just didn't have enough!'

This set off another round of hearty laughter, but they soon sobered up when Vanessa Palfreyman, putting her fingers to her lips and trying to regain control of herself, said, 'Shhhh! If he hears us, he'll come in to see what's so funny, and *I'm* not telling him.'

That produced a more sober mood, in more ways than one, and they applied themselves to the challenge of a new piece of music – a very rare event, since the last but one Musical Director had fled the drear of English weather for sunnier climes.

As Dashwood had been appraising the awful caterwauling of the strings, he had been aware of doors opening and closing, and the scraping of what sounded like a chair. With his suspicious mind on red alert, he headed straight for the woodwind room, and found exactly what he had concluded, from the noises, that he would find.

Wendy Burnett sat with her double reed in her mouth, keeping it moist, so that it was ready to play. Gayle Potten was adjusting the three parts of her flute to get it into perfect alignment, giving it a little blow between each minute adjustment. Geraldine Warwick had the new piece on her stand, and was gently fingering her way through it with a stately slowness, blowing only very gently, so as not to disturb the others, who were listening to Myles holding forth.

He was still intermittently sucking at his reed to moisten it sufficiently to play. 'I don't see why we have to learn anything new, when we've got such a large repertoire already. There are plenty of pieces we've already played, that would serve perfectly well for this concert, and …'

'Good evening, ladies and gentleman.' Dashwood had made a swift entrance, so as to catch them all by surprise. 'Not playing yet? Tut tut! And where is our Mr Westlake? I did emphasise that the saxophone was to be in its correct section, and yet I see no sign of him in here.'

'He's gone in with Harold, so that he won't have to sit all on his own. There is a social element to band meetings, whatever you may think to the contrary, and he didn't come here to spend the evening alone in a little room, with nobody to talk to but himself.' This explanation came from Gayle Potten who, being his current girlfriend, was always concerned for his welfare.

'Contrary to what seems to be common belief, he would not have needed anyone to talk to. The idea of using these practice rooms is so that you can play in your separate sections, without getting put off by any of the others. He should be spending all his time in there playing, which I can patently see, that you are not. Now, why would that be?'

'Reeds, old boy,' explained Myles with an infuriating smile, and putting his reed back into his mouth, to make noisy sucking noises on it.

'Get those reeds onto your instruments, and put 'Cornelius' on the stands. I want you playing that to me within ten seconds, and no more of the dumb insolence and downright defiance that I've been faced with this evening.'

As in the strings' room, Dashwood made copious use of his notebook and pencil, stopped the piece after two lines, and bade them put their new piece out to play at sight. As sheet music rustled in the changeover, a voice could be heard muttering, 'You'll be lucky, mate!'

'Who said that?' Dashwood demanded, his face reddening with anger, but no one owned up, and they began, at various different speeds, and wildly differing competence in sight-reading, to murder the piece he had selected to be the jewel in the crown for this, his first concert as Musical Director.

'Stop, oh stop that dreadful racket!' His patience did not last long, and he swept out of the room, reminding them to be in the largest of the rooms at eight o'clock, so that they could all play together.

Entering the room that had a piece of paper taped to the door reading 'Brass', he found Lester Westlake reading the newspaper, and Harold Grimes, busy with a pencil, writing on his copy of the new piece of music.

'What the hell's going on in here?' Dashwood asked in disbelief. 'Why is neither of you playing?'

'Well, Harold here can't concentrate if I play while he's thinking, so I thought I'd let him get his prep done first, then we'd have a go together,' explained Westlake, looking even more superior and supercilious than usual.

The saxophonist was immaculately turned out, as usual, with not a hair out of place, his teeth looking as if they had been professionally whitened, had recently taken to wearing a variety of coloured contact lenses. Tonight his eyes were of a turquoise hue. In his job, although no one knew exactly what that was, one had to look smart at all times, in case one was seen by one of one's clients.

Dashwood let his gaze stray over the younger man, sneering slightly, as he had deemed the saxophonist to be rather 'naice', then glared at Harold, whose pencil was still working away, writing all over what had been a pristine piece of music.

'And what the hell do you think you're doing, Mr Grimes?'

Harold looked up. 'I'm marking in my notes, squire. Haven't quite got the hang of this music-reading yet, so I mark my notes in, then I know which fingers to use, to get the tune right.'

Dashwood eyes turned up so much they nearly disappeared into his head. He struck his forehead with the palm of his right hand, and merely said, 'Eight o'clock. Don't forget!' before slamming shut the door, and disappearing off to hear the pianist run through his paces.

As he walked down the corridor, he became conscious of a totally unmusical sound and, muttering, 'What the hell is that cacophony?' hurried along to the hall.

'That cacophony' was Edmund Alexander, who was trying out the accompaniment for the new piece. At the moment, the music was well ahead on points, and the entry of Dashwood gave Edmund the excuse he needed, to call off the fight and declare the music the winner.

'What was that bloody awful racket I just heard?' asked

Dashwood without preamble.

'I was just having a go at my new part – I'm afraid it rather got the better of me, but I'll get it under control eventually.'

'But I thought you could sight-read. You played perfectly well for the last two rehearsals.'

'Oh, I can sight-read, but not at FIRST sight. It takes me a while to sort it all out between my eyes and my fingers, and then everything's just fine and dandy.'

'And just how do you propose to accompany the band for tonight's joint practice at eight o'clock?'

'Blimey! It's going to take longer than that, before I'm comfortable with it.'

'And?' asked Dashwood, urging him on to the inevitable conclusion.

'And – I suppose I'm not going to able to manage it. Sorry.'

'And what do you propose we do without the piano accompaniment?'

'Don't know, Mr Dashwood,' apologised Edmund, looking down at his feet in embarrassment.

'I'll tell you what we're going to do, Mr Alexander. You're going to turn round all those chairs until they face the piano, and I'm going to play the damned thing. It won't be easy, trying to conduct with my head, while my eyes and fingers are trying to give of their best to the music, but it'll just have to do for tonight.

'You must practise like the very devil before our next meeting, because I can't be doing with this on a regular basis. Do I make myself understood, Mr Alexander?'

'Perfectly, Mr Dashwood. Sorry, Mr Dashwood.'

At exactly eight o'clock, a rather more subdued straggle of players wandered into the main room, showing a modicum of surprise to see that the configuration of chairs had been rearranged to face the piano, and Edmund Alexander, normally the most cheerful of characters, sitting in a chair to the left of the piano stool, a glum expression on his face.

Looking at his watch, as he noted their punctual arrival,

Dashwood, aware of their curiosity at the change of seating, addressed them thus. 'I have decided that I shall provide the piano accompaniment for this part of the rehearsal. As you yourselves are no doubt aware, Mr Alexander is not a gifted sight-reader, and I am giving him the opportunity to familiarise himself with the work, during the next week.'

(What he had, in fact, said to Edmund was, 'You will no longer play for the rehearsals, I have decided. You're suspended until you know the accompaniment by heart.')

'I shall take his place for tonight, leaving the keyboard, if I feel it necessary, if the timing goes adrift. I'm sure you will all be most cooperative at this temporary arrangement, and try your hardest to produce the most accurate playing of which you are capable.

'Now, if you'll all find your places, I'll play the piano introduction, and you can take your tempo from that? What was that? I didn't quite catch it?'

There was no reply to this, as someone had mumbled, 'Pompous old git!' just loud enough to be heard, but not loud enough for the words to be distinguished.

Seating himself on the piano stool at the keyboard, he nodded to Edmund Alexander, who had found himself cast in the role of page-turner for the rest of the evening, and prepared to play. At his opening notes, Harold winked across at Myles, acknowledging that, even if no one else had identified the speaker of the *sotto voce* insult, he had, and was congratulating him in on his naughtiness.

At the appointed bar, only the violins played, the rest of the strings joining them on the third beat, others joining in throughout the next two bars. With an angry crashing of notes, Dashwood stood and faced his band.

'I assume you all took the time to run through your parts in your separate rooms?' he enquired angrily. There was a subdued mutter of assent. 'Then what the hell was that shambles?' he asked, piqued, as only a fussy little man of his bent can be.

'It's too fast.'

'We weren't ready.'

'I've got my music upside down.'

'There are too many flats in it. Can I ring them in pencil? I'll only be a minute.'

'We're not used to the introduction. All we've got is the number of bars' rest.'

With a murderous expression on his face, Dashwood addressed these issues one by one. 'First of all, I'm already playing it at half speed, so it is definitely *not* too fast. If I play it any slower, I'll fall asleep on my stool with boredom.

'Secondly, no, you were not at all ready, which is an absolute disgrace for a band that claims to have been playing together for *ten years*. Thirdly, I shouldn't have to check that you've got your music on your stands the right way up.' Here, he sucked air in through his teeth, the way a car mechanic does when he lifts the bonnet of one's car, and is deciding how much he can get away with charging one.

'As for the key signature, it's only four flats. I should have thought you'd have been able to cope with them with relative ease, given what I said in point two. And as far as the introduction goes – *count*! You've got the number of bars that you are at rest: bloody well count them, then you'll have no trouble coming in on time. Now, let's try it again, and I'll try to play it even slower.'

Their second attempt staggered its way through the first four lines – that was, the first four lines for some of them. Others were still on line three, and Myles Midwynter had managed to sprint ahead to halfway through line five, before Dashwood exploded again.

'Have you performed much in public?' he demanded in a loud voice, and without waiting for an answer, went on, 'I understand that you collect for charity at Christmas by playing carols at various venues. Do you make much?'

'Five or six hundred pounds a year, old chap,' Myles informed him with pride.

'How? Do people pay you to shut up and go and play somewhere else? It's unbelievable to me, that anyone could

44

stand the cacophony you make for more than a few minutes.'

'Now, look here, guv, a lot of people get real enjoyment from our carols at Christmas,' Harold shouted, in defence of them all.

'Then they must either be stone deaf or tone deaf. I'm going to go through you, one by one now, and offer a little friendly advice to improve your playing. After this utter waste of an evening, we've got very little time left, and I'm not going to waste what little there is on listening to you slaughtering a beautiful composition.

'I'll start with you, Mr Midwynter. What number reed do you use?'

'A three-and-a-half,' answered Myles, looking a little smug, as this was a rather hard reed, that many people who only played for fun were unable to blow.

'Then I suggest that you return to a number two. Not only do you go purple in the face when you're playing, which, apart from anything else, can't be good for your blood pressure, but you squeak and squeal like a whole colony of mice. Not only is that an unpleasant sound, it is very jarring to the nerves, as well.'

Myles's face had only just returned to its normal tanned hue after the effort of playing, and began to redden again at such harsh words. He was secretly very proud of his playing, and the little man's criticism had cut him to the quick.

But Dashwood hadn't finished with him yet. 'You also need to learn to count accurately. In that last debacle, you were a full bar-and-a-half ahead of everyone else. Pay attention, and listen to the other players. If you don't listen to each other, we'll never get anywhere.'

Finished with victim number one, their new Musical Director moved on to Myrtle. 'How long have you been playing the cello, Mrs Midwynter?'

'Fifteen years. I have a lesson every week, without fail.'

'Then may I suggest that your teacher is just cynically making money out of you? Have you looked at the passage on page two, that goes into the alto clef? No? Can you read in the alto clef?'

'No.' This was more whispered than spoken, for Myrtle couldn't believe he could say such harsh things to her.

'And when is your next lesson?'

'Monday.' Again a whispered answer.

'Then get your teacher to explain the workings of this thing that is, at present, a mystery to you – that is, if your teacher is, in fact, musically competent enough to understand it himself, and pass on the information, for we shall, please God, move on to that page next week.'

There was now a susurration of whispers in the room, as players exchanged horrified opinions of what was being said.

'Silence!' shouted Dashwood. 'I'm only saying this for your own good. You want Swinbury Abbot to be proud of its band, don't you? Well, don't you?'

'Yes.'

'Well, let me help you to reach that point. If you work hard and take my advice, you could be the best village band in the area. And while we're at it, the vicar told me what you call yourselves, letting me in on the little joke, and I must tell you this – I do *not* approve. It is a negative title, inviting negative criticism of your performances. I suggest that from now on, you should style yourselves 'The Swinbury Village Band', and give people exactly what it says on the label.

'Silence! Quiet, I say! I haven't finished yet! We've still got a quarter of an hour. Mr McKnight, I would like you to swap parts with Ms Radcliffe. No, don't protest. I have listened to you play, and although you play with a great deal of panache, your tuning leaves a lot to be desired. May I suggest that you work very hard to play in tune, or I shall have no further need for you in this band?

'And Ms Radcliffe, although you show no style with your bow, and do not even attempt any vibrato, at least you play accurately, and I should like you, for now, to take over the part of first violin. Now swap parts, and let's have no argument about it. If it doesn't work, we can always swap back – that is, if I detect any improvement in your tuning, Mr McKnight.'

The tirade worked its way through all the members of the band. Little Wendy Burnett was upbraided for not having a small glass or eggcup of water beside her, so that she didn't have to constantly keep the double reed in her mouth, to keep it moist.

Fern Bailey was informed that her bow was not sufficiently anointed and consequently squealed on the strings, which didn't matter too much, as she hardly moved her bow at all, and would have to learn to do so if her part was ever going to be sufficiently loud to be heard. 'Your instrument should sing like a rich contralto. With your bowing, it's more like the croaking of a drunken old crone in the pub at closing time on a Saturday night,' he informed her, causing her to wish a hole would open up in the floor, and swallow her up,

Vanessa Palfreyman, unfortunately, had not noticed that her entrance was marked 'arco', and she had plucked it. 'The devil is in the detail!' she had been informed, a comment that had been accompanied with an acid little smile of superiority that didn't reach Dashwood's eyes. 'If you paid more attention, and spent less time joking and clowning around, you might sound as if you actually know how to play your instrument,' he upbraided her acidly.

To Geraldine Warwick, whose piccolo had had no parts written for it for some time, and who felt desperately underused, he upbraided her, 'Miss Warwick, for goodness sake watch your music and count. You don't have many entries, and you missed all of them. As you finally have a printed part to play, I should think you ought to be grateful, and play every note with great accuracy and skill. Pay attention!'

Lester Westlake, who hadn't yet mastered playing any other volume than 'molto belto', was asked to bring a spare pair of socks with him in future, so that they could be put in the bell of his saxophone to act as a mute, until he had mastered the technicalities of dynamics.

'I have also noted, from a little chat I had with Mr Midwynter, that you miss a lot of rehearsals, Mr Westlake. I would ask you to arrange your affairs more efficiently, to ensure that this does not happen under my baton. Thank you!'

He turned his attention, next, to Gayle Potten and her flute, although the flute didn't even get a mention in his criticism, as he addressed his contumely entirely to her attire. 'Ms Potten, may I ask you to, for God's sake, wear something that covers your body. You look like you've just come from a burlesque performance, and have done every time I've seen you. You need to dress more appropriately, my good woman, to be a member of this band.'

Harold Grimes had been left till last, as Dashwood was in a state of utter disbelief as to how he had ever been allowed to join the band, and had made his mission for this evening, to find out. 'Mr Grimes,' he started. 'How long have you been a member of this band?'

'Two years – no, I tell a lie. Two and a half years.'

'And how long have you been playing the trumpet?'

'About the same time.'

'Pray, tell he how that is so, that you could become a member, when you had just commenced playing the instrument?'

'I used to come along to practices with my lady friend, Gayle – plays the flute – and Myles suggested I had a go at an instrument, then I could join in, instead of just sitting on the sidelines.'

'And how long was it before you were able to participate in the rehearsal sessions?'

'Oh, not long.'

'And yet I found you marking in the notes on your part, earlier in the evening. Can you explain that to me?'

'Easily. Once I got the hang of some of the notes, the last Musical Director but one wrote very simple parts for me, for all the pieces they were likely to play, and spent some time going through them with me, until I knew them off by heart. That's what I said earlier. I'm not used to 'reading' music. I can play it if I know it, and it's not too difficult, but this thing you've given us this evening just looks like a load of hieroglyphics to me.'

A silence fell, after this little speech, and Dashwood stood absolutely still, his eyes clamped tight shut, for a good ten seconds. Then he opened them again, and with a falsely bright smile, said, 'There is just one announcement, before we finish for the evening. I need to get a feel for the acoustics in the church for our performance, and I want to do this as soon as possible, so that I can work out the instrumental seating for the actual performance.

'I should like you to come along after the Sunday morning service, if you're not already there, with your instruments, and we'll just play through something that you're familiar with – God willing that such a piece exists! It shouldn't take up too much of your time, for those of you who have luncheon appointments. And just one more thing – if there are any of you who would like some private tuition, I am available for hire, at very moderate rates. Thank you very much for your attention this evening, and I shall see you all on Sunday. And remember – practise, practise, practise!'

That ten seconds of silent reflection with his eyes closed must have done him the world of good, as he had ceased to be the power-crazed dictator that they were just getting used to, and suddenly, butter wouldn't melt in his mouth. He either had a dual personality, or it was the mention of making a few bob out of some of them from lessons. Who could tell?

As they filed outside, Myles piped up with, 'Back to ours again?' to be answered with a resounding 'Yes'. They had an awful lot to get off their chests after enduring such a harangue, and, at least when they got back to The Grange, Acker gave them such a joyous welcome, as if he'd been alone for days instead of for a couple of hours, that he raised a smile from everyone.

Chapter Four

Saturday 10th July – conversations

'He's an absolute pill,' declared Myles to Myrtle, gathering things together for a barbecue, as the weather was so glorious.

'I know, Myles, but we've got to stick it out until after the concert. The vicar would be so disappointed, and you know how he looks when he's been let down – just like a kicked puppy. Anyway, it's a point of honour, and you agreed,' she replied, assembling the various utensils needed for handling food over real flames. 'And put your apron on; you'll frighten the horses.'

'No one can see me out there. You'd need a step ladder to see over those hedges, and I don't give a fig, if anyone wants to go to that much trouble, just to have a look at little old me,' was his unconcerned answer. 'And as far as the band goes, I'm already gritting my teeth so much, that I think they'll be worn down to the gums, by the time we get to the concert.'

'He was particularly horrid last night, wasn't he?'

'Horrid? He was positively poisonous! I've been using a three-and-a-half reed for years. How dare he! And as for what he said about you, I could have throttled him.'

'Well, at least he was fair, and verbally crucified each and every one of us, I suppose. Just try to stick it out, then we can tell him that we no longer require his services, and we can go back to the way things used to be,' said Myrtle, offering her husband words of comfort in his time of need.

'Have you got that meat out of the fridge? Ah, the way things used to be; and just a few short weeks ago. Sometimes it feels like a lifetime ago, and those times are just distant memories.'

'Don't get maudlin. I'll just take this tray of stuff outside, so that it's ready for you to get started. The charcoal should be hot enough by now.'

As Myrtle disappeared through the back door, there was a knock at the front door, and Myles trotted off to answer it, making sure he had his apron tied on securely. 'Hello, old chap. What can we do for you, on this sunny summer's day?' he asked, finding Edmund Alexander standing on the doorstep looking particularly glum.

'I need someone to sound off to. Sorry to bother you and all that, but the most ghastly thing's happened.'

'Come through and tell us all about it,' offered Myles. 'We're just starting a barbecue, and I always cook far too much for just the two of us. Why don't you join us for a bite to eat, and get whatever it is off your chest?' As he said this, he turned round and started to walk through the house,

Staring after him in disbelief, Edmund realised that Myles had got something off more than his chest. His back view exposed, it became obvious that he was stark naked under his apron, and the keyboard player was mesmerised as he trailed in his wake, by the bobbing of the brown buttocks beneath the apron strings, their colour confirming that nakedness was no new fad for Myles.

'I hope I haven't called at an inconvenient time,' he said, wondering what on earth was going to meet his gaze when he got outside. Would Myrtle be similarly un-attired?

But he was soon relieved of this worry. Myrtle met them at the back door, modestly attired for the hot weather, their golden retriever, Acker, bouncing round her legs, and welcomed him, explaining that Myles simply didn't like wearing clothes in the house or garden. He made an exception for band nights, but, if no one was expected, this was how a visitor would find him. 'And at least he's wearing an apron,' she concluded, with a little smile.

Myrtle was sensibly clothed in a sleeveless tee-shirt and shorts, and totally dispelled the aura of the bizarre that Myles' near-nakedness had lent to the trek through the house.

Moving over to the barbecue, Myles asked, 'So, whatever's got your goat, Edmund, old fellow. You looked about as jolly as the angel of death when I opened the door to you.'

'I've just had a phone call from the vicar.'

'What's so dire about that? At least he wasn't standing on your doorstep, actually bleating into your face – I say, old chap, no offence meant; always glad to see you and all that.' Myles was quick to identify a faint nuance of disapproval in his comment, at Edmund's visit, and was quick to dispel it, as it had been quite unintentional; just an unfortunate wording on his part. 'You know what the old blether's like.'

'I do now!' answered Edmund, his voice deeper than usual, and his face clouding over. 'Do you know what that bastard's done – sorry Myrtle, not fit language and all that, but I'm really steamed up.'

'Don't apologise, Edmund. I said an awful lot of equally bad words yesterday evening, when everyone had gone home, so be my guest. What *has* the vicar done? He's usually as mild as milk.'

'The bastard has only gone and sacked me as church organist.'

'Never!' exclaimed Myles

'He can't!' declared Myrtle, shocked into speech.

'He damned well has!'

'Well, who's going to play the organ on Sundays, now?' Myles was first to enquire.

'Can't you guess? Someone, perhaps, who can actually play the thing, and not mess up every hymn?'

'No!' Myrtle had worked it out.

'Not that Dashwood horror?' So had Myles.

'Got it in one! And I'm just discarded like an old rag, after all these years of service. Not even a proper 'thank you and goodbye'. Just a brush off, and his reverence was sure I'd be relieved, as it had been such a struggle for me, etc. I'm so furious, I could throttle both of them!'

'And we'll bloody well help you,' offered Myles. 'It was

that smarmy dog-collared bugger who foisted Dashwood on us in the first place. I never thought he could be so two-faced, and here was us, talking about not disappointing him about the concert.'

There was a full minute of silence, as all three were lost in thought, then Myrtle spoke. 'We've still got to go through with that. I don't give a flying fig about disappointing the vicar any more, after this, but we mustn't disappoint the charity. Of course, I don't give a damn about his church restoration fund now, but we can't let the Air Ambulance suffer because of pettiness. Yes – I know this isn't petty, but we ought to rise above it, just until after the concert, then we can tell them both where to stuff it.'

'Wise words, my dear; wise words.'

'But what about *me*?' wailed Edmund. 'What am I going to do? He's taken over the accompaniment at the band practices as well.'

'You're going to turn the pages for him like a good little boy, and leave the rest to me; that's what you're going to do. I have the nugget of a plan forming in my head, which I'll have to refine, but I'll tell you about that, when I've figured it all out.'

'Oh, come on Myles; don't be mean. What are you thinking of doing?'

'Not yet, my pretties. I need to work out the details, then I'll let you in on it. Fear not, for help is at hand,' he declaimed, brandishing a barbecue fork in the air like a sword.

'Silly sod!' said Myrtle. 'Now you've dripped fat all down your apron. It's lucky you were wearing it, or you'd have basted your own sausage!'

As Edmund wandered disconsolately round the walled garden, waiting for the food to be served, he found himself approaching the south-east corner, where the wall that divided the front garden from the back, joined the perimeter wall, and just stared, surprised out of his glum frame of mind.

'Myles,' he called in astonishment. You've got a positive jungle over here. These surely can't be those plants you put in a few years ago: the ones we said would never survive, because they were sort of tropical.'

'They are, old son,' called back Myles from his position in front of the barbecue. 'The walls protect them, and the bricks hold the heat, like a night storage heater. I told you all they'd grow, and no one believed me. Well, look and believe now. Look and believe!'

'It's astonishing. I'd never have thought it possible, but they're magnificent,' called back Edmund, staring at two palms, a whole cluster of large-leaved plants that looked very alien in such temperate climes, and a variety of large ferns and other exotic growths, obviously flourishing in their position, and with no intention whatsoever of curling up and dying.

'It's always good to be proved right,' returned Myles, turning a row of sausages and considering them done. 'Come on, Edmund! Grub up!'

Lester Westlake entered The Clocky Hen, feeling instantly battered by the volume of the music from the jukebox, and the babble of conversation, and was glad of it. He was still smarting about being asked to put, not 'a', but a pair, of socks in it – his saxophone, that is – the night before.

He knew that this particular pub was always heaving on a Saturday lunchtime, due to the amount of custom it got from the Wild Flowers Estate, and he craved the noise and the crush, to curb the incessant ranting of his brain, about how unfairly he had been picked on. He was egotistical enough to have ignored the cutting and acerbic comments that had been levelled at the others, remembering only his own embarrassment and ire.

As he approached the bar, a voice hailed him, and he saw Harold Grimes perched on a stool, a nearly empty pint glass on the bar top, in front of him. 'Hello there, me old mate, Lester. What'll you have? I was just about to order?'

'A pint of best,' he responded automatically, and then couldn't make up his mind whether he was glad or not of the familiar company. Granted, he had sought anonymity by not going to The Leathern Bottle, but the sight of Harold, one who would understand how he was feeling, was a positive, rather than a negative. Sitting together at practices had forged a bond between them. Their instruments were different from the others, and that made them kinsmen, in Lester's eyes.

'Come and prop yourself up next to me here, and tell me what's up,' called Harold across the tops of the heads of the people who still separated them. 'You look like you've lost a shilling and found sixpence.'

'It's just last night,' Lester replied, finally fighting his way through to the bar, and settling beside his comrade. 'That bloody, pompous dipstick! Socks? I'll give him bloody socks, and not where he's expecting them either.'

'Don't let him get to you. He'll get his comeuppance when we drop him like a hot potato after the concert.'

'Do you think so?' Lester had not considered this idea.

'Of course he will. Can you see Myles and Myrtle putting up with all this shit once we've done our bit? No, we'll go back to practices at theirs, and it'll be just like before.'

'I don't know how many more rehearsals I can put up with,' Lester admitted. 'It's worse than being at school. There's not another person on this planet who could speak to me like that and not get a bunch of fives.'

'Just let it all go over your head. Unless he's speaking to me personally, I tune him out, and think of something else. Why don't you do the same?'

'I can't! I can't! I just can't! He's so damned superior that he makes me feel like a five-year-old who's not done his homework.'

'So, have you been practising, then? To make Sir happy?'

'Well, no, actually, I haven't. Every time I look at the music case, I can feel my temper rising, and I don't want to play a note, because it'll make me think of him again, and then I just get so full of rage. Who does he think he is?'

'A little man, with nothing else in his life but making other people's a misery.'

'You're right! I've got to get a grip, otherwise I'll just pack the whole thing in, and there's nothing else around here that I enjoy so much.'

'You can't do that! We need you! *I* need you! Who am I going to sit with if you bugger off? And you're right about Dashwood. I could have wrung his scrawny neck for him last night. It's just as well we went off to old Myles's, or there might have been murder committed, and that wouldn't be good for the village's reputation, now would it?'

'Well, I'll come tomorrow, because it's not a proper practice, but I'm not coming next Friday,' Lester announced somewhat aggressively.

'Sulking or hiding?' Harold asked, genuinely curious.

'Neither,' Lester replied. 'It's business, actually. I have a prior engagement.'

'Ooh, prior engagement. Mr Hoity-Toity, are you, now?' Harold was in just the mood to pull the younger man's leg.

'Don't be silly, Harold. I've just got something else on, and I can't make it. It's not because of him, because if it'd been at Myles's, I still wouldn't have been able to make it. You know I have to miss a session now and again, because of work. It just can't be helped, but this time, I'm really glad to have an excuse not to go.'

'Well, at least you won't have to listen to Myles going on and on about his time in the RAF,' comforted Harold. 'I found out that he only spent three years in it. From the way he talks, you'd think he'd been a career man. Sometimes it makes me sick! Me, I spent my whole life in the army – never got anywhere, because I was always getting into scrapes and getting busted down whenever I got promotion, but I never talk about it. Him, he's all talk and no 'do'. You'd think he'd joined as a beardless boy and only recently retired, the way he goes on about it all the time.'

'I know what you mean,' Lester agreed. 'It does get a bit much sometimes, but I always take that as a signal for another glass of wine. It might mean that I drink rather too much, but it gives me that relaxed feeling, where I can just let it all go over my head.'

'Well, that's exactly what you should do with our rather less

57

than charming MD.'

'You're quite right there. He just seems to be able to get to me. I need to develop a thicker skin, before I have to spend any more time in his unpleasant company – tomorrow excepted. Do you want a refill in there?'

'Good lad!' said Harold, handing over his again empty glass.

The take-away food shop on the High Street always put a few battered metal tables and chairs on the pavement outside during the good weather in the summer, and served teas, coffees, cold drinks, and slices of shop-bought cake, enlivened by a squirt of artificial cream on the top to give it a more home-made look.

Myrtle Midwynter sat in one of these chairs now, a cup of frothy coffee and a plate with a half-eaten slice of Battenberg cake on the table in front of her, completely lost in thought. Myles had decided that he would do the decent thing, and was practising his clarinet with the sort of gusto that had driven her out of the house to seek some peace and quiet.

So completely abstracted was she that she failed to notice a familiar face approaching, and only became aware that she was about to get company when a voice called, 'Coo-ee, Myrtle. Order me a coffee, will you?'

Damn and blast it! It was Vanessa Palfreyman: the last person she wanted to see or talk to at the moment, but she'd have to invite her to sit down, and try to discourage her from talking about the one subject that she considered absolutely and undisputedly closed. 'I'll just go in and order another one for myself, as well. This one's gone cold,' she answered, and then swore under her breath. Why did she have to indicate that she was going to linger. She could just have drained her cup, and said she was in a hurry, and had to be somewhere else. See where good manners got you, these days? Up shit creek without a paddle, that's where they got you.

Returning to the table, she found Vanessa sitting there with a look of determination on her face, which was slightly marred by the fact that she kept having to hold a handkerchief to her nose, into which to sneeze. Myrtle's heart sank when the first words the other woman uttered were, 'Why won't you come hiking this year? We've always done it. You've had a good time, haven't you? Why stop now?'

'Because I simply don't want to do it anymore, Vanessa, and that's the end of the matter, as far as I'm concerned.' Be firm; that was the way to handle things.

'But why? I don't understand. Have I done something, or said something, to upset you? If I have, I'm sorry, and I'll do anything to put it right.'

'It's nothing like that, Vanessa. I just don't want to do it anymore, and that's that. Oh, for Heaven's sake, don't start crying,' Myrtle said, in an exasperated voice. 'There'll be other people that will want to go hiking with you, and we'll still see each other at band practice.'

'But that's not the same, and you know it. Oh, what am I going to do?' she wailed into her handkerchief.

At that point Myrtle lost her rag, and snapped, 'You're going to start acting like a grown-up, and you're going to accept my decision without any of these stupid histrionics, and if I hear that you've been going around crying on anyone else's shoulder, you'll have me to reckon with. Now finish your coffee and leave me alone. I'm going home now, and I don't expect to be disturbed again today. Do I make myself clear?

Now, go home and get some practice in on that double bass of yours. The way that man went on last night, anyone listening would've thought we were all Grade One, and getting a good dressing down from our teacher.'

'You're right, Myrtle,' replied Vanessa, blowing her noise in a very noisy fashion. 'He made me feel completely incompetent, and everyone else, as I remember it. I could've throttled him at the time. I'm glad we went back to yours for a good old bitch. It made me feel much better. Thanks. And I will try to find someone else to come hiking with me,' this last uttered in a voice without a shred of hope in it.

'That's the ticket,' replied Myrtle, relieved that she had managed to change the subject. 'See you tomorrow morning, after service.'

'You know I can't attend the service, don't you? That vicar doesn't like me, and I'm not going there to be glared at all the way through the sermon.'

'Don't be so sensitive, Vanessa. Either grow a thicker skin, or get a life. Or both!' on which prickly advice, Myrtle turned her back, and headed home to The Grange, her craving for peace and quiet totally unfulfilled.

When Myrtle arrived back at The Grange, Myles was, unusually for him, wearing a pair of shorts and sitting on a chair in the kitchen. 'Hey!' she called, 'You've got your togs on.'

'Well, I've got one tog on, to be accurate,' he retorted, 'I've been waiting for you, because I want to talk about something, and putting the shorts on sort of added dignity to the fact that I wanted to ask you something quite serious.'

'What's that?' asked Myrtle, pulling out a wheel-backed chair and sitting down opposite him.

'You know what we've been discussing lately?'

'Of course I do. How could I not?'

'Well, I just wanted to make sure that you're absolutely sure you want to go ahead with it. I mean, it's a huge step to take, and I don't want you feeling pressurised into it.'

'It was *my* idea, if you think back. And no, it's what I want to do, whatever the consequences.'

'And you're absolutely positive? Once we do it, there's no going back.'

'I couldn't be more positive. Now, stop looking all serious, and let's take a jug of Pimm's and lemonade out on the lawn, and have a little sit in this glorious weather. It just seems to be getting hotter by the day. I know it's summer and all that, but it is England, too, and hot weather and England don't often go together. Come on! Off with those serious shorts, and let's get ourselves outside again.'

In the back garden of 3 Columbine Cottages, which backed on to the large grounds of The Grange, sat three figures, sipping (maybe even gulping a little, at times) glasses of sangria. The garden was Gayle Potten's, and her guests were Wendy Burnett (minus her oboe for once) and Geraldine Warwick (who may have had her piccolo concealed in her handbag, it was so small), and was there reluctantly, as she and Gayle were not exactly bosom buddies.

Gayle had phoned them up that morning, and suggested that, as the woodwind section, they should have a small council of war. 'Why didn't you ask Myles to come round?' asked Wendy Burnett, who knew a little more about Myles than most people in Swinbury Abbot, and wanted to see how Gayle would react.

'Because I thought he might strip off as soon as he got into the shelter of the garden. You know what he's like, and I didn't want to spend all afternoon being confronted with his dangling "charlie",' answered Gayle truthfully.

'Harold and I asked him and Myrtle round for supper one evening, and as soon as he got through the back door, he was pulling off his tee-shirt, and by the time we got to the table, he was buck naked. It quite put me off my cannelloni.'

'Well, I wouldn't mind,' commented Wendy Burnett, a sort of dreamy look coming over her rather pointy features.

'Forget it, sister,' Geraldine Warwick advised. 'Those two are set for life. I don't fancy your chances there at all.'

'You never know,' Gayle opined. 'If you've got a couple of tricks up your sleeve, seduction-wise, you just might pull it off.'

'So long as you don't turn them too fast,' added Geraldine Warwick, a bitchy smile on her face as she looked over at the flautist.

Returning, not exactly to the same subject, but to the same area of interest, Wendy asked Gayle, 'Why don't you and Harold move in together? He only lives a few yards away, in Honeysuckle Terrace. It would a lot cheaper to have just one household to run.'

'It would,' answered Gayle, with a little smile, 'But I like my own bed at night, and I have no intentions of sharing it again. I don't mind spending the odd night at his, or him staying over here now and again, but nothing else. Besides, I've got my garden to think of. His is just grass – not a shrub, or a tree, or a

61

flower in sight. His garden reflects the sort of life he's lived. Me, I like colour and variety, so I'm staying put here for the foreseeable future, and that's definite.'

And in any case, she thought, Harold was OK for marking time with, but if a better offer came along, she might just take it. Myles, for example, was rather yummy, and she did so like men with moustaches.

'Anyway, that's not why we three have met again, and not in thunder, lightning, or in rain.' She used a cracked and high-pitched voice for this sentence; a sop to the play from which she had adapted the words. 'We're here to discuss what the hell we're going to do about our darling band. It's been absolute ruined by *that man*, and I, for one, have had enough of it. What do you two suggest?'

'Take out a contract on him,' suggested Geraldine Warwick, with a smile. 'We could get a hit-man – I've got all of three pounds and twenty-seven pence in my purse, right this minute, that I'm willing to donate.'

'I don't think that'd get us very much,' commented Wendy Burnett, glumly. 'I think we're just going to have to do what Myles suggested last night, and put up with the miserable bastard until after the concert. Then we can tell him to sling his hook.'

'Perhaps we could rig up the organ to electrocute him at tomorrow morning's service? Did you hear that the vicar had given Edmund the elbow as organist?'

'Yes. It's all over the village grapevine, and don't be an ass, Geraldine. With our luck, the old sod would call in sick, and then someone else would get the benefit of God knows how many volts through their body.' In a more practical vein, Gayle briefly hinted at a boycott of rehearsals, but that was a non-starter, as they really did need to improve, and improve considerably, before their performance in the church.

'We'll just have to wait it out. It's not that long, now. Just grit your teeth, and try to ignore what he says,' was her final bit of advice. 'Tell the others to hang on in there, and if Cameron McKnight throws a hissy fit, offer to grit his teeth for him –

they're false, anyway, so at least we could save him the trouble.'

This raised a small titter and, as Gayle refilled their glasses, ice tinkling in the jug, drops of condensation dripping off it, as it was tipped, to pour the refreshing liquid, they sat back in their chairs to enjoy the sunshine and put all thoughts of Campbell Dashwood out of their heads, on this lovely, lovely afternoon.

In the back garden of The Limes, on the Stoney Cross Road, Gwendolyn Radcliffe, who could be a martyr to her arthritis, was taking advantage of the sun warming her bones and easing the pain, and weeding a border in front of the trees that stood at the end of the garden. She had just managed to remove what she hoped was every trace of the roots of a particularly stubborn dandelion, when she heard a car draw into her drive, and a car door slam.

She was still struggling to her feet, when Cameron McKnight marched round the side of the house, and stood still for a moment, staring at her belligerently. 'What do you want?' she asked, equally confrontational.

'I want you to refuse to take the part of first violin. You know I'm a better player, and I've been 'first' ever since we started this band.'

'I shan't! You weave about, and flourish your bow like some virtuoso player, but your tuning's rotten, so it is. I'll do a much more tuneful job as 'first', and you know it,' she retorted.

'I know no such thing!' he replied, in challenge. 'You haven't got the first idea about vibrato, which really gives the music soul.'

'And you do so much of it it's hard to tell exactly which note you're supposed to be playing. The composers would turn in their graves if they heard the wibbly-wobbly mess you made of their melodies.'

'You poisonous old bag! I do not play out of tune!'

'Yes, you do!'

At this point, both of them stopped and looked at one another, and fell silent.

After a short while, Cameron spoke again, only in more reasonable tones. 'You know who's put us at each other's throats, don't you? It's that pill, Dashwood. We've always got on perfectly well before.'

Seeing her face, he corrected this by adding, 'Well, most of the time. But we've never been at daggers drawn in the past, have we?'

'No, Cameron, but I still want my turn at 'first',' Gwendolyn stated adamantly.

'And you shall have it, but you'll find the part much more difficult than 'second', and I don't think you'll be able to cope.'

'We'll just have to find that out, won't we, eh?'

'Fair enough, and if you're anything like me, you're probably still smarting from the insults that old bugger rained on us last night.'

'Too right, I am! What a stinker that man is! And could he do any better? I doubt it. I phoned Fern Bailey this morning, and she was in tears, the poor girl, and all because of what *he* said to her last night. But we'll not let him unsettle us, will we? Truce?'

'Truce, you stubborn old besom.'

'Do you fancy coming inside for a cup of tea?'

'I'd love to. And we can have another good bitch about our so-called Musical Director.'

'Delighted! Follow me,' she instructed, and made her way slowly towards the back door. They'd all been together too long to squabble like this. Really! That horrible man was destroying the camaraderie that it had taken a decade to build, and it just wasn't on.

Campbell Dashwood sat on the very edge of an armchair in the vicar's study, sipping tea daintily from a china cup, his little finger stretched out as far as it would go, as a demonstration of his refinement in such matters.

'They really are an awful shambles, Vicar. If you hadn't asked me to intervene, I doubt whether there would have been much of a concert, if there was any concert at all.'

'They've always muddled through in the past,' replied Rev. Church, slightly defensively. 'I had no idea thing were in such a bad way. I mean, we've always collected goodly sums for the Air Ambulance, and there's been no sign of the donations flagging.'

'That's Christmas, Vicar, if you'll excuse me pointing out the obvious. People are more generous at Christmas, and will give to a good cause just because the season makes them feel more generous. Put the same quality of music before them at the end of August, and you'll have a riot on your hands, I can assure you.'

'Oh dear, so it's serious, then?' Rev. Church put down his cup and saucer and stared worriedly at the little man sitting on the other side of his desk.

'Very serious. Did you ever go to one of their so-called band practices?'

'No, Mr Dashwood – er, Campbell. I usually take a confirmation class on a Friday evening, and it doesn't finish until half past eight. That was why we called round at the time we did the other Friday. I was only just free, and available for our visit.'

'Did you not notice how much alcohol was being consumed?'

'Not really,' replied the vicar, blushing as he remembered his own glass of wine, that had been thoughtfully put on a small table for him. 'Do you not approve of alcohol?'

'Never a drop touches my lips, Vicar.'

'Not even at Communion?'

'That is the one exception to my rule; but other than that, I do not drink a drop. It's the devil's instrument, is alcohol, and causes all sorts of terrible behaviour as a result of too much being taken.'

Rev. Church had left the door of his study slightly ajar, and could see his wife, Olivia, hovering there, waiting to see if she was needed. And she was, and realised it, tapping gently on the door, before entering the room with an apologetic look on her face.

'I'm terribly sorry to disturb your discussion, but I'm afraid there's someone at the back door that you really ought to talk to,' she informed her husband. 'I think they could be in need of your services, and I could hardly turn them away.'

'I'm sorry, er – Campbell, but I shall have to go. So much pastoral work to be done, even in a rural community. If you would please excuse me, I'll see you out.'

When he had closed the front door, he made his way through The Parsonage to the back door, but found no one there but his wife. 'What's going on? Have they gone away?'

'No, they're still here,' she informed him, wrapping her arms around his neck and pulling him towards her. 'It's me that's in need of your services. Now you've got rid of that horrid little man, you can give me a kiss.'

Which he did – with gusto! Although their children had grown up and left home, and they were both in their late forties, they were still in love, and a fine example to many others who lived in Swinbury Abbot.

As they drew apart, Olivia said, 'I don't think I like that Dashwood man very much. A few of the band members have been talking to me on a Sunday after church, and he sounds very spiteful and cruel, from what I've heard.'

'I don't like him either, now. I thought, originally, that he'd been sent from above, as the answer to the band's lack of musical direction, but I'm coming round to the opinion that he was sent by a completely opposite supernatural being, from rather hotter climes. I shouldn't have interfered, but I don't know how to put things right.

'And as for replacing Edmund with *him* as organist – I must have been out of my mind. Granted, Edmund doesn't play very accurately, but he's always been there when needed, for weddings, baptisms and funerals, without a word of dissent. This cove wants to introduce all sorts of fancy organ voluntaries to the services, says he'll have to consult his diary for anything other than Sunday services, and I've had a nasty premonition that he's after the post of choir master,' replied her husband, ending with a deep sigh of resignation.

66

Chapter Five

Harry Falconer wandered downstairs, late for once, as it was his day off, and headed straight for the kitchen to brew a cafetière of coffee. Stopped in mid-stride, however, he looked at the mess that greeted him on the kitchen floor.

Strewn across its usually shining tiles, which had been pristine when he went to bed, were the bodies of a bird, a vole, two mice, and a baby rat, all partly consumed. Since he had adopted Cadence, he had come down in the morning to the occasional smear of blood, and a tiny organ from some minuscule mammal that he could not identify, but obviously did not make good eating, and was, therefore, scorned by this new addition to the household.

With a sigh, and a muttered, 'You wasteful, murderous little beast!' he put on the kettle, then filled a bucket with hot soapy water and disinfectant, gathered up the remaining body parts and deposited them in the dustbin, before commencing to obliterate the evidence of their presence from his usually immaculate kitchen.

He was not used to this sort of behaviour, as his other cats spurned anything that didn't come out of a tin or a packet of dried food, and he was surprised at how annoyed he felt. It was only natural, after all, but 'natural' behaviour did nothing for the state his floor had been left in, and he wondered if this sort of thing was going to be a regular occurrence.

As he finished the mopping, the cat flap opened a fraction, and a little grey face peered through at him, something alive and squeaking in its mouth. 'Get out of here, you furry killing machine!' he shouted, brandishing the mop at it, and dropping water all over his nice clean floor. 'Damn and blast you!' he finished, squeezing out the mop once again, to soak up what he had just dribbled on the floor in his anger.

After morning service, Vanessa not entering the church until the congregation had dispersed, the band was entrusted to set out chairs for the 'sound practice', although those instructions included setting out the chairs in sections, according to instrumental grouping.

As they played through the 'Cornelius' March, Dashwood rushed from place to place in the church, his notebook out, busily scribbling in it wherever he stopped. At the end of the piece, he just shouted, 'Again!' and carried on with his perambulatory note-taking.

After the second rendition, he suddenly stopped dead, turned to the players and, singling out Gayle Potten, asked, 'Do you think you could moderate your breathing to something that is more appropriate to playing the flute. You are overblowing, and changing register willy-nilly, without a thought for the written pitch, and I will not have it. If you can't play the instrument competently, I suggest you leave the band temporarily, and have some lessons.'

Fixing them all with his beady eye, he added, 'And that goes for the rest of you. If you can't play your instrument properly, for God's sake find someone who can teach you how to, and show some mercy for anyone who has to listen to you. I shall expect much more from you on Friday than I've been getting. I just won't put up with people in *my* band who don't practise. Please accept this as due warning!'

At that, he turned on his heel and walked briskly out of the church without a word of farewell, leaving behind him a shocked silence. Rev. Church, who had been in the vestry disrobing, and dealing with the coinage from the collection, put his head round the door and asked, 'Did I really hear that?'

'You did, Vicar,' replied Marcus. Can you imagine what it's like for us, for the best part of two hours, on a Friday night?'

'Beastly!'

'Exactly!'

'I'm so sorry! I thought he was a godsend. It would appear that I couldn't have been more wrong.'

'Don't worry, Vicar. We've decided that we'll stick it out until after the concert, for the sake of the charities, but after that, we're going to give him the elbow. He's ruined all the fun we used to have, but if he gets us to play better for the performance, then it'll have been worth the suffering.'

'That's very charitable of you,' replied Rev. Church, genuinely relieved. 'And I think you've made the right decision. I'm just so sorry that I put you in this position.'

'These things are sent to try us, Vicar. Now, who's for a drink over at The Leathern Bottle?' suggested Myles.

'But what about our instruments, dear? We can hardly drag those into the pub on a busy Sunday lunchtime, can we?' asked his wife, sensibly.

At that moment, Harold Grimes exclaimed loudly and crossly, 'Pissed and broke.'

'Not again!' Gayle called over to him.

'Language,' retorted the vicar. 'You are in God's house, after all.'

'I said that one of my pistons was broken – as in 'piston broke'.'

'Oh, I'm so sorry. I totally misinterpreted what you said, Mr Grimes,' apologised the vicar.

'I'm staying on here,' decided Harold. 'I think one of these here valves might just need oiling rather than being actually broken, so I'll just take a couple of minutes now, and do the lot of them, before I put the thing away, or the next time I play, another one, or even both of the others, will act up. I've also got to tidy the hymn books and ASBs [Alternative Service Books] before I go.

'Tell you what, Vicar; you give me the key to the church, and we can all leave our instruments here for the time being. I'll finish off and lock up, then, when we've had our drink, we can come back and collect them, and I'll put the key through your letterbox. If you need it in the meantime, I'll be in the pub with the others.' Harold was a sides-man.

'That's very decent of you Harold. Many thanks. Well, I'll be off now, if that's all right?'

'Off you go, Vicar, and put your feet up until lunchtime. We'll make sure that no one steals the candlesticks.'

Harold dealt with all his necessary chores, and joined the others, only twenty minutes later, participating in with the latest Dashwood-bashing bitchery with the greatest of relish.

Monday 12th July

After they had finished their evening meal, Myles got out his clarinet and erected his music-stand, putting on it the new piece of music they had been given. 'Going to join me, my little flower?' he asked.

'What? You're going to practise? I don't believe it!'

'Oh, come on,' urged her husband. 'If we're going to go through with things the way they are, the least we can do is make the best of them, and how would it look if we turned out to perform, and simply couldn't play the music, because we'd been sulking like children?'

'You know exactly how to play me, even if the old bugger moans about your ability to play the clarinet.'

'I've even put a two-and-a-half reed in, just to satisfy the miserable old sod.'

'I'll get my music and cello, if you'll put up my stand for me. You know what a tangle I always get into. It's like some people and deckchairs. Me, I can't do music stands. They're like the worst kind of Chinese puzzle, as far I'm concerned,' she agreed, opening her cello case, from which she removed her instrument, looked at it in a rather perplexed manner before stating, 'My spike's not here. How the hell can I have lost that? In fact, *where* the hell can I have lost that? It doesn't seem possible.'

'Maybe it fell out in the church,' Myles suggested.

'Well, I don't see how I wouldn't have noticed.'

'We were all steaming mad when we left there. You just may not have noticed because of what that little prick said, so you mislaid your bigger prick while distracted. Sorry! Bad joke! Are you sure it's not in the case somewhere?'

'Absolutely! I've looked in every nook and cranny, and it's nowhere to be found.'

'Well, let's wander over to the church and take a look. It could be sitting there on the floor between the choir stalls now, just waiting for mummy to come and fetch it home.'

'Don't be silly, Myles,' she admonished him, but she smiled as she said it. 'Come on, let's get a move on, or there won't be any time left to practise.'

But there was no trace of the missing cello spike in the church, although the vicar came with them with the key, and searched alongside them. They checked in the choir stalls, in case someone had kicked it, and the vicar said he'd had nothing handed into him by the cleaners, who always came in on a Monday, to clear away any mess left by the regular tramping of Sunday feet.

'That's that then,' said Myrtle despondently. 'I'll just have to get straight on to the internet, and order another one. If I'm lucky, I should have it by Wednesday, and then I can get down to some proper practise, because I certainly can't use it as it is.'

'Never mind. It's only a couple of evenings without it. We'll just have to work extra hard on Wednesday and Thursday, to get up to snuff for Friday night's harangue.'

Chapter Six

Myrtle's new cello spike arrived, punctually, on Wednesday morning and, that evening, she and Myles ran through the new piece, first inaccurately and hilariously, then with a little more confidence, actually managing to be playing in the same bar at times, even if not on the same beat of it. After an hour they took a break, but neither made any comment whatsoever on how they were playing.

They followed the same routine on Thursday night, but neither of them could keep from commenting after they had finished. 'I think we've more or less got the hang of that,' offered Myrtle, both surprised and reluctant to admit that Dashwood had been right.

'I'm afraid I have to agree with you, old girl. We seemed to have improved no end and that's just two night's practise. Think what we could sound like if we did this more often.'

'I can't bear to think that the old bugger was right, but it would seem that we have been rather lazy in the past.'

'Much as I hate to say it, I have to agree with you,' said Myles, shaking his head in disbelief. 'I'll tell you what, kid; we'll dump him like we said we would, because I don't think there's any chance of him mellowing. If he treats us like that when he's only just met us, think how much worse he'll probably be in another year's time.'

'There wouldn't be any band left in another year. He'd have driven everybody away.'

'That's true enough. I say, Myrtle – here's an idea: we get rid of him, like we agreed, then we go back to having the practices here, but not like they used to be. We'll play first; still start at the same time, and rehearse for between an hour and a half and two hours, then we eat, and it doesn't matter how long we take over the meal, or chatting afterwards. We'll have done our playing, and we'll be free to indulge ourselves. What say you?'

'Myles! That's absolutely brilliant. That way, we benefit from playing more, *and* we get our social time. Would we still meet once a week, or go back to once a month, like we did before?'

'Oh, once a week, I think, but we could circulate between each other's houses: that way you wouldn't have to cook every week, and miss out on playing time.'

'Or,' suggested his wife, 'we could order food in from that take-away place in the High Street, if someone didn't feel like cooking. I mean, none of us is living on the breadline; we could all afford to chip in.'

'Even better, my sweetie. Let's get together in the pub after tomorrow night's practice, and put it to the others; see what they think of the idea.'

'I'm sure they'll love it. Oh, Myles, it's all going to be all right, and we shan't lose our beloved band after all.'

'Correct! Just that ghastly man'

Friday 16th July

The temperature had continued to rise since the weekend, and Friday was an extremely warm and beautiful day. The evening was exceptionally balmy, and Myles was surprised not to have received any phone calls with excuses not to spend the evening shut up in the meeting rooms. He knew they would have called *him*, because nobody wanted to speak to Dashwood, and would only have done so if their life depended on it.

Nearly everyone arrived at the hall well before seven o'clock, eager to set out the chairs and stands, and be ready for a prompt start. From the conversations that were being indulged in, it would seem that everyone had done exactly the same thing

74

as the Midwynters, giving practice at home a try, and had realised how beneficial it could be.

The last to arrive was the piccolo player, Geraldine Warwick, who puffed her way in at four minutes to seven, apologising for being late, which she, in fact, wasn't. 'I wanted to get here earlier, but I was having a little play through, and I totally lost track of the time,' she explained, then looked around her and asked, 'Where's Dashwood? I'd have thought he'd have been at the front, his baton poised, matches at the ready, waiting to roast the lot of us.'

A chorus of 'don't know' greeted her question, and silence descended, as they all took a moment to think.

'Perhaps the phone caught him on the way out,' suggested Gayle Potten. After all, it was always happening to her, and she often arrived at her destination a few minutes late, and out of breath.

'I'll conduct,' offered Edmund. 'He's taken me off keyboard – well, I assume he has, as he said I was suspended after last week, and that business with the church organ. I don't need to do anything fancy. We'll just have a run through while we're waiting for him. Knowing what he's like, he probably looked in the mirror to check his appearance before he left the house, and started having a row with the chap that looked back at him.'

'Ha ha! Very funny!' said Myles, slightly sarcastically, then continued, 'OK, old son, you're on. Everybody got their music ready? Beat us in then, Edmund, there's a good chap.'

'One, two, three, four … No, no, no! You've got to watch me, otherwise it won't work,' Edmund chided them.

'You're starting to sound like *him*,' called out Harold, ready to pull his leg if the opportunity presented itself.

'Oh, no I'm not,' their temporary conductor denied. 'Now, watch everybody. Here we go again, and concentrate. One, two, three, four …'

This time they managed to get all the way through the piece, admittedly with little tangents here and there by some individuals, but they had begun together, they had ended together (more or less) and had made contact with each other, at certain points, in between.

Edmunds congratulatory words were drowned in cheering from the rest of the band, who couldn't believe they'd done what they could not even have attempted the previous week. 'That was fun!' exclaimed Fern Bailey.

'Yes! Let's do it again,' urged Lester Westlake.

And so they did. And again, and the next thing they knew, someone looked at their watch and called for attention. 'Does anyone realise that it's a quarter past eight?'

'Good God!'

'Good Grief!'

'How did that happen?'

'What, already?'

'So where the hell's Dashwood?' Lester asked. 'Has anyone got their mobile with them? I think we really ought to give him a ring.'

Myles did the honours, but the answerphone cut in after eight rings, doing the same thing when he tried another two times. 'I know, ring the vicar, and see if he knows anything about where Dashwood's gone. He may have said something to him: might even have asked the vicar to get a message to us. You know what a scatterbrain the Rev. can be at times,' Myrtle suggested.

There was no answer from the vicarage either, but then Myrtle remembered that he would not quite have finished his confirmation class, and had probably unplugged the phone, so that they would not be interrupted. 'Why don't we just go round to his house?' she asked.

'Rather you than me,' interjected Geraldine Warwick, who lived next door to him.

'Why's that, then, Gerry?' asked Myles, wondering if the man had taken, like himself, to naked sunbathing.

'There's such a ghastly smell, every time I go out in the back garden. It's been like that for a couple of days now. The bins aren't emptied till Monday, but it smells as if he's got a dead cat in his, and I wouldn't put it past him, putting down poison for the little darlings as if they were vermin. He's got a real cruel streak in him, if you ask me. You've only got to look at the way he treats us, and we're human beings.'

'I wouldn't put it past a man like that to put poison down, either. There's not a sentimental bone in the man's body,' Myles agreed.

'Well, let's go and take a look, shall we?' suggested Wendy Burnett, hurriedly packing away her oboe.

'We can go round to the back and check that bin out, if he's really not in, and make sure he hasn't done anything absolutely beastly.' This suggestion came from Fern Bailey, who was very sensitive to criticism, and hadn't got over what Dashwood had said to her in earlier weeks. She'd quite like to see him reviled for some sort – any sort – of other unacceptable behaviour.

Myles took charge of the situation. 'We'll go to the front door first, and approach this situation like civilised people, just calling round to see why he didn't turn up for band practice. If nobody answers, we'll cut round the back way to his back garden, and see if we can't just get a peek into his dustbin. Without evidence, this is all just conjecture.'

Once out of the rehearsal building, their instruments locked in for safety, they decided to approach from the rear, as it would look odd to anyone who was out and about, to see a straggle of a baker's dozen of people making their way down the High Street at this time of day.

Off down Dark Lane they went, not knowing whether they felt foolish or confrontational, silent with thought, as they passed the back of the hall, The Parsonage, and St Back-to-Front's, finally reaching Back House Alley, which, after a right hand turn, took them on to the Stoney Cross Road. A left hand turn, and they were outside the front door of Wheel Cottage.

At this point, Geraldine Warwick owned up that she had brought her instrument with her, in case they didn't manage to resume playing that evening. It was, after all, only a piccolo, and not heavy or bulky, like a cello or a double bass. 'I'll just pop it through the door,' she said, guiltily, knowing that she would not have to trudge back to the rehearsal hall, now, 'And then I'll be right behind you.' Geraldine always felt better when she was behind someone else, being shy, self-effacing and easily upset.

Myles rang the doorbell and banged on the knocker, but there was no answer to his summons. He tried again, with a similar lack of success. 'The curtains aren't quite together, even though it's early for them to be drawn. See if you can see through the bit where they don't meet. You'd think he'd have the windows wide open on a sultry night like tonight, wouldn't you?' he asked, also wondering why the man had already drawn his curtains, when it was still perfectly light outside.

Gayle Potten, always up for a bit of nosy-parkering, squashed her face against the window pane and peered inside, suddenly pulling back with a look of disgust on her face. 'There seem to be an awful lot of flies in there,' she said, wrinkling her nose. It's not easy to see, because it's rather gloomy, but I can just make them out, crawling all over the place, and I can hear their buzzing through this window. It's only single-glazed, and hardly any use as a sound barrier.'

Myles gave the door one more hammering, then suggested they made their way round to the back of the house. 'We'll have a look at that dustbin, then see if we can't make ourselves heard at the back. If he's skulking in there for some reason, he might have taken refuge in the kitchen, never thinking we might advance from the rear.'

Although Wheel Cottage's frontage was right on the edge of the road, and had a fine privet hedge all round its boundary, it was easy to see where Campbell Dashwood's predecessors had pushed a way through where the hedge met the house, and it was still visible, although a little more overgrown than it must have been when he first moved in. 'I'll go first,' volunteered Myles, 'and hold the branches back for the ladies. When we're all through, regroup, and we'll approach en masse – a united front – to show our disapproval of his non-appearance after all the fuss he made about us not starting on time, and arriving promptly.'

It didn't take long to wriggle through the gap in the hedge, although Vanessa Palfreyman had a bit more trouble than the others, being rather, as her mother put it, 'big-boned'. Once more all together, they began to pussyfoot round to the back door, but soon the smell hit them, and they variously covered their noses, or fished out handkerchiefs to use as filters. The further they went, the stronger the smell became, and when they reached the back garden, one or two of them gagged.

'Check the bin,' ordered Myles, forgetting for a second about the foul smell just long enough to put up his hands and twiddle the ends of his moustache – in his mind, he was back in the RAF.

'Bin's empty,' reported Lester Westlake, none of the women having the stomach to look, in case there was something gruesome under the lid.

'It seems to be coming from the house. Look! He's got the top light of the kitchen window ajar. We'd better try to get inside and see what the hell's going on.' Myles was in his element, having his troops obey him without question, and taking charge of the situation without challenge.

'But it's not even locked,' gasped Gayle Potten, trying to ignore the signals from her stomach that it couldn't stand much more of the stench it was being asked to cope with. 'The door's open!'

That stopped them all in their tracks. Someone would now have to go in there and find out what was making that ghastly smell. It was Myles to the rescue again. 'This is no job for a lady,' he announced, with great bravado. 'You stay out here, and we men will go in and track down the source of the smell, and what exactly the situation is.'

'Too right we'll stay out here, and what's more, I, for one, am going back round the side of the house where it doesn't smell so bad. If I stay here another minute, I'm going to throw,' exclaimed Gayle.

'Me too,' agreed Wendy Burnett. The other women nodded their heads, not wanting to open their mouths again with that filthy whiff in the air, and they all retreated back round to the hedge to await developments.

From the relative fresh air of the perimeter, they heard the creak of the back door, as it was pushed open, and then there was absolute silence for a few seconds, followed by a positive bellow. 'Bloody hell!' echoed round to the side of the house, followed by, 'Let's get out of here! We've got to phone the police.'

Within seconds, the herd of men arrived to join them, with the exception of Edmund Alexander, who had had to have a quick peek, and then proceeded to be sick by the side of the house, heaving until he ran out of ammunition.

'Myles, you look as white as a sheet. What the hell did you find in there?' asked Myrtle, observing the faces of the other men, which were also pallid, and screwed into a variety of expressions of disgust and nausea. 'Tell me! Tell *us*, before we explode!' but there was suddenly an unseemly rush, in which she instinctively joined, to go round to see what all the fuss was about, then a general regret, as they wished they had not been so precipitate.

'He's dead!' said Myles, in a voice that sounded as if it did not believe itself, as the group reappeared at the side of the house, each looking as nauseous as Edmund. 'He's in there, dead as a doornail, the place full of flies, and there are maggots in his eyes and … I can't even think about it at the moment. It's just too ghastly, and I truly wish you ladies hadn't gone off like that to have a look. It was bad enough for us men. You will have nightmares for the rest of your lives, now.'

'We know! We saw!' said Myrtle, in a strangled voice, regretting giving in to her curiosity.

'I think I'm going to have nightmares, anyway,' declared Lester Westlake, fighting to retain the contents of his stomach. 'I don't think anyone, man or woman, is ever prepared for a sight like that. God, it must have been the heat this week that made him look that bad: that, and the fact that he hadn't shut that little window, letting in the flies, to do that to him.' He shuddered, and gave an enormous swallow, still engaged in the fight with his insides. 'What are we going to do about it?'

'Well, the first thing we're going to have to do is inform the police. Can we use your telephone, Geraldine?'

'Of course you can,' she agreed, 'but there's not much room in my little cottage for all of us to wait for them.'

'Agreed! I suggest, as our instruments are all safely under lock and key, that we close the back door – don't worry, I'll do it – then adjourn to The Grange for a stiff brandy or two, and wait for them there. There's no benefit in us hanging around like a gang of teenagers in a bus shelter, is there? I'll go in next door with you, Geraldine, and make the phone call, and you lot can get off to The Grange – you do have a key with you, don't you, Myrtle?'

'In my shorts pocket,' she confirmed.

'Right, well, off you go, and we'll join you in a few minutes. It shouldn't take long to report this, but it may take rather longer to get someone here to take charge, so I'll tell them to call at The Grange, and we'll all be waiting there for them. What's the time now?'

'Ten past nine.'

'Then we should be back at the house by half-past. See you then.'

Practicalities taken care of, Myles and Geraldine entered Tile Cottage to make the fateful telephone call – the one that would make this nightmare a reality, and bring God knows what in its wake.

Chapter Seven

Friday 16th July – telephone conversations

Duty Sergeant Bob Bryant: Hello, Market Darley Police. How may I be of assistance?

Myles Midwynter: I'd like to report finding a body.

BB: A dead body, sir?

MM: Of course, a dead body!

BB: Of an animal or a person, sir?

MM: Of a person – a very dead person.

BB: And who is this calling, sir?

MM: Mr Myles Midwynter from Swinbury Abbot.

BB: And who exactly is dead, sir?

MM: His name's Campbell Dashwood, and he lives – lived – in Wheel Cottage on the Market Darley Road.

BB: And how did he die? Was there an accident?

MM: No, we just found him dead at his home – in the kitchen, to be precise.

BB: And who would *we* be, sir?

MM: The members of the village band.

BB: So, let me get this straight, sir. You, and all the members of the village band, went round to this Mr Dashwood's house, and found him dead in his kitchen? Is that correct?

MM: Perfectly!

BB: This wouldn't be a joke, would it, sir? Or something you're doing for a bet?

MM: No, it bloody well *isn't* a joke! I've sent the women back to my house, and at least one of our number has lost the contents of his stomach, at what he saw in that kitchen.

BB: Sorry, sir, but I have to ask. There are so many hoax calls these days, you wouldn't believe it.

MM: Well, you'd better believe this, because I've seen it with my own eyes, and smelled it with my own nose. He's very dead, and it must have happened some while ago, because of the insect infestation. *Hurmmm*! Excuse me, but I felt a wave of nausea just describing it.

BB: I'll get some officers on it right away, sir. Are you staying there, or is there a number where we can reach you?

MM: No, I am *not* staying here. Nobody's likely to pinch that thing, nor pass by it to pinch anything else. The back door's not locked, so you won't have any trouble getting in. I'll be at home with the other band members. My number's Market Darley 717507. I'll be waiting for you. Oh, yes, how stupid of me. My address is The Grange, Beggar Bush Lane. It's easy enough to find. If you go to The Leathern Bottle in the High Street, there's a small road right opposite its car park. I'm the second house down, on the left.

BB: I've got that. Thank you very much for reporting this, sir. We'll be right on to it. Goodbye.

MM: Goodbye.

DI Harry Falconer: Hello, Falconer speaking.

Bob Bryant: Sorry to bother you on a Friday evening, but it seems we've got an unexplained death on our hands.

HF: Accidental, natural causes, or murder?

BB: We don't know yet.

HF: Where is it?

BB: Swinbury Abbot.

HF: Well, that's a new one on me. Who found the body?

BB: If you can believe it, the whole of the village band.

HF: Oh, bloody hell! It's going to be one those mad village cases again, isn't it?

BB: Looks like it. The address is Wheel Cottage, Stoney Cross Road, and I understand that the back door isn't locked.

HF: Do you have the name of the informant, and a contact number?

BB: It was a Mr Myles Midwynter, telephone number Market Darley 717507.

HF: And where does Mr Midwynter live?

BB: The Grange, Beggar Bush Lane.

HF: Where in the name of God is that? Oh, never mind, I forgot I've just installed a sat-nav, so I'll never get lost again. I'll get in touch with Carmichael, and you get a SOCO team and Doc Christmas out there. Have you phoned old Jelly? *(This reference was to Detective Superintendent Derek Chivers, who had earned the obvious nickname.)*

BB: Will do. Have done. Apparently it's a squelchy one, so have fun.

HF: Have fun yourself, Bob, and thanks a blinking bunch, for landing me with this at the start of another weekend. Why can't criminals work office hours? That's what I'd like to know.

BB: There's no answer to that one. Goodnight, Harry.

HF: Bugger off, Bob.

Detective Sergeant 'Davey' Carmichael: Hello.

DI Harry Falconer: Is that you, Carmichael?

DC: Oh, hello, sir. I didn't expect to be hearing from you, at this time on a Friday night. What can I do for you?

HF: We've got a body in Swinbury Abbot.

DC: Oh, blast!

HF: Are you in the middle of something?

DC: Yes, but it doesn't matter. It's not something that has to be finished tonight. I can easily slip out of it.

HF: I'm not even going to ask what that means. Look, I'll pick you up; save taking two cars. Bob Bryant says it's a nasty one, so a few minutes aren't going to make any difference either way.

DC: Righty-ho, sir! That means I don't have to stop until you arrive.

HF: Please, Carmichael; the mind boggles. No, no; don't explain, or I'll probably end up sorry that I asked. Just expect me sometime within the next twenty to thirty minutes. Bob's already getting on to sending out a SOCO team and Christmas.

DC: OK, sir. See you soon, then. Goodbye.
HF: Goodbye.

Back at The Grange

Rev. Church: Good evening. The Parsonage. Rev. Church speaking. How may I help you?

Myles Midwynter: Hello Vicar, Midwynter here. We've got a bit of a tricky situation up here at The Grange, and I wondered if you would come over and lend a hand. There are some of your flock in need of some comfort.

Rev. C: Is it absolutely vital, Myles? I had to go into the school to give a talk to the infants this morning, I had choir practice this afternoon, the confirmation class overran, and this is the first bit of free time I've had all day.

MM: To state it bluntly, Vicar, Campbell Dashwood is lying dead in his kitchen, and the band found him less than an hour ago. Some of the ladies are very shaken up.

Rev. C: Not another word, Myles. I'll grab an apple, and I'll be right with you. You can explain everything to me then. I'll go now, and get out my bicycle. Goodbye.

MM: Goodbye, Vicar.

Chapter Eight

Friday 16th July, 2010 – evening

As DI Harry Falconer drove over to Castle Farthing, he wondered how he would find his DS attired this time. During their last case together, Carmichael had become enthralled with old American police and detective shows on the television satellite channels, and had done his best to emulate them, to the immense disapproval of his inspector.

Falconer had originally been surprised to find his colleague coming into work with his head shaven, and sucking a lollipop – that had been Kojak – the first of many. He had managed to forbid him to wear false facial hair to emulate Hercule Poirot, to dress like a cowboy (*McCloud!*) or to wear a deer-stalker hat – Sherlock Holmes – and had made it clear that there were to be absolutely no violins, ever.

Well, Carmichael should have his violins tonight, along with a host of other instruments.

When he knocked on the cottage door, Carmichael's wife, Kerry, answered the door, with her mouth full of pins. Instead of risking several unscheduled piercings, she motioned him inside, and pointed to Carmichael, who was standing on a stool in the middle of the room, his head bent so that it didn't bump against the ceiling. He was draped in a long, black garment, which was in the middle of construction.

'Oh my God, Carmichael! Not Miss Marple. surely?'

'No, sir,' answered Carmichael, but before he could offer any other information, Falconer carried on with his speculations.

'Well, if it's Cagney and Lacey, don't expect me to play the part of Mary-Beth. If, for any reason, and I can't think of one off the top of my head, I should be unlucky enough to have to dress like a woman, there's no way I'm playing the part of a frump, so you can count me out now.'

'Don't be silly! I'm making him his Hallowe'en costume. I've started dead early, because I've got to make one for all of us, and he's the one I don't have constant access to. He's always off somewhere with you. Honestly, if you were a woman, I'd think you two were having an affair.' Kerry had removed the pins from her mouth, and was now capable of speech.

'Ha ha! Very funny!' said Carmichael sarcastically.

Falconer merely made a disgusted face, then tried to cover this up by clearing his throat, partially covering his face with his hand, as he did so. 'Come along, Cinderella: you shall go to the ball,' he urged, to cover his embarrassment.

'Don't be so daft, sir.'

Meanwhile, back at The Grange, the players were in various stages of shock. Gayle Potten had fastened herself on to a bottle of gin, and was drinking it, diluted only with a little water, at an alarming rate. The strings had gone into an exclusive little huddle, and shut up immediately anyone from another section approached them.

The only one missing from their numbers was Myrtle, who was bustling around the room, offering hot or cold drinks and distributing plates with little nibbles on that she had prepared for after the practice; but no one seemed very disposed to eat, which wasn't surprising, after what had happened earlier.

The woodwind players had gathered round the unused fireplace, and were discussing whether it could have been natural causes, or an accident, that had caused Dashwood to peg out. Harold Grimes joined them, a glass in his hand, and gave it as his opinion, that it was murder. 'I've got a strong stomach,' he informed them, 'and I went to have a little look-see when Myles came out. I just had a peek, while he was leaning against the wall. I thought I could see something sticking out of his chest, but I don't know if Myles noticed it. Hey, Myles …' he called, as the man in question drifted over in their direction, from his previous post by the front window, where he had been watching for the arrival of Rev. Church.

'What's that, Harold?'

'Did you see anything sticking out of Dashwood's chest? I was telling these here ladies that I thought I did – you know, when I went in for a couple of seconds, after you'd come out.'

'You must have damned good eyesight, old chap. I just got a general impression, then I high-tailed it out of there as fast as my legs would carry me: so, no, I didn't notice anything other than how absolutely ghastly it was, and how much I didn't want to be looking at it anymore.'

'The police will tell us what did for him when they arrive, and that shouldn't be too long. In the meantime, does anyone fancy a game of cards? Do you have a pack or two handy, Myles?' But no one else felt in the mood, and a slightly queasy Wendy Burnett was actually taken upstairs by Myrtle for a little lie down. The poor woman was shivering, as if it were midwinter, (*ha ha!*), and Myrtle ushered her up to one of the guest rooms, where she tucked her up under an eiderdown and told her to lie there until she felt better.

Back downstairs again, she discovered that alcohol was doing a better job of nursing than she could have managed herself, so she poured herself a giant gin and tonic and perched on the end of a settee, waiting for something to happen.

The only thing that did occur in the next few minutes, however, was the squeak, squeak, squeak of an approaching bicycle in need of oiling, and Rev. Church's voice calling a welcome as he let himself in and joined them.

After suitable greetings had been exchanged, the vicar asked them exactly what had happened – or what they knew of it, anyway. At first, all of them spoke at once.

'Dashwood's dead.'

'We found Dashwood dead in his kitchen.'

'Someone's done for that miserable sod, Dashwood.'

'That's not true! For all we know, he could've died from

natural causes.'

'There weren't nothing natural about that man!'

'Harold reckons he saw something sticking out of his chest.'

'There were flies everywhere, and the smell was indescribable. We thought it was a dead cat in his dustbin before we found him.'

'It was you suggested it was a cat.'

'I think Harold only said that – about something sticking out of him – to scare the ladies.'

'Well, he scared me, right enough.' This admission was from Edmund Alexander, who had already lost the contents of his stomach, but looked like his insides might be ready to search for anything they'd missed, the last time round. 'Do you mind if we stop talking about it until the police arrive? I feel really nauseous again.'

At this point in the proceedings, the men retired to the kitchen en masse, and the ladies regrouped themselves so that they made a semi-circle in front of the vicar, who had just plumped down into an armchair. The sexes had divided, as they did at many a lackadaisical party: the men, to chew the fat in the room where the refrigerator was situated, and the ladies, in this case, to seek comfort from their spiritual adviser.

'I'm afraid I don't quite know what to say,' Rev. Church began. 'I gather he's been an awful pain in the neck to all of you …'

'Arse!' interrupted Gayle Potten, rather drunkenly. 'He was a pain in the *arse*, not the neck. Neck's too polite for that bastard!'

'Hush, Ms Potten, you don't really mean to speak like that of the dead.'

'Yes I do! And, no, I won't regret it in the morning. With any luck, I won't even remember it in the morning. That piece of, oh, I don't know – he nigh on ruined our band, and we've been together for so long. Why did you foist him on us? What had we ever done to deserve *him*?'

'I had no idea what he was like. He came to see me with such sparkling references, I didn't see how there could possibly be a problem,' declared the vicar, blushing at his own lack of character judgement.

'I'll bet he only got those references so that he'd go away, and leave some other poor people in peace,' piped up Gwendolyn Radcliffe. 'You stretch out and have a little nap, Gayle. You look all-in.'

'More like rat-arsed!' commented Myrtle, who had just returned from upstairs.

'Myrtle, that's not very kind, and I'd be grateful if you'd moderate your language. Someone has died, if you've forgotten.'

'I haven't forgotten, Vicar. And I think it proves absolutely that there is a God, for he couldn't have chosen a more worthy person to strike down.'

There was a general murmur of agreement at this comment, quickly stifled, as the vicar looked around him, scandalised. 'I think we should sit here in silence, and say a little prayer, instead of making cruel comments. Now, eyes closed, please.'

'Dear Lord, thank you for removing a pariah from our midst, and delivering us from our only evil.' Myrtle could be heard to mutter, as she obediently closed her eyes and bowed her head.

Despite a SOCO team and the police doctor already having been summoned, and the inspector having to go via Castle Farthing, Falconer and Carmichael were the first to arrive at the locus, and made their way round to the back of the cottage, where they believed the door to be unlocked.

The first thing Falconer did, before even leaving the car was to make a brief phone call. 'This place is going to need someone on duty overnight, and I've decided that PC Proudfoot is due for something, in apology for spreading that rumour about you having cancer. I've just told him to get his arse out here right away, because he's on night duty right now, and told him that he can't be tired, as he spends most of his daytime duty hours asleep behind a broadsheet in various hidey holes at the station.'

'Good!' said Carmichael with feeling. 'He's actually had the nerve to start calling me 'Baldylocks', and I was stopped by one of the collators the other day, and she said she was glad to see my hair was growing back, and asked when had I finished my treatment.'

'What did you say?'

'Just that I wasn't ill, and Proudfoot had got things all wrong, then I scooted off back to the office to hide for a bit.'

'I don't blame you. I could cheerfully wring that man's neck sometimes. He's about as useful as a chocolate fire-screen, but at the end of the day, he's still an extra body when we need one.'

This deed done, they were both smiling as they got out of the car, Carmichael, as usual, looking like a living ironing board as he unfolded himself carefully out of the cramped (for his size) seat of the inspector's Boxster, but those smiles were soon to be wiped off their faces.

As they turned the corner to the rear of the cottage, the smell began to get to them, and both removed a handkerchief from their pockets, and clamped it against their mouths. 'Cor, that's a whiffy one!' commented Carmichael, as Falconer opened the back door and flicked the light switch.

'Good grief!' he exclaimed, in horror. Dashwood's body was slumped in a chair at the kitchen table, his head drooping backwards over the back of the chair. His face had made a good meal. Flies buzzed everywhere, and he had maggots squirming from every facial orifice. 'It doesn't take long for decomposition to set in in this heat, Carmichael. Carmichael? Where are you, Carmichael?'

A pathetic figure, its face pale and beaded with a cold sweat, re-entered the kitchen from the garden, trying to speak, but not quite managing it.

'Whatever's the matter, man? You look like death.'

'I know, sir. Sorry, sir,' said the figure, its capacity for speech now returning.

'Where the devil have you been?'

'Being sick in the dustbin, sir. You know I've got a weak stomach!'

'That was very enterprising of you. And I suppose if I asked you to hose it out, you'd be sick again, wouldn't you?'

'Yes, sir.'

'My day just gets better and better,' muttered Falconer, silently fuming, and sighed deeply.

But his mood slid back to that of the professional when he took a closer look at the body and saw that there was an object embedded in its chest. Whatever it was, it seemed to be made of metal, and he presumed that it went in quite deeply.

'SOCO's here, sir,' announced Carmichael unnecessarily, as they had heard two vehicles pull up outside, and figures were already entering the kitchen via the back door.

'Ah, my good Dr Christmas!' exclaimed Falconer, spotting the first of them. 'How the devil are you, Philip?' Dr Philip Christmas had worked on all the murder cases with them since Falconer and Carmichael had first been partnered together; at first because he was available, later, because he had been appointed Police Surgeon for the area.

'I'm fine. It's all them other buggers,' was his irreverent reply, followed by, 'That's a bit of an ugly customer. I wonder how long he's been there.'

'That's your job. You're supposed to tell us that.'

'I know. I was only speculating. Can you get that thing in his chest photographed *in situ*? I rather want to get it out, to see what it is'

'Same old Christmas,' commented the SOCO with the camera. 'Always wanting first dip into the bran tub, to try to get the best prize, aren't you, Doc?'

'Oh, I live for it, man. I live for it.' Christmas was in a frivolous mood, and Falconer wondered if maybe he'd had a drink before he received the call to come out here. If he had, it would only have been the one, for he was a scrupulous man, and would never have driven if there was even the slightest possibility that he was over the legal limit.

A camera flashed several times, as the photographer moved from place to place, recording the unidentified object from all angles, before he was ready to hand over to the doctor.

'There you go, Doc,' he said at last, and moved away from the grotesque object that sat in the chair, staring at the ceiling with squirming eye sockets.

'Where's that sergeant of yours?' Christmas asked. 'I haven't seen you without him once during the last year.'

'He's been sick in the dustbin, and Muggins here is going to have to be the one to clear it up. Our Carmichael has a weak stomach, you know. Anyway, I've sent him outside to get some fresh air. If he's going to be sick again, I'd rather he did it at as great a distance from me as he can get.'

'Good thinking. Now, evidence bag, please,' he requested, pulling on gloves. 'There she goes,' he said, putting gentle pressure on the object to remove it slowly. 'Here it comes. Now, what, in the name of all that's holy, is that thing?'

'That thing,' Falconer informed him, 'is a cello spike. And the band came here to find him earlier on, because he hadn't turned up for band practice. I wonder if one of them knew they would find him in less than glowing health? I think I'll borrow that, if you don't mind. I'll book it in as evidence tomorrow but, for now, it's mine.'

At ten o'clock, Falconer rang the doorbell at The Grange, and was greeted by Myles. 'You must be the police. Please come in and meet everybody. I'll introduce you. I'm Myles Midwynter, by the way.'

'Thank you, and I'm Detective Inspector Falconer, and this is my partner, Detective Sergeant Carmichael. Lead the way, if you would be so kind.'

At that moment, a golden retriever lolloped into the hall, examined those present, and headed immediately for Falconer, where the dog began to smell the inspector's crotch with great interest. Grabbing Acker by the collar, Myles finally managed to drag him off and deposit him in the dining room, shutting the door, so that he wouldn't be able to get out and resume where he had left off with his investigations of the inspector's trousers.

'I'm so sorry about that,' said Myles, looking, not shamefaced, but rather as if he were trying hard to suppress his amusement. Myrtle, who had followed the dog, and was now standing in the doorway of the drawing room, suddenly snorted, and began a real belly laugh.

'That dog goes right to the point doesn't he? He knows where all the interesting bits are!'

Falconer blushed a deep red with embarrassment, not only at what had just happened, but at the coarseness of Myrtle's remarks. Carmichael remained in the background. He was trying not to snigger but, nonetheless, he had a huge grin spread across his face from ear to ear, making him look quite insane, and possibly dangerous.

To break the ice that had metaphorically just materialised round the inspector, Myles said, by way of pertinent information, 'His name's Acker.'

'Like the clarinettist?' Falconer asked, recognising a life-line when he saw one.

'That's right. Not a lot of people remember Acker Bilk now, and assume it's just a weird name.'

'He's unforgettable, but then my taste in music is quite catholic, and spans all styles and eras.' Falconer was back on form now, and ready to get on with his job. A little return to the modicum of pomposity that was part of his character always restored him to a better humour.

'Oh, that's rather pertinent, given that you're both in the village band,' he said, pointing to a coloured steel engraving, hung on the wall. It showed a large open trunk, with inside it, a donkey, with a man on his back dressed garishly in blue, red and yellow, and written underneath was the phrase, 'My ass in a band box'.

'It's absolutely perfect,' their host answered. 'Especially as the rehearsals used to be here. I got it at an auction, for a song. I know it's a trifle foxed, but it's rather good, isn't it? We love it!

Myles led them into a room of chattering people, drinks in hands, the vicar plumb in the middle, looking a little bit embarrassed at the party that seemed to have erupted around him. When he had introduced everybody, Falconer asked if everyone was present, and if they had a room he could use, just for a short while, to speak to people alone.

'I won't keep any of you for very long,' he informed them. 'I just want to get an idea of who you are, and take your names, addresses, and contact numbers. DS Carmichael and I will call on you tomorrow in your homes, to take statements. I'm sure you're completely exhausted with what has happened, and could all do with a good night's sleep.'

When informed that Wendy Burnett, their oboe player, had gone upstairs to have a lie down, as she had suffered physically from the shock of finding Dashwood's body, Falconer requested that she be asked to re-join the others, and asked them to, perhaps, spend the intervening time trying to remember everything, no matter how small and insignificant it might seem to them, about finding the body.

At the end of his request, there was a chorus of groans. 'Do we have to think about it? I know I'm going to have bad dreams as it is,' asked Vanessa Palfreyman.

'I shall be relying on you to give me as accurate a report as it is possible for you to give. I'll speak to Mr Midwynter first, and then I want you to come along, one by one, to speak to me. There is, however, something that I'd like to show you first, he said, removing the cello spike, carefully protected by its evidence bag, from his pocket, and held it out for all to see.

'This was found embedded in Mr Dashwood's chest, and will no doubt prove to be the murder weapon. Myrtle gave a little cry of recognition and disgust, and her husband pointed unnecessarily, and said, 'But that's the cello spike that you lost, Myrtle!'

Myrtle was almost incapable of speech, after this shock appearance of her lost cello part, but managed to splutter out an explanation. 'We've looked high and low for that, Inspector. We nearly tore the house apart, then we went to the church and gave that a good old going over too. I had it when we played there, after morning service, but when I opened the case to get my instrument out on Monday, so that Myles and I could have a bit of a practice, it had disappeared.'

At the end of this dramatic statement there was a sudden rap on the front door, which made several of the women jump, and, on opening it, Myles found the intimidating figure of PC Merv Green – who was, in actual fact, a pussycat, but was just a little scary at first sight, due to his muscular build and his shaven head.

'Great!' thought Falconer. 'Good old Bob Bryant!' This paragon at the station had anticipated his need to be in two places at once, and had sent Green out, so that Falconer and Carmichael could get on with the interviews, and Green could sit in with the others, to make sure that no one had the chance to conspire with one of the others to spin a yarn.

'Come on through, Green,' he called. 'Your arrival is very timely. Myles here was going to conduct us to a room where we can interview people in private and, now you're here, you can sit in with this lot. They look as if they could do with a few of your hilarious tales of life in the Force, although I have advised them to go over, in their minds, everything that happened earlier on at Wheel Cottage.'

Green squeezed himself down on a sofa, between Gayle Potten and the not inconsiderable bulk of Vanessa Palfreyman. 'Well, that's me nicely settled then, between two beautiful ladies.' Gayle giggled drunkenly, which brought a frown of disapproval from Harold, and Vanessa blushed scarlet, and, pulling her arms close to her body, she clamped her knees together, as though that would make her appear less bulky than she actually was.

Myles led Falconer and Carmichael through the house to what appeared to be his study-cum-library, where there was a desk and several chairs, both hard and softly upholstered, and waited for them to settle themselves.

Falconer nodded to a Jacobean-style chair near the window for Carmichael to transfer to the other side of the desk, fingers crossed that it was a reproduction, as it looked like a toy in his sergeant's enormous hands. He, Falconer, went behind the desk, sat down in what must be, in more normal circumstances, Myles's chair, and beckoned for Myles to sit opposite him, in the chair that Carmichael had so recently repositioned.

Carmichael took himself off to the back of the room, where he was out of the sight-line of the other two, and extracted his notebook and pen, before settling in an upholstered wing chair, ready to take notes, but being as invisible as it was possible, for someone of his great height and breadth, to be.

Chapter Nine

Friday 16th July – continuation

'I asked you to come along first, sir, not only because this is your home, but because you reported the finding of the body, and I supposed that you have some sort of standing with the others.'

'I've more or less been in charge of things since our last Musical Director moved to France – actually, it was I who started the whole shebang, ten years ago. That's three in a row – Musical Directors, that is – that have done that to us. It's barely credible, that each and every one of them could have deserted us to go to the same damned country.'

'Very coincidental, Mr Midwynter,' agreed Falconer, then urged him to continue.

'The vicar brought along that Dashwood chap – it was only a few weeks ago, but it feels like forever – and he took over the position.'

'Was Mr Dashwood a popular man?'

'My big fat hairy arse, he was! He was a bully, with no tact or diplomacy, and publicly humiliated us all in the few weeks he ran the practices. And he disrupted the whole flow of rehearsals.'

'We can go into that further tomorrow, Mr Midwynter. Now, about this evening?'

'For once, we all arrived early, at the new village meeting rooms – that was his latest place for us to rehearse. I think we'd probably all taken on board some of what he said to us – I know Myrtle and I had – and we were all eager to put our practise into, well – practice. But he didn't show up.

'He was always there first, wherever *there* proved to be that particular week … I know, I know,' he said, as Falconer put up his hand to divert him. 'I'll leave that for tomorrow. Anyway, he didn't show up, so we started without him, and it was pretty damned obvious that everyone had done the same as Myrtle and I, because we sounded not half bad, instead of bloody execrable. Please excuse my language, only this thing's left me in a bit of a stew, mentally.'

'No problem, sir. When did you decide to go looking for him?'

'Not until a quarter past eight. We'd got so involved in what we were playing, and it sounding so much better, that we just lost track of the time.'

'So you all made your way to Wheel Cottage? With all those instruments in tow?'

'No, we decided to lock up, and leave them there, expecting to find out that he'd forgotten about rehearsal, or something like that, and that we'd return once we'd bearded him in his den. I suppose, like little kids, we were anxious to show him what we could do.'

'And did you all go into the house?' Falconer asked, remembering the waft of corruption that had assaulted Carmichael and him, when they had arrived.

'No fear! You must have smelled it when you got there. We thought, at first, there was something ghastly in his dustbin, but when we had a look, it was empty.'

There is now, thought Falconer, and it's not empty any longer!

'Then we noticed that that dreadful smell seemed to be coming from the house, and when Harold tried the door, it was unlocked. That's when the ladies made their exit. Harold and I – that's Harold Grimes, plays trumpet – stepped in to have a look, but one look was enough, as far as I was concerned.

'All we brave men made our retreat with alacrity, the only straggler being Edmund Alexander – keyboard accompanist for the band. He stopped off to be sick, and I don't blame him. I could feel my gorge rising as soon as we saw what was sitting in that chair, and the condition it was in. And then all the others came tottering round to see what the fuss was about, I regret to say.'

'Did you touch anything, when you were inside the house?'

'Absolutely not! I mean, if you're talking about fingerprints, you may find mine on the door or the door frame, but I never laid a finger on anything else, and the others, when they herded round, just took a look from outside, from what Myrtle told me afterwards. It was all so sordid, with flies everywhere. The air was thick with them, until we opened the door, and let a whole swarm of them out. That wasn't very nice either, and rather a harbinger to the doom that lay just inside that kitchen.

'And then we all high-tailed it back here, like a bunch of scalded cats. Myrtle dished out the drinks, to help with the shock, and got out some nibbles for anyone who wasn't feeling queasy, and I phoned the station in Market Darley: except, I didn't! I did that first, from Geraldine Warwick's cottage, next door to Dashwood's – that's Tile Cottage. My head's so muddled, I can hardly remember what order things happened in,' Myles apologised.

'Don't give it a thought, and thank you for your time, Mr Midwynter. You've been very helpful. If you'd just make sure my sergeant has your telephone number, I'd like you to send in your wife next.'

Myrtle Midwynter looked shocked to the core, when she entered the room, and felt her way on to the seat of the chair, as if she were in a trance.

'Are you all right, Mrs Midwynter? You look very pale,' said Falconer, solicitously.

'It's the shock! Oh, not just the shock of finding Dashwood dead, and turned into that 'thing' that was sitting at his table. No, the biggest shock was that it seems to be my cello spike that was used to kill him, and that really sickens and disgusts me. When the case is over, I don't want it back. I never want the thing in my house again. Throw it out, or put it in your black museum. Do whatever you want with it, but I never want to see it again – ever.'

'I can imagine how you feel and I shall dispose of it, one way or another, at the end of the case if you still want me to. But tell me, when do you think it could have been stolen?'

'It must have been while it was in the church. I know Harold – Harold Grimes – he's the trumpet player – says he locked the door before he came across to the pub, but did he? Or did he forget, and then feel too embarrassed to say anything about it afterwards, when there were no instruments missing when we went back to get them?'

'Did you actually see him unlock the church door?'

'I saw him fiddling around at the lock with the key, but that doesn't prove anything, does it? If he'd forgotten to lock it, he'd hardly say anything, unless anything was actually found to be missing.'

'Whose idea was it to go round to Mr Dashwood's house?' Falconer asked her.

'I've no idea. I mean, we did try to ring him first, but it just kept going to the answerphone. We, or at least, *I* thought that maybe he'd had an unexpected visitor, and been delayed. I even wondered if he'd just completely forgotten that it was Friday, although I knew, in my heart of hearts, that he wasn't that sort of man at all. It just seemed like a joint decision to me, as the next logical step to take. Aren't you going to ask me for an alibi or something, considering it was my spike that he was killed with?' she asked, in a slightly challenging manner, considerably recovered in spirits, since she had entered the room.

'Absolutely not, Mrs Midwynter. We don't know when he died yet, so I wouldn't know when to ask you for an alibi for – that was very clumsily phrased, but you know what I mean.'

'I do, and it was a silly question for me to ask, really. I'm still not thinking straight. Sorry!'

'That's perfectly understandable, under the circumstances. Can you tell me one more thing: did you touch anything when you were at Wheel Cottage, even if it was just the door or its frame?'

'No way! The place was swarming and crawling with flies.

As soon as I saw what was in there, I just wanted to get away as fast as I could. The smell of corrupting flesh was everywhere, and it turned my stomach.'

'You're aware, then, of the smell of decomposition, are you?'

'I've come across it from time to time: usually when I'm walking Acker – that's our dog. I believe you met him earlier,' she said, turning her face away from him, as she suppressed a smirk. 'And he quite often smells out dead animals, when he's off the lead, then I have the unpleasant job of trying to distract him, to get the lead back on, and take him somewhere else so that he doesn't remember it and go straight back when I let him off for a run again.'

'Thank you very much, Mrs Midwynter. That will be all for now. I'll speak to you in more depth tomorrow.'

As she rose, she asked, 'You're going to be here for some time yet, aren't you? Would you and your sergeant like a cup of coffee?'

Two voices, one tenor, one bass, announced their gratitude at the offer, and when she asked about sugar and milk, Falconer answered, 'Just black for me.' Carmichael, on the other hand, asked if he could have his milky, and with six sugars, at which request Myrtle's eyebrows rose, though she managed not to make any comment as she left the room in pursuit of the offered refreshments.

With coffee to sustain them, they dealt very efficiently with the other band members, but they all had something to say about Dashwood and his abrupt manner, and it wasn't until nearly midnight that they were finally able to make their farewells to the Midwynters and get off to their beds.

PC Green had left in his patrol car when the last of the band members had left their details with Carmichael, so the two detectives were the last to leave The Grange that night, both grinning widely at the sight of PC Proudfoot standing outside Wheel Cottage, doing his duty, as every policeman should, no matter what the personal inconvenience.

When Falconer had dropped Carmichael off in Castle

Farthing, and finally reached his own home, it was to find a message on his answerphone from Dr Christmas.

'I can't possibly give you an accurate answer to time of death, or even day of death, given the upturn in the weather, Harry,' the message ran, without preamble. 'The best I can do at the moment is to say somewhere between five and nine days. I know that's not much use to you, but corruption had begun, and the flies and maggots had done a good job. Maybe you can shave the ends off that a little by finding out who saw him last, and when. It's a bit like that case at Stoney Cross, isn't it?'[3] 'Well, I'd better get off. I'll speak to you, if I learn anything new. Goodnight.'

The message was timed at eleven forty-five, so he and Carmichael weren't the only ones not home until the witching hour: not that that made him feel any better.

---

[3] See *Choked Off*

Chapter Ten

Saturday 17th July

Carmichael had phoned Falconer at half past seven that morning, to report that his car wouldn't start, and would the inspector mind picking him up on the way to Swinbury Abbot. 'I know it's not really 'on the way',' he apologised, but you called for me last night, and it didn't add very much time to our journey, did it?'

'No problem, Carmichael, but please tell me, do you actually know when I'm in the shower?'

'No, sir. How would I know that?'

'Because every time you call,' explained Falconer, dripping water all over his bedroom carpet, and using one hand to hold on to the towel that was wrapped insecurely round his waist, 'I am in that cubicle. I know it's you, because you have such impeccable timing, that I'm beginning to recognise your ring.'

'Sorry, sir. See you shortly. Goodbye.'

'Goodbye, Carmichael,' snarled the inspector, and cut the line with a certain amount of unnecessary temper.

As Falconer approached the diamond-shaped village green in Castle Farthing, he could see that Carmichael was up and about. Whether he was dressed or not was another matter. Today, the sergeant seemed to have rediscovered a couple of Hawaiian garments that the inspector had not seen for some time.

A red-, orange- and pink-patterned short-sleeved shirt adorned the top of the huge young man's body, and a pair of green, blue, and yellow shorts the bottom half, only a little of which was visible, as he was involved in an activity that demanded a lot of scrunching up.

'Carmichael! You're far too big for that bicycle. Whose is it? Return it to its rightful owner this very minute!'

'It's Dean's, sir,' called back Carmichael. Dean was one of his two step-sons, for his wife had been married before, then widowed, before becoming married to Carmichael. Carmichael was making tentative enquiries about adopting Dean and Kyle, so that they could all share the same surname, but Kerry, his wife, was not convinced about the idea as yet. 'Both the boys bet me I couldn't ride such a small bike, so I'm just proving to them that I can.'

'Well, just make sure that you don't come to work on it while your car's out of commission. Get off it this minute. Someone might see, and we've got people to interview.'

'Do you want to come in for a glass of something cold, first, sir? It's awfully hot,' asked the sergeant, always solicitous of his superior's welfare.

Realising that he was quite thirsty, Falconer agreed, and locked his car, approaching the front door with caution. 'No, don't open it too wide,' he almost shouted, as Carmichael put his hand to it.

'It's all right, sir. The dogs are out in the back garden.'

'Thank God for that!' commented Falconer, for he had had several run-ins with Carmichael's dogs, a Chihuahua and a toy Yorkshire Terrier – Fang and Mr Knuckles by name – and didn't want another one at the very start of a working day. 'I haven't got my 'old Harrys' on,' he explained, 'and I simply can't afford to have another pair of trousers ruined.'[4]

'You'll be quite safe. We'll just grab a glass of orange squash and be off.'

As they approached the kitchen, there was a squeak of hinges, Falconer's heart gave a great lurch, and he turned and fled back outside the cottage. That was the sound of Kerry, opening the back door, to let the little darlings in for something – they'd probably smelled Uncle Tasty-Trousers

---

[4] See: *Murder at The Manse*

from outside, and were anxious to re-make his acquaintance.

Well, they'd just have to wait until he was suitably attired, in the chewed and clawed trousers he now reserved especially for visits to Carmichael's household. This morning he didn't think there'd be a chance of meeting the toothy little terrors, but he'd been wrong. Knowing how acute their senses were, they probably recognised the sound of his car engine before they'd even got a whiff of him.

Carmichael came out with two glasses of orange-coloured liquid, clinking with ice, and drank his off, pausing only to say, 'Sorry, sir. Kerry didn't think. She sends her apologies, and she's put them back outside.'

As Falconer drove, Carmichael described the most efficient route round the addresses he had been given the night before.

'We'll start at Tile Cottage, right next door to Wheel Cottage. That's Geraldine Warwick – plays the piccolo and percussion.'

'At the same time?' asked Falconer sarcastically. 'I should like to see that.'

'Don't be silly, sir. It's out of character, and it's a bad example to me,' commented Carmichael, with a smile in the driver's direction.

'Sense of humour coming along fine, then, Carmichael?'

'Just fine and dandy, sir. Next we go to 3 Columbine Cottages – Gayle Potten who plays the flute – that's almost opposite. Then we go into Groat Lane, to 2 Honeysuckle Terrace for Harold Grimes – him that plays the trumpet. Then we back up a bit, and go up Dark Lane to The Old Manor, for that Palfreyman woman who plays the double bass. I think she must've chosen the instrument to go with her size, sir, don't you?'

'That's very impertinent, sergeant. But, nevertheless, I agree wholeheartedly with you. Go on.'

'No, I've missed one. The first call in Dark Lane is at The Old Orchard – Fern Bailey on viola. Then we turn into the High Street for The Old Bake House, for Lester Westlake and his saxophone.'

'That sounds like lunchtime to me. What does that leave us for the afternoon?'

'Dunspendin on Mill Race, for Mr Edmund Alexander – Les Dawson, pianist, from what I picked up last night – then The Hurst, Chopping Knife Lane for Cameron McKnight – ex-first violin. That was a little diversion, so we go back down the High Street next, for the vicar at The Parsonage, then back to Stoney Cross road for Gwendolyn Radcliffe at the Limes – ex-second violin. Then next door to Thistle Cottage, for Wendy Burnett, the oboe player, and then finally, down Beggar Bush Lane, to The Grange again.'

'We'll be exhausted after all those people.'

'Absolutely knackered, in my opinion, sir.'

'Carmichael, language!'

'Sorry, sir.'

Halfway there, Carmichael asked in a rather desperate voice, 'Do you think we can stop somewhere? Somewhere there are trees or bushes?'

'Why? Do you want to make a den, or something?'

'No, sir. but I'm absolutely busting!'

'Didn't you go before you went out? I'll bet you always remind the boys to 'go', before taking them anywhere,' Falconer commented.

'Of course I do, and I did go before we left, but I had three cups of coffee with my breakfast, and that great big glass of orange squash, and now they've gone right through me and are desperate to get out again.'

'Three cups!' thought Falconer. 'Three of *Carmichael's* cups! He knew that cup, and it must hold the better part of a pint. *And* what must have been nigh on a pint of orange squash! He had no option but to find a convenient place, and fairly quickly. There was no way he wanted his sergeant leaking all over his car's immaculate leather upholstery.

Pulling up abruptly by a stand of trees, he left Carmichael to conduct his business behind one of the trees, and leant on the bonnet of his car, his back to the stand of trees, and observed nature going about its business, all around him, on this glorious day. There was barely a breath of wind, and the sky was a clear blue, and cloudless. The good weather was obviously getting itself out of the way before the children broke up for school holidays, as it seemed to every year, and the children were, consequently, left trapped indoors, bored and driving their parents mad for six whole weeks.

Just above tree level, he spotted a kestrel hovering, and kept it in his sights, because of its connection, no matter how tenuous, with his name; and then feathered death, on silent wings, dropped softly down, and another tiny life was extinguished, somewhere in the field opposite him. Well, that was nature for you: beautiful, miraculous and enchanting, but full of death and suffering, just like the human world. With a sigh, he stopped his daydreaming, and got back into the car to wait for his sergeant.

When they arrived at Tile Cottage, there was still crime tape across the boundary of Wheel Cottage, but there must be someone from the police in there searching, for Falconer noticed that all the windows had been flung open, not only to disperse the smell, but the flies as well. It had struck him, the night before, as akin to a particular scene from 'The Exorcist', and it had sent an unexpected shiver down his spine.

'Funny,' Falconer said to Carmichael. 'I'm sure Proudfoot should be on duty here this morning'

Suddenly the said John Proudfoot emerged, red-faced, from the ancient privy at the side of the house, clutching the local newspaper and a crumpled pack of cigarettes.

'Get back on duty, man!' snapped Falconer to the hapless DC. Carmichael shared his boss's ire and glared at Proudfoot as they strolled back to the main road, to continue their enquiries.

It was lucky for them that it was a Saturday, and most people would be at home, rather than at work. It was a double-edged 'lucky' though, as all their investigations seemed to start at the weekend. Maybe the weekend was a time when frustrations, after a bad week, were vented, sometimes in violence. Maybe people just drank more at the weekend, in the relief of a couple of days off from the daily grind. Falconer didn't have the explanation, but he knew only too well what the outcome was, as far as he and Carmichael were concerned.

Geraldine Warwick opened the door at their first knock, and, getting a better look at her in daylight, they saw a pale-skinned woman, with hair of an anonymous colour that was less like brown than it was dead mouse. It was cut short and straight, and her face had a dissatisfied expression on it, as if life had never quite lived up to her expectations.

'Come on in,' she invited. 'I remember you from last night. Would you like a cold drink? It's scorching out there.'

'That's very kind of you, Mrs Warwick.'

'Take a seat in the sitting room, and I'll bring some lemon squash through.'

The sitting room proved to be small, the furniture anonymous, not showing any particular style or character. The walls were painted a bland magnolia, the floors, of old-fashioned flagstones. The oatmeal curtains were pulled closed at the front of the room to banish the heat of the sun and keep the room a little cooler, and the general atmosphere was of utility.

No ornaments were displayed on the mantelpiece, or on either of the two simple wooden tables that were set by two armchairs, a sofa making it a trio of seating, but in a miniature sort of way. The suite had obviously been chosen to fit the room, and must have been quite difficult to find, given the sofas on offer to customers today that would not even go up the stairs or through the door of most modern-build apartments.

Come to think of it, how on earth did young couples buying brand new houses get wardrobes into bedrooms that would barely contain a double bed? And then Falconer remembered that there was a 'credit crunch', and no one could get a mortgage, nor sell their house, in a market that seemed to move only in a downwards direction. And there was always Ikea, for that life-shortening experience of self-assembly furniture.

Returning with a tray of condensation-bedewed glasses,

Geraldine put down the tray on one of the small tables and handed out the tumblers, stopping to smile, as she surveyed Carmichael's huge bulk squeezed into one of her miniature armchairs.

'I hope we don't have to call the Fire Brigade to get you out of that, or that'll make all three emergency services within twenty-four hours, with the ambulance, last night ...' Her voice trailed off, as she remembered what the ambulance had been summoned for, and then dismissed in favour of a coroner's vehicle, and her pale face, if possible, became a little bit more pallid.

'Of course, that's what you're here for, isn't it?'

'Yes,' confirmed Falconer, but I'd like to ask you to tell me a little bit about the individual band members first, to give me an idea of their characters, you see? You don't mind, do you?'

'Oh, no. I'd be glad to.'

Surreptitiously removing his notebook and pen from the pocket of his Hawaiian shorts, which had, so far, received nothing more than a surprised stare, Carmichael did his best to become invisible, and prepared to take notes.

'There's not much to tell really, except that, until Mr Dashwood arrived, we used to meet once a month at The Grange, have a nice meal and a few drinks, and then play for a while afterwards, then he – Dashwood, that is – changed the practices to once a week, and I wasn't quite so keen. I mean, I feel under-used as it is.

'Since the musical director before last, no one's been able to write me any parts, and the only thing I can do to join in is a bit of schoolkid maracas, and other silly basic percussion instruments, or play the flute part an octave higher. I would play the melody, but that woman on the flute refuses to play 'second' flute, and I can hardly play 'second' at a higher pitch than her 'first' so I'm stuffed either way. And I have, personally, been stuffed by that woman in a lot of ways.' Here she broke off, and her eyes swam with tears.

'Whatever's the matter?' asked Falconer, pinned to his seat, as he usually was when any emotion of this sort was displayed.

Carmichael, more practical, managed to wriggle out of his armchair without actually having to trail it behind him, like a snail with its shell, and went to sit with her on the tiddly sofa: there was just about enough room for both of them, even though Geraldine was of a small build. Putting an arm round her that was ape-like in its length, he spoke quietly to her until she sniffed, and wiped her eyes with a tissue. 'I'm all right now', she said in a slightly tremulous voice, 'and I'd better explain that little wobble.'

Carmichael slotted himself back into the armchair – it was a bit like Lilliput in here – and took charge of his notebook once more. 'I used to be married, you know, and I lived here with my husband, and we were very happy. That is, until that fat cow, Gayle Potten,' she almost spat the name, 'got her claws into my husband, Peter. They met at band practice, as it happens: he played second clarinet to Myles's first.

'I don't know what it is about her, but Peter fell for her, and they had been having an affair for six months before Muggins found out about it. Then, when I faced him with what I knew, he cleared off, leaving both of us behind. We went for a quickie divorce, and I believe he's remarried now, and living somewhere up north.'

'Did you have children?' Falconer asked, surreptitiously scanning the room for any evidence of toys.

'No. Peter didn't want any, so I went along with it, thinking I had a companion for life so it didn't matter,' she explained, somewhat sadly.

'But you stayed in the band?' Falconer was somewhat surprised at this.

'How could I not, and let her see that she'd ruined my life and broken my heart? It became a matter of principle, but I don't know how I'm going to able to face it now the meetings are every week. I don't know if I can stand it! And it really turns my stomach when I see her canoodling with Harold Grimes. She got over Peter just like that.' Here she snapped her fingers. 'And within a month or so, she'd taken up with Harold.

'She's a right old slapper. She's divorced too, you know.

Twice! So she certainly knows how to get through men. Oh, and this is something that isn't common knowledge, but I know about, because I went round to The Grange one day, for something or other – I forget what – and when there was no answer to the door, I went round the back, and there they both were, Myles and that Potten woman, and they were both stark naked, him taking photographs of her.

'I mean, I know he likes the whole naked scene, but for her to join in, with him a married man – well, I think it's disgusting. I haven't said anything to anyone else about it, and I slunk off that day without being seen, but it made me hate her even more. What if Myles is her next target? She'll drop Harold, who is older, and doesn't have such a fine house, and steal Myles from under Myrtle's nose, without a thought to what she's doing to other people.

'I was invited round to hers last Saturday, and I had to really steel myself to go, but I got through it, and even though someone else had caught Myles strolling around in the buff, I kept my mouth shut about seeing those two together, and with a camera. And I only made one bitchy comment, so I ended up like a wet dish-rag emotionally, but proud of myself, for not screaming, or crying, or doing any of those thing that I really wanted to do.'

Here, she stopped, almost out of breath, so worked up had she been during her rant, and Falconer was able to turn the subject back to the previous evening, but they learnt nothing they hadn't already heard, except for the fact that she had brought her instrument with her when they went to Dashwood's house.

'Why did you do that? Did you think you wouldn't be returning to the practice, or did you *know* you wouldn't? You didn't go round to see Dashwood sometime between Sunday midday and last evening, did you?'

'Certainly not!' she denied, vehemently. 'I brought it back with me because it's very small and light to carry, and because I hadn't heard any noise from the house for a couple of days at least. I thought we'd find he'd gone away on holiday, and just forgotten to let us know. So, of course, there was no point in having to go back to the meeting rooms, if I lived next door to him.'

'Did you have a music stand? That's not quite so easy to carry.'

'No, I usually share Wendy Burnett's. The oboe doesn't have a lot to do either, so, when everyone else has four sheets we've usually only got one each, with dozens of bar's rest to count.'

'So you just thought Dashwood had gone away?'

'Yes.'

'Can you remember when you first thought that this might be the case?'

'No. A couple of days – no – longer. Oh, I don't know. I don't spend my time listening, to see if my neighbour's at home or on holiday.'

'And you didn't call round there for anything?'

'Call round on *him*? You must be joking. I'd rather stick pins in my eyes.'

'Well, thank you very much for your time, and please let us know if you remember anything else. I'll give you my card, so that you can contact me if anything comes back to you.'

Chapter Eleven

Saturday 17th July, 2010

Their next call, by coincidence of geography, was actually to the much-maligned Gayle Potten, who lived just a few steps further down the Stoney Stile Road, but on the opposite side, at 3 Columbine Cottages, a row of eight dwellings that used to be accommodation for farm labourers, long ago, before the machines took over and the farmers had to diversify, lest they succumbed to being the victims of a dying breed.

Gayle, as mentioned before, could have done with losing a good deal of weight, but this did not prevent her answering the door in a skimpy bikini top, and a matching, almost invisible, thong-style bikini bottom. In fact, there was so much of her actual bottom visible, as she wobbled off into the house in front of them, that Carmichael didn't know where to look, he was so embarrassed, and things just got worse when she turned round again and presented them with an eyeful of her ripe melon-like breasts, the nipples barely covered by her minuscule top.

Taking off her sunglasses, she took one look at Carmichael, and hooted with laughter. 'And what have you come as, today?' she asked, between guffaws. 'Is it "befriend a clown day"?' she asked, addressing this remark to Falconer, who summoned the dignity to ignore her rudeness, and said:

'I wonder if you'd mind putting on a bathrobe or something, Ms Potten. My sergeant, young as he is, is subject to sudden rises in blood pressure, and it would be a kindness to him, if you would just cover yourself rather more than you are at the moment,' requested Falconer, a totally innocent expression on his face.

'No problem,' she answered. 'I was out in the garden soaking up the sun, but now I'm indoors, I'm rather chilly, so I'd have had to get a robe anyway. Won't be a minute,' she assured them, and disappeared off upstairs, to cover her largesse.

'Thanks, sir. I thought I was going to be sick. You know how dodgy my insides can be. But why was it me that had to have the high blood pressure? You're older than I am,' he complained.

'Because I'm an inspector., that's why. Quite simple, really.'

'Thanks a bunch, sir. She was awfully rude about my summer gear, wasn't she? Shhh – here she comes, thundering down the stairs like a baby elephant.'

Gayle re-entered the room wearing a thin cotton bathrobe, but the effort was better than nothing. At least less of her was actually visible, and Carmichael's stomach was no longer in any danger of rebelling. Although she wore the robe loosely, she still managed to reveal some cleavage, but her hair, now falling over the front of her shoulders, covered a multitude of sins.

And, in fact, her hair was a real shining glory of very long, thick, dark tresses, with individual hairs of pure white shining here and there. It was natural, but looked like the most expensive highlighting job in the world, and she knew it, and was justly proud of it; as good a reason as any, not to have it all hang down her back, out of sight.

'Would you gentlemen prefer to sit in the garden?' she asked, receiving a vehement and unison 'no' to this question, Carmichael's eyes bulging at the thought of her removing the robe to catch a bit more of the sun.

'Can I perhaps interest you in some refreshments? Tea or coffee? Perhaps a cold drink?'

'No thank you,' said Falconer. 'We've just had something, so we're all right for now.'

While she had been upstairs, he'd noticed how different this home was from the last one they'd visited. It was very feminine, the sofa and chairs being upholstered in a cheery lilac, the scatter cushions a hot pink. Abstract and colourful framed prints adorned the walls, which were painted in a muted wheat colour, making the room fresh and bright, and very inviting.

'We'd like to start by asking you when you last saw Mr Dashwood.' Carmichael, taking his cue, made himself as unobtrusive as a man of well over six feet in height and wearing Caribbean-coloured clothes can, and prepared himself to take notes.

'Until last night, I hadn't laid eyes on him since last Sunday lunchtime,' she answered.

'You didn't call round to see him at any time in the meantime?' Falconer asked.

'Absolutely not! I wouldn't have gone to visit that man about anything, even if you'd paid me. I know it's not right to speak ill of the dead, but he was completely obnoxious. He picked holes in everything I played, and he even had the unutterable nerve to ask me to dress more modestly. Bloody cheek of the man!

'I dress how I like, and my clothes reflect who I am. Who was he, to say I ought to cover myself up. That's suppressing the real me, that is. I mean, it was only for practices. We don't have a uniform or anything, and we always wear black clothes when we perform in public. I could have throttled him. Oh!' she exclaimed. 'I didn't mean that literally. It's just a figure of speech.'

'I know, Ms Potten. We all do it, and don't think anything of it until something like this happens, but I gather you weren't on good terms with the deceased when you last saw him.'

'I certainly was not! I detested him, and so did everyone else in the band. Take poor Edmund Alexander, for instance.'

'What about him?'

'He always played the piano or keyboard accompaniment for rehearsals, and for performances. We've got one of those portable Yamaha things that we can transport easily, you know. He also played the organ for the church services every Sunday, and never minded turning out for weddings or funerals, or anything else.

'Then Dashwood tells him his sight-reading's not good enough to play for the band in practices – he'd given us a new piece of music, and we were all sight-reading – so he took over that. Then, the next thing Edmund knows, the vicar tells him he won't be required to play the organ any more. He's devastated, you know. Lives with his old mum and dad, and, apart from his garden, he lives for his playing.

'I don't know what he's going to do with all the spare time he's got now. It got him out of the house and meeting other people. There are only so many people you can meet in your own garden, aren't there? At least he's still got that, and I must say, if you'd said Dashwood had been poisoned, I'd have sent you straight round to Edmund's house. He's got loads of foxgloves, and his bit of wild garden is full of deadly and woody nightshade, and goodness knows what else. I always refer to that bit of the garden as the Killing Fields. He doesn't like it, but I enjoy teasing him, and bringing him out of himself a little.'

'So, you never visited Mr Dashwood in his home and, in your opinion, everyone in the band had a good motive for murdering him.'

'I said no such thing!' she said, scandalised. 'I said that no one liked him. That's rather different from wanting him dead, I'd say.'

'Point taken, Ms Potten. Do you know if Mr Dashwood socialised with anyone else in the village, apart from those he met through music?'

'I've no idea, but I got the impression that, apart from the band and the church, he was pretty much a recluse.'

'One last question, if I may? You live very near, and almost opposite him. Did you see him out and about, anytime between Sunday lunchtime and yesterday evening?'

'No. I spend a lot of time at Harold's – that's Harold Grimes; plays trumpet – and when I'm here at this time of year, I tend to spend as much time as I can in the back garden, working on my tan.' Here, she pulled down the material of her robe, to reveal a meaty shoulder with no strap marks of any kind. 'It gets more of the sun out there. Who needs an expensive electric beach when you've got a south-facing garden?'

'That'll be all for now. I'm asking everybody if they could find the time to call into the police station in Market Darley to sign printed statements sometime in the next few days, if you'd be so kind.'

'No problem. And don't look so worried, sergeant. I shan't turn up in just my bikini.'

Carmichael blushed when she said this, and when they were safely outside again, commented to Falconer, 'That was no bikini. There's more material in three sticking plasters than there was in that. How can she? And answering the door like that – brazen as you like!'

'Carmichael, you have a very prudish streak in you,' opined Falconer.

'Yes, sir. And I'm proud of it. I don't hold with loose living, or flaunting your body like that, especially at *her* age, and with *that* body.'

'Good for you, Sergeant.'

They called next on Harold Grimes, who lived at 2 Honeysuckle Terrace, up Groat lane, and finally roused him from his back garden, where he was mowing the lawn. He escorted them straight through the house and onto a patio, where his collie, whom he'd introduced as Dolly, lay flat out on the flagstones, panting, a large bowl of water just beside the back door, and bade them sit down on cast iron chairs that surrounded a matching table.

Falconer eyed the dog with mistrust, but she was too old and too heat-drugged to take any notice of him, sleeping on with the dedication to this activity which only dogs and cats can achieve. He was safe for now.

'Let me get you a frappe,' Harold offered. 'I do iced coffee, Greek style, and it perks you up a treat.'

'That's very decent of you, Mr Grimes,' Falconer thanked him. Both he and Carmichael were a little dry, having accepted nothing at their previous visit, and Falconer felt they could do with the fluid on such a hot day.

As he left them to make the drinks, Falconer gave his sergeant an appraising look, and said, 'Your hair's growing through nicely now. You don't look like a thug anymore, and you're starting to look as if your hair is like that on purpose.'

'Well, it is now, isn't it? I wish I'd never shaved my head. All those people thinking I'd got cancer, and feeling sorry for me. I could strangle that John Proudfoot. I'm glad you sent him out to guard that cottage all night. Serves him right, the filthy, rotten rumour-monger! I should have wrung his neck when I first found out what he'd done.'

'There you go. You've used that sort of expression now, but you wouldn't actually go through with it, would you?'

'Probably not,' answered Carmichael, 'but with Proudfoot, I'm not absolutely sure. I'll get back to you on that one, sir.'

At this point, Harold trotted out of the back door carrying a tray with three tall glasses on it, all of them with straws. At their looks of surprise, he commented, 'Best way to drink them. Gets the cold liquid down the throat a little bit quicker, and cools you down miraculously fast.'

As they sucked away at the deliciously cold coffee, Falconer appraised what he knew about this man. That he was retired was obvious, for he certainly looked old enough. He knew he played the trumpet, and was Gayle Potten's beau, although he couldn't see the attraction in either direction, if he was honest. He had a dog called Dolly, and that was about all. He'd have to get digging.

As Carmichael made loud slurping noises with the straw in the very last dregs of his drink, Falconer got out his metaphorical spade. 'I understand that you stayed behind at the church on Sunday?'

'Yes, that's right. I'd got a problem with one of my trumpet valves, and I wanted to give all three of them a good oiling. And I'm a sides-man, and I needed to tidy away the hymn and service books properly. And then I locked the church doors and went over to the pub to join the others. They all wanted a

Sunday lunchtime drink, and they couldn't take their instruments with them at a busy time like that, so I said to leave them in the church. I'd get the key from the vicar, and lock up, then join them in the pub. Then, when we'd had our drink, we could go back to the church to get them, and I'd drop the key through the vicar's letterbox.

'I do have a little confession to make, though. I did actually forget to lock the doors, and it was only when we were on our way back over there that I remembered. Rather than own up, and look a fool, leaving all those valuable instruments available for anybody to half-inch, I fiddled around at the lock with the key, pretending to open up, and just kept my mouth shut. Nothing seemed to be missing, so I thought, least said, soonest mended.'

'But something had been taken, hadn't it, Mr Grimes? Someone had gone in there, opened Mrs Midwynter's cello case, and stolen the spike from her cello, and then used it to stab Mr Dashwood,' said Falconer.

'I know! I realise, now, that I didn't quite get away with it, did I? You could have knocked me down with a feather when you produced that thing last night. I thought I'd seen something sticking out of his body, but it was difficult to see, what with all the flies, and I didn't want to get too close because of the smell, and, of course, not wanting to contaminate the crime scene – I believe that's what you call it, isn't it?'

'Perfectly correct, Mr Grimes, and very sensible.' As if this acted as some sort of forgiveness for his carelessness, the grey-haired man stood up, and stretched his stocky five-foot-seven frame, before asking if they'd like another drink.

Carmichael looked wistful, but Falconer declined on both their behalves, and merely carried on with his questions. 'Did you call on, or even possibly see Mr Dashwood out and about on any occasion after that Sunday lunchtime?'

'Not at all, and if I had, I'd probably have thumped him one.'

'Why was that?'

'I was thoroughly fed up with his sneering derogatory

comments about my playing. I haven't been playing the trumpet for very long, and I have a lot of trouble with reading the music, so I mark in the notes. He was scandalised when he found out, but, as I thought, it's either that, mate, or I don't play at all. It wasn't only me, though. He ripped everyone in that band to ribbons, and treated all of us like naughty school children.

'Then, when he'd finally nagged and needled us into practising between rehearsals, and we sounded a hell of a lot better, the bugger's lying dead in his kitchen, and can't even congratulate us on all the time and hard work we put in. Not that he would've, of course. He'd just have said that that was what we should have been doing all along. I couldn't stand the man, and nor could anyone else, if you want my honest opinion.'

'So you've no idea who could have committed this murder?' This was Falconer's final question.

'It could've been any of us, or someone completely unconnected with the band, who had known him before, perhaps, and had an axe to grind. No point in asking me. I don't know nuffink!'

Deploring the use of the double negative, Falconer concluded the interview with, 'Thank you for your time, Mr Grimes, and for the delicious drink. If you could call into the station sometime, we'll get a printed statement for you to sign. Anything you remember in the meantime, feel free to give me a ring. Here's my card.'

'Good luck!' Harold called after them, as they saw themselves out through the house, and he returned to mowing his grass, eager to get it finished before lunchtime so that he could loll about and watch sport on the television in the afternoon.

Executing a turn in the road, Falconer drove the few yards to the turning into Back House Alley, then took a left turn into Dark Lane, where The Old Orchard was their next target. This was the home of Fern Bailey, the viola player, and she was to be found playing with her Jack Russell in the side garden by the drive.

'Oh, not another bloody dog!' Falconer declared, as they pulled off the road.

'Language, sir!'

'Sorry, Carmichael, but you know how attractive I seem to be to anything canine. So many people living in these country villages have dogs that I'm getting quite paranoid about it.'

'Have you got your old trousers with you?'

'My 'old Harrys'? Yes, they're in the boot.'

'Well, why don't you change them in the pub loos at lunchtime, and then if we meet any dogs this afternoon, you won't have another pair of trousers ruined,' suggested Carmichael.

'Good idea! But it's the embarrassment of being sniffed that really gets to me. Come on, let's get on with it.'

As Falconer parked the car, the slightly plump figure of Fern Bailey ceased her game with her Jack Russell, and approached the car, the dog trotting excitedly at her heels at the thought of more people to play with. Their first impression of her the previous evening, as just like of an overgrown schoolgirl, was confirmed. She appeared to be in her mid-thirties, but still wore a hairband, her face was devoid of any make-up, and her nails were unpainted.

'What-ho!' she greeted them and, as they got out of the car, called her little dog to heel, as it had made straight for Falconer, like an iron filing to a magnet. 'Down, Mickey,' she called, then went over to him and grabbed him by his collar. He had affixed himself firmly to one of Falconer's legs and was having a jolly old time, biting the material and growling away to himself.

'Sorry about that,' Fern apologised, dragging him away. 'He's just awfully playful, you see. Just like a child really. I'll pay for any damage he's done, of course.'

'That's perfectly all right,' answered Falconer, through clenched teeth and a forced smile. 'No harm done, I'm sure. Can we have a word about Mr Dashwood's demise? I'm sure it won't take up too much of your time.'

'No probs! I'll just put this little fellow out of the way, and we can talk in peace.'

'What was that, sir?' asked Carmichael, having heard the inspector mutter something under his breath.

'I just said, 'thank God',' he replied, trying to keep his smile fixed in place, until they had got away from the demon trouser-muncher.

'There, that's him shut up out of the way. Do come in and sit in the cool. Can I get you anything? It's such a hot day.'

'Only if we can use your facilities,' was Falconer's reply, as he was very conscious of the diuretic properties of coffee – and he had just drunk a very large glassful back at Honeysuckle Terrace.

'Into the hall and first on your left,' she directed him, and disappeared into what, presumably, was the kitchen.

Her cry of warning coincided with Falconer's cry of dismay as, on entering what turned out to be a downstairs bathroom, he was immediately assaulted by Mickey again, who thought he had come for the express purpose of his amusement.

'I'm so sorry! Must be losing my mind. I forgot I'd just corralled him in there. Come on out, Mickey, there's a good dog, and come into the kitchen with Mummy.' She grabbed the dog by its collar, and headed back towards the kitchen, dragging the reluctant animal behind her. 'Oh, and I forgot to ask you what you'd like to drink. Tea or coffee?'

'Tea,' stated Falconer firmly, feeling just a little bit wary of more coffee, and examining his trouser leg anxiously.

'Tea for me, too,' called Carmichael, and Fern was able, at last, to imprison the dog in the kitchen with her, safely out of trouble, for the time being.

When they were all seated in the drawing room, and Carmichael had loaded his cup with his usual six sugars – something that produced an expression of amazement on their hostess's face – Falconer got down to business.

'I believe you play the viola, Ms Bailey. I thought I heard someone mention that yesterday evening.'

'That's right, and it's Miss Bailey. Haven't managed to snare my man yet, but one mustn't give up hope, what?'

'Precisely, Miss Bailey. I wondered if you'd called round to Mr Dashwood's house between Sunday and yesterday, or if you'd seen him out and about – anywhere really – between those days?'

'Would've run a mile if I had seen him. Couldn't stand the sight of him, and you wouldn't catch me visiting him for all the tea in China,' she stated vehemently.

'So, the last time you saw him was when you were all in the church after morning service?'

'That's right! I must say, he really ruined band for me. It was a lovely social evening once a month, and when he took over, he turned it into a weekly military camp. Very bad form, the way he treated everyone. No tact; and absolutely no manners whatsoever. Noisome little oik, in my opinion.'

She had a curious clipped way of speaking, omitting many of the pronouns deemed by others to be necessary in their speech, and she continued now, 'Met people like that before. The man acted like a power-crazed jellyfish. If he hadn't been done in, I was going to leave. No fun anymore! Couldn't put up with that on a weekly basis. Surprised it wasn't one of the band that did for him.'

'Well, that's something I'd like you to help me with. I've already spoken to Harold Grimes, and he's admitted that he actually forgot to lock up the church on Sunday, and only made a pretence of unlocking it when you went back to get your instruments. That means that anyone could have got in there and removed the spike from Mrs Midwynter's cello.'

'Crumbs! That puts things in a different light, doesn't it?' she replied, surprised at such duplicity on the part of one of her musical colleagues.

'It certainly does. Can you remember if anyone left the pub, or disappeared for a while on Sunday, perhaps claiming that they were going to use the facilities?'

'Not off-hand, no, but I could have a jolly good think about it. Know it's not cricket to rat on one's chums, and all that, but it's hardly cricket to do someone in, either, is it?'

They learnt nothing more from Fern that they didn't already

know, and managed to leave the house without any further run-ins with Mickey.

'Where next, Carmichael?' Falconer asked. 'And why isn't it lunchtime yet?'

'Too early,' he replied, 'and we're just going to the next house along – The Old Manor – to speak to Vanessa Palfreyman, who plays double bass.'

'I remember her. She looks like she chose the instrument to match her figure, we decided, didn't we? Right, here we go again.'

The elderly woman who opened the door to them at The Old Manor proved to be Vanessa's mother, on introduction. 'Sorry I took so long to answer the doorbell, but I was sitting in the garden with my husband, discussing what bulbs we'd have to lift in the autumn. You know what a pain dahlias can be, I expect?'

Falconer, who wouldn't know a dahlia if it bit him on the bum, nodded his head sagely, then said, 'I wonder if we could have a word with your daughter, Vanessa. It's about that dreadful business with Mr Dashwood.'

'So horrible!' the old lady declared, and tottered into the house and called up the stairs with lungs of brass, 'Vanessa! Police here to see you! Come on down!' then explained to them, 'I have to shout. She's up there practising her double bass, and if I don't shout, she simply doesn't hear me. She'll be down in a minute, never you fear.

'Step inside, and I'll leave you to it. Archie gets upset if I leave him alone for too long. Thinks I'm going to run off with a door-to-door salesman. Silly old fool! There aren't any of those left. He'd be much better off worrying about the pharmacist, who's a bit of a hunk, and I have to see a lot of him because of all our pills and potions. Getting old is miserable, gentlemen. Don't do it – that's my advice.' And with this, she tottered off back into the depths of the house, leaving them to their own devices, while Vanessa took her time in coming downstairs.

The hall was a large one, in keeping with the dimensions of

the house and, looking around them, they could see what looked more like a Victorian entrance hall, with its framed etchings on the walls, a long-case clock, and one or two little tables covered in silver frames, most of them with photographs of long ago people, represented in black and white.

'It looks rather like this place could have come down the family,' said Falconer, still staring around him like a prospective burglar. I bet it's stuffed with antiques.'

'You could be right, sir, and one of them's just gone out into the garden,' replied Carmichael, with a twinkle in his eye.

'Ha ha, very funny, Sergeant. I'm doubled up with laughter – not. Hush up, I think I can hear movement upstairs.'

And he was not mistaken, for almost immediately the robust figure of Vanessa Palfreyman clumped down the stairs towards them. From the gloom of the hall she looked more like a man than a woman against the light from the landing.

'Wouldn't fancy meeting her on a dark night,' hissed Carmichael out of the corner of his mouth, and Falconer quite rightly ignored him, and stepped forward to greet their next interviewee.

Vanessa escorted them into a very old-fashioned room that, in a smaller and more humble dwelling, would have been called a parlour. Referring to it as the morning room, as it caught the early sun, she bade them sit down, and asked them if they would care to partake of any refreshment.

'No, thank you very much, Miss Palfreyman. We're just following up on our very brief meeting last night, at The Grange. There are a few questions that we need to ask you,' the inspector said, and then, when her face showed alarm, added, 'They're the same questions we're asking everyone who was there. There's nothing to be alarmed about. These are just routine enquiries.'

This seemed to reassure her, and she settled more comfortably in her chair, looking at him expectantly. 'Fire away, then!'

It was getting very tedious now, but Falconer just had to grind out the same old questions, to learn the same old things:

that everyone in the band had reason to dislike Dashwood, and that he had nearly been the means of said band's destruction.

While Carmichael slavishly took notes, Falconer let his attention wander, and looked around the room, surreptitiously admiring the fine old Adam fireplace, the ormolu clock on the mantelshelf, the pair of Sevres vases at either end of it, his attention finally being dragged back to what Vanessa was saying by the words, '... so she was particularly out for his blood.'

'Would you mind repeating that, Miss Palfreyman,' he asked politely, receiving a knowing glare from his sergeant, who had realised he wasn't really concentrating, and was feeling slightly resentful that he had to keep on scribbling, no matter what.

'I said it was Myrtle Midwynter who really had her knives out for him. He criticised her, I believe, more than anyone else. Always pulling her up for playing out of tune, or not noting the key signature. The last straw for her was when he had a go at her for not being able to read the alto clef, which appeared in her part for the new piece. He even hinted that her teacher was a charlatan. Yes, I think she hated him more than any of us, and so she was particularly out for his blood. I think that's what I said last night, isn't it Sergeant?'

'Word for word, Miss Palfreyman,' said Carmichael, taking another sneaky peek at her. She was tall for a woman, he had noticed before: probably about five-foot-nine, and she was very well-built; well-covered was a slightly more feminine way of putting it. She had short-cropped, dark hair which was just beginning to show signs of grey at the sides – certainly no spring chicken anymore – and still living at home with Mummy and Daddy.

Mind you, in his opinion, it would be a brave man who took on a woman like this. Perhaps if the man had a penchant for Shire horses ... Carmichael had to leave that thought unfinished, but he knew one thing well enough – he certainly wouldn't have wanted to pay the dowry on that one! Although he'd certainly make a good profit if he were to sell it by the pound. (*warning: non-metric author at work!*)

128

When they left The Old Manor, about ten minutes later, Falconer's first words were, 'I heard what you said to me as she was coming down the stairs, and it was all I could do not to burst out laughing. You'll have to suppress any similar remarks ...'

'Sorry, sir.'

'No, I'm not looking for an apology. What I was going to say was, in future, wait until we're finished, then I can laugh to my heart's content without hurting anyone's feelings.'

'OK, sir! Will do! So that's another one who neither visited him nor saw him between Sunday and Friday. Do you think they're all telling the truth?'

'At least one person saw him during that time, Carmichael – his murderer. It is possible, though, that he was murdered on Sunday. Until I get more detailed information from Doc Christmas, we've got to leave the window of opportunity wide open,' were Falconer's final words on the matter, as they drove just a few yards to The Old Bake House, in search of Lester Westlake.

Lester Westlake answered the door dripping wet and with a towel round his waist. 'Sorry, gents, I was in the Jacuzzi when I heard the doorbell. I haven't got the room or the dosh for a proper swimming pool, so I just turn the old temperature down in the summer months, so that I can still get a nice, wet cooling off,' he explained, fastening the towel a little more securely.

Falconer heard Carmichael mutter, 'Lucky sod!' but ignored it, and determined to have another word with him when they'd finished here. Mr Westlake would probably have taken it as a compliment, had he heard it, but that was not the point. Imagine what would have ensued had Vanessa Palfreyman heard his hissed comment when she came down the stairs. She'd have been so insulted that she wouldn't have said a word to them and she had at least independently given them the information that Myrtle Midwynter had a particularly strong dislike of Dashwood.

'Keep it buttoned, Carmichael,' he hissed, as they followed

Westlake into his back garden, thus breaking his own rule unthinkingly.

'Help yourselves to a lounger, gents, or would you rather I got you out some rather more upright seating?' asked the saxophonist, the wet hairs on his chest glistening in the bright sunlight. His garden faced south-east, and was a real suntrap.

Carmichael was already down on a lounger, but Falconer gave him a glare, and asked if they could have something a little more conventional to sit on while they questioned him. When Westlake went off to fetch some ordinary folding garden chairs, the inspector looked at his sergeant, and asked, 'And just how do you think you're going to be able to take notes from that position, may I ask you?'

'It is a bit silly, I suppose, but I just wanted to see what it felt like, to lie on a sun lounger in my summer gear, beside a real Jacuzzi. Yes, sir, I'm just getting up. It's just that there's so much length to actually get up, that it takes a bit longer than you'd expect, and this lounger's a bit of a tricky one to get out of.'

Westlake returned with chairs, having also taken the time to pull on a tee-shirt and shorts. 'Here we are gents – two prim and proper police chairs. And I also got some togs on. It doesn't seem right to be interviewed wearing just a towel, does it?'

'You mean you had no drawers on under that towel? asked Carmichael, scandalised, and not for the first time that day.

'I most certainly did not! I'm not overlooked, and I wouldn't mind if I were. Wearing swimming trunks in the hot tub feels so wrong you wouldn't believe it.'

'No, sir,' replied Falconer, leaving their interviewee to wonder what exactly Falconer was saying no to, but the inspector knew. He wouldn't get into a Jacuzzi without wearing swimming trunks, even if the Jacuzzi was an *inside* one and there was absolutely no chance that he could be caught out by unexpected visitors.

'I'd like to ask you a few questions about the late Mr Dashwood, if you'd be so kind as to indulge me. How did you and he get on?'

'Like a couple of fighting dogs. And when he found out that I'd probably have to miss rather a lot of rehearsals, he'd most likely have hit the roof. It wasn't so bad, when we only met once a month, and I could fit my work round it, but with them being once a week – well, fat chance!'

'And what exactly is your work, Mr Westlake.'

'I don't like to talk about it,' Lester answered, becoming rather flustered.

'Anything you tell us will be in the strictest confidence, I assure you.'

'It mustn't get out, if I tell you. I don't want the whole village to know what I do for a living. I make good money, I've got a nice house and a nice car, and I want things to stay as they are. People envy me my lifestyle. If they found out what I did for a living, though, I'd become a laughing stock overnight.'

'Unless it's pertinent to the outcome of our enquiries, the information will be safe with us. It will be looked on in a very unfavourable light if you refuse to tell us,' Falconer informed him.

Westlake lounged for a few moments in silence, pondering his quandary. Even in a tatty old tee-shirt and frayed shorts, he looked like a Greek god lying back on a sun lounger with his deep tan, and his no doubt expensively barbered locks.

'All right! I'll come clean, but only if you don't tell another soul.'

'That's not how we work, sir; but go ahead,' Falconer encouraged him, ambiguously.

'I'm a male escort. I escort ladies to parties and functions, if they haven't got a partner, and I get paid for it, and very generously.' Noting the gleam in Carmichael's eye, he added, 'And if there are any 'extras', that's between me and the lady, and nothing whatsoever to do with the agency, and it's not a criminal offence, as far as I know.'

'Thank you very much for your candid explanation, Mr Westlake. Now, let's get back to Mr Dashwood.'

'Silly old fool told me I ought to stick a pair of socks in the bell of my instrument, because it was too loud. He also told all of us we ought to get back to having lessons, and needed to spend a whole lot more time practising. I'd just about had it with him, and I was going to leave after the charity performance.

'I know we've been together a long time, but what we've been doing lately was not what I expected from being a band member. We used to have such good times, and then that pocket-dictator comes along, and turns everything from a fun evening, once a month, into a weekly trip to hell. Nah, I'd had enough of it, and was going to pack it in.

'Old Harold used to try to cheer me up – he's one of the good guys, ex-soldier and all that, but it didn't make any difference, I couldn't stand it any longer. And before you ask, no, I didn't see Dashwood between Sunday and Friday. I knew you were going to ask that, because old Harold gave me a bell after you'd left his place.'

And that was all they got from Mr Westlake, amateur saxophone player, and professional gigolo!

Chapter Twelve

'Come on, Carmichael. Let's go and get some lunch. I'm all hot and bothered, and starving and parched as well. That young pup didn't even offer us a cold drink. Thoughtless little upstart,' said Falconer in an aggrieved tone.

'You're only jealous, sir. He's not that much younger than you, and he doesn't have to put much effort into escorting ladies, and gets well-paid for it into the bargain,' Carmichael retorted.

'Shut up, Sergeant. What are the options for lunch in this place? Any ideas?'

'There are apparently two pubs, sir: one at each end of the High Street. There's The Clocky Hen, at the end we're about to come out on, or The Leathern Bottle, at the other end. Which one shall we try?'

'Where's our next call?'

'Dunspendin', sir, just opposite the Clocky Hen,' Carmichael informed him, consulting his list of interviews to be conducted.

'Well, we'll try that one first then, shall we?' asked Falconer.

'If you say so, sir.'

Falconer found them a space in the somewhat crowded car park, and they headed towards the entrance. As soon as they'd passed through the doors, Falconer knew he couldn't eat there. It was crowded beyond belief, with a lot of people who looked like bricklayers, and members of other blue-collar callings; it smelled appallingly of body odour and stale beer, and although

133

smoking had been banned in public houses, there was a distinct whiff of marijuana in the air.

Turning to Carmichael, who was surveying the heaving mass of people, he said, or rather, he shouted, so that Carmichael could hear him above the thumping of the jukebox, 'I'm leaving, and I'm leaving now,' and he about-turned, and exited, relieved to see that, as he approached the car, Carmichael was only a few steps behind him.

'It was a bit too hot in there,' the inspector explained, as they headed down the High Street towards The Leathern Bottle, 'and I didn't see a garden.' Thus did he cover the feeling of revulsion that had swept over him as he had entered The Clocky Hen. It was too much like finding all the cons he'd ever arrested, all gathered in one place, waiting and ready to give you a nice 'thank you' party, for all the times he'd arrested them and put them behind bars. Not that crime was exclusively a working-class thing, but in his opinion, people from that walk of life were more likely to give *their* opinion of *you* with a knuckle sandwich, rather than with words.

When they got to The Leathern Bottle, there did prove to be a few tables and chairs down the side of it, set beside the wall of the hairdresser's next door, but Falconer chose to go inside first – to have a look at the menu, was his excuse.

The interior of the pub was certainly much less crowded, and it was cool and quiet. 'This'll do me, Carmichael. Shall we go to the bar and order something to drink, then have a look at the luncheon menu?'

Having ordered a pint of lemonade each, for which Falconer paid, ('Thanks very much, sir.' 'Don't mention it, Carmichael.'), they retired to a table to choose their food. 'We'll ask for separate bills for this,' decided Carmichael.

'Why?'

'Because I eat so much more than you, my lunch will probably cost twice what yours does. I have been known to have double portions, if it's pub grub. Nobody feeds me right but Ma and Kerry.'

Falconer ordered smoked trout and new potatoes with salad, Carmichael, a double portion of burger-in-a-bun with chips, and a side order of four slices of white bread and butter, and a bottle of ketchup – he might not use the whole bottle, but, when it came to Carmichael, it was a case of 'better safe than sorry'.

As Carmichael was mopping the last traces of ketchup from his plate with a smidgeon of bread, he reminded Falconer about his proposed change of attire. 'Don't forget to change into your old trousers before we leave. You said you had them with you in the car.'

'Thanks for that, Carmichael, but shall we have a coffee before we go? I don't feel as if I've had a sufficient break yet.'

'Fine with me, and while we're drinking them, I've got something to tell you that I found very interesting.'

Coffees served, Carmichael set off on his story. 'Do you remember the church for that weird sect, in Steynham St Michael?'[5]

'I think so,' answered Falconer, furrowing his brow in an effort of recall.

'It was the Strict and Peculiar Baptist Church,' offered Carmichael, as an *aide memoire*.

'"Strict and *Particular*," you doughnut, the inspector corrected him, now remembering perfectly well the dilapidated little building with its sad, neglected cemetery, its headstones noting the passing of many generations of the same local families. 'What about it?'

'They're going to renovate it, as some sort of historical exhibit. Some committee's been collecting for it for some time, and they're going to start work in a few weeks. It'll take ages, of course, but the thing that interested me, was the fact that – do you remember that they had a great wooden cross, that the congregation used to take it in turns to lug through the streets of the village on Good Fridays? In the olden days, of course.'

'I seem to remember something like that being said. So what?'

---

[5]See *Inkier Than the Sword*

'So, they're going to move the cross, for safe-keeping, to the church in Castle Farthing. I know we haven't, as yet, got another regular vicar, but it's always kept locked, except for when there's a service or something there, although you can always get the key if you want a look around, from the village shop – Allsorts: you remember.'[6]

'Of course I do, but why move it at all?'

'Because the old chapel will be wide open when they start working on it, and anyone could get in and nick it. It's a valuable local religious symbol.'

'But who on earth would want to steal a bloody great wooden cross?'

'Builders, perhaps, for nice beams above a fireplace in a renovation job. Kids, just for a lark. It could even be kidnapped – or would that be cross-napped? – and held for ransom. Leave anything open and accessible, and someone will have it on their toes and away with it, these days.'

'I suppose so, Carmichael, but what makes you so excited about them moving the cross to Castle Farthing?'

'I want a real close look at it. It's a bit of real local history, and I wouldn't mind taking a couple of photos of it, so that the boys remember its history when they grow up.'

Carmichael could be unexpectedly sentimental at times, and seemed to be interested in so many different aspects of his adopted village.

'Oh, and don't forget that I asked you to be godfather to the boys, sir. Kerry's come round to the idea, so we've started the process,' the sergeant prompted, the mention of his step-sons bringing this subject to mind.[7] 'We're getting on OK with the adoption papers, and once that's finalised, and their names are changed, we're going to arrange the ceremony, and get a locum vicar to come and do the service in Castle Farthing.'

'I hadn't forgotten,' stated Falconer, with a sudden hunted look in his eye. 'I've finished my coffee, so I'm going out to the

---

[6]See *Death of an Old Git*
[7]See: *Murder at The Manse*

car to get my 'old Harrys' so that I can be wearing them if we meet any more members of the canine species. There's at least one more to come, as the Midwynters have got that sniffy monster, Acker.'

'I'm glad we had lunch here, sir,' was Carmichael's last comment before Falconer went to get his old trousers.

'So am I. To be bluntly honest with you, the sight of that crowd in The Clocky Hen frightened the bejesus out of me,' admitted the inspector, looking a little shame-faced.

'Me too, sir. It wasn't just you.'

Thank God for that, thought Falconer, glad that he had owned up now. Given the professional life he'd lived in the army and the police force, he'd thought he was losing it, when that wave of apprehension had hit him as they entered the other pub, but if Carmichael felt the same, it didn't seem so bad.

Chapter Thirteen

Saturday 17th July – early afternoon

Their next quarry was Edmund Alexander, the one-time pianist for the band, and they headed back up the High Street to its very end, where 'Dunspendin' sat opposite the car park of The Clocky Hen.

'I bet it's noisy on Friday and Saturday evenings. I saw a poster for live music at the weekends, and you know how loud the jukebox was when we looked in there,' commented Carmichael as they pulled into the drive.

'I see they've got double glazing, and that's probably why. It'd be unsalable, otherwise,' Falconer replied, pulling on the handbrake in a most un-masculine way. (*Most men just haul up the brake, and make that ghastly pulling against the cogs sort of noise. Falconer, however, always pressed in the button at the end of the thing, so that engaging it was a silent affair. It was only a tiny thing, but it did help to mark him out as a more refined specimen of his sex.*)

For the second time that day they were greeted by a very elderly person, this time a man, who had the slightly cross look of one whose post-luncheon nap has been disturbed.

'What d'yer want?' he asked brusquely, looking them up and down and appearing to be unimpressed by what he saw.

'Detective Inspector Falconer and Detective Sergeant Carmichael, from Market Darley CID,' announced Falconer, holding out his warrant card in one hand, the other outstretched in greeting. After shaking both their hands, and examining the two warrant cards minutely – he had left his spectacles indoors – he turned, made a 'follow me' gesture with his head, and retreated back into the house, and into the back garden by the way of a pair of French windows.

'They're both in the garden; Edmund and his mother. I presume it's Edmund you want to talk to? You'll find them beyond the roses, near the wild section, working in the herb beds,' the old man, who was presumably Mr Alexander Senior, directed them, holding out an arm in the appropriate direction. He never spoke another word to them, but stumped off back into the gloom of the house, no doubt to resume his interrupted forty winks.

Falconer and Carmichael looked about them, at a garden that was the perfect cottage garden, full of already-gone-to-seed foxgloves, carnations, sweet peas, roses, hollyhocks, and delphiniums. Beds edged with local stones had their edges softened by lobelias and aubrietas, and any number of sound ground-cover plants that filled in the gaps and kept weeds at bay. The buzz of voices, one high-pitched, the other deeper, floated across the garden, born on the slight breeze from the very rear of the plot.

Both men headed in that direction without a word, both captivated by the atmosphere created by a garden that looked so natural and higgledy-piggledy with plants, but which must have taken an awful lot of time and attention to achieve that relaxed, random look.

Before they were noticed they could see two figures, both with their backs to them, bent down, examining something in a herb bed, and with each silent step on the well-kept lawn, their voices became more audible.

'I really think we could do with another apple mint. I mean, look at this one, Mums. It's really curling up its toes, and I don't think it'll recover. What do you think?'

'I sort of agree with you, but I'd like to give it one more chance. If I can't do anything within a week, we can go to the garden centre and get one, but only if we can get a Russian tarragon plant as well. We'll be able to squeeze it in somewhere, and if not, I'll put it in a pot for now.'

'When do you think we should collect the foxglove seeds for

next year? I was thinking of sprinkling some of them at the back of the wild garden. What do you say, Mums? Is that a good idea, or not?'

Falconer cleared his throat as they drew near, not wanting to eavesdrop any more than was necessary on what was a wholly gardening conversation between mother and son.

'Good afternoon, Mrs Alexander, Mr Alexander. I hope you don't mind us turning up like this, but your husband ushered us through the house, and told us where you were working.'

'Do call me Grace,' requested Edmund's mother, graciously.

'Thank you very much, Grace,' replied Falconer, returning courtesy for courtesy. As he explained their presence, both held out their warrant cards for inspection, to have them waved away by Edmund, who had met them the previous evening at The Grange. 'It's OK, Mums,' he assured his elderly mother. 'These are the two gentlemen that I told you about, who are looking into Mr Dashwood's … sudden passing,' he finally finished the sentence, obviously not wanting to mention the word 'murder' in front of his mother.

'Why don't you stay out here for a while, and let Edmund show you the garden, and I'll go inside and make a pot of tea. We could certainly do with a drink. Gardening is very thirsty work, in this heat. I'll give you a call when it's ready, and put it in the living room, and if I find your father in there, sleeping a lovely day like this away, I'll give him what for,' and with that, she turned quite smartly on her heel, and stumped off back to the house, looking a jolly sight more spritely than her husband had when he had answered the door.

'Mums is actually the official band librarian,' explained Edmund, 'but she doesn't have to go to practices; just keep the instrumental parts in some sort of order, and issue them when needed. She has a little book where she records each instrumental part that is lent out, so that there's no quibble if anything goes missing.

'The vicar used to call her the Grace of God, as a joke, when he first moved here, but he once borrowed a piece of music and forgot to return it, so now he calls her the Wrath of God, for she gave him hell until he hunted it out and returned it to her. Now, I suppose you want to ask me some questions,' said Edmund, suddenly becoming more serious-faced. 'I can see Mums waving from the French windows, so why don't we go in and do this over a nice, refreshing cup of tea?'

As they walked back to the house, Falconer took a good look at Edmund Alexander. He was no longer young, nor was he old, but he looked older because of his typical male pattern baldness, and had only a short fringe of hair left round the sides and back of his head. He was tall, but not as tall as Carmichael – probably about six-one. He wasn't an ugly man, and he seemed well-brought up and nicely mannered, and yet he still lived at home with Mums – and, no doubt, Pops would be how he referred to his father.

Nearly everyone in Swinbury Abbot seemed to be either single or divorced. They hadn't come across more than one married couple, except for the two pairs of elderly parents they had met. Was it just a coincidence? Falconer wondered, or was it because of a general shortage of choice in a place where most people moved away when they were young, to seek more exciting surroundings? And some just got left behind. But lacking an answer to this question, he abandoned it, as they went into the house for tea.

Settled in the shady living room, Falconer explained that he only wanted to know two things at the moment, and these were: what Edmund's relationship was like with the deceased, and whether he had visited Dashwood at his home, or seen him, between Sunday lunchtime and Friday evening. 'Once we can get those two questions answered, we can chat more generally, Mr Alexander.'

Edmund set down his dainty china cup in its saucer, and gave himself to think, preparing to choose his words carefully. 'We didn't get along at all, I'm afraid,' he started. 'He was brutally honest about my sight-reading, but I've never been any different. It was all right with the old band. We were all just playing at it, really, and by the time we were due to perform anything, we all more or less knew our parts, and we got by.

142

'Dashwood took a totally different attitude. He didn't seem to be able to comprehend that the band was a part of our lives, not the be-all and end-all of it, as it obviously was to him. At the last rehearsal he attended, he actually suspended me as accompanist until I could prove myself worthy. Can you believe that?

'And he had me ousted as church organist. He'd evidently done a good job of soft-soaping the vicar, and 'bigging' himself up, and just smarmed his way into the position.'

'And how did you feel about that, Mr Alexander?' Falconer butted in.

'Oh, I was furious at first: I'd been in both positions for so long. In fact, it was because I played the organ that I was asked to be the accompanist for the band, and that was ten years ago now. But then I got to thinking, and realised that I still had the most important things in my life – my parents and the garden – so it was a case of 'just get on with it', as far as I was concerned, and I decided not to lose any sleep over it.'

'Brave words!' thought Falconer, taking the man's story with a pinch of salt. Of course he cared. How could he not?

'Then Dashwood was done away with. I won't say it was the answer to a prayer, because that would be blasphemous, but it means that things will probably just go back to the way they used to be, which suits me fine.'

'And did you see him or visit him?'

'I don't think he ever went out, except for shopping in Market Darley, or musical things. He certainly didn't seem to have made any friends here. Quite the opposite, really! But, to answer your question, no, I didn't see him again after Sunday lunchtime, and I never visited him, nor wanted to. Does that about cover it?' he finished.

'Is there anything you can tell us about how he got on with the other band members?' Falconer enquired, looking hopeful.

'I don't think so. He got everybody's dander up; that I can tell you. He tore our playing to shreds at the last proper rehearsal, and I think he was close to finishing us off, if truth be told. But I expect we'll just drift back together in the old way, now, or something very close to it.'

'Thank you for being so frank with us,' the inspector thanked him, then said, 'There is one question I'd like to ask, but it's got nothing to do with Dashwood's death.'

'Fire away,' replied Edmund, leaning forward in his chair, his elbows on his knees and looking attentive.

'It's about the name of this road. I noticed it as we pulled into the driveway. It's called Mill Race, but I don't see any signs of running water hereabouts, so how did it get its name?'

'Now, that's an old story, but a good one, and if you've got the time, I'll tell it. There are the ruins of a mill in the grounds of The Hurst.'

'That's where we're going next, sir,' chipped in Carmichael.

'And once a year,' continued Edmund, un-flurried, 'there is a wheel-barrow race – in fact, round here, it's called a beer-barrow race – where people enter, one in the barrow, and one pushing, and in some sort of rustic fancy dress. They start at The Clocky Hen, drinking a pint of beer each before they set off, then, before that new estate was built, they used to race off past The Hurst, cut through a back road, across what used to be fields, finally joining the Stoney Cross Road, where they had to stop at The Leathern Bottle, where they had to drink another pint.' Edmund was back in the past now, having changed the tense of his narrative, and his eyes shone with nostalgia.

'They had to go round six times, changing places after each round, and finish off back at The Clocky Hen. First pair back in the pub had to drink another pint each before they were declared the winners.

'Of course, the route's changed now, and they still do it, but there's no back road across the fields anymore, so they just come straight through the new estate, turn left into Chopping Knife Lane, and get to the Stoney Cross Road that way. It's always held on a Saturday night in September, and it needs to be evening, because those lads are fit for nothing after all that beer. There's always a few who throw up on the way, and the parish council has had complaints from people on the new estate, but they've stolen part of our countryside for their tacky development; we won't let them steal our old traditions as well.'

'Do you go along to watch?'

'You bet your boots I do! I even entered it myself once, when I was a teenager, along with one of my cousins. My parents used to let me stay up especially for it when I was a kid, and I still find a lot of amusement in the second half of the race, where co-ordination really starts to deteriorate. Yes, that race is part of Swinbury Abbot, and always will be, if I have my way.'

'Well, you certainly sound passionate about it. Thank you for that information, and now, we really must go. As DS Carmichael pointed out, we have other people to interview this afternoon, but thanks for the tea – and the story. It's been a pleasure. Do you mind if we have one last wander around your lovely garden before we go?'

'Not at all! Help yourselves. I'll just clear these tea things away, and see what Mums and Pops (*!*) are up to.'

Once more in the garden, Carmichael asked Falconer why he had asked that last question about the name of the road.

'One, because I really wanted to know,' replied Falconer, 'and two, because it gives us an insight into how passionate he is about his village, and how much he dislikes change. Motive for murder? Quite possibly! Now, look at all those deadly plants he has, in both the cultivated garden, and in the wild garden. Means? You bet your life! Opportunity? Definitely! He seems very much a loner, apart from his musical activities, which have just come to an abrupt end. Do you understand what I'm getting at, Carmichael?'

'Crikey! I'd never have thought of all that. You're a marvel, sir; a real marvel.'

The entrance to The Hurst was down Chopping Knife Lane, and the easiest way to get to that was by going back down the High Street and turning off where the lane bisected the parade of shops. between the post office and the junk shop. Their destination had the benefit of the local village green and pond opposite it, but the downside was that the rather less up-market

Wildflowers Estate had been built right up to its western boundary wall, presumably devaluing the property considerably.

For once, the occupant did not have to be disturbed in the garden, and after the first ring on the doorbell the door swung open to reveal Cameron McKnight. He was of medium height, his only distinguishing features a rather long nose and a thick mane of white hair. His eyes were hidden behind light-sensitive glasses, the lenses of which began to darken while introductions and reminders of their meeting the night before were made. The only comment unrelated to this that the man made was to Carmichael, to whom he said, 'See you're dressed for summer, Sergeant. Are you, perhaps, off on your holidays later today? I wonder that the powers that be allow it.'

Leading them into the gloom of the hall, he carried on through the property until he reached a bright room with enormous picture windows, where the light flooded through. With the lenses of his glasses still trying to cope with two changes of light, they were for the moment still dark, and they gave him a slightly sinister air, as if he were blind, and had something to hide, although this furtive look didn't leave his eyes, when he removed his glasses, to clean them.

They were settled in rather modern, minimalistic armchairs, which were quite uncomfortable, Falconer noted, inwardly chuckling as he watched Carmichael squirming to try to find a position that suited.

'Dreadful business!' McKnight opened the conversation. 'I still can't believe it actually happened. I mean, what a barbaric thing to do to another person. There must have been a great deal of hatred in that act, and it must have taken courage to carry it out. I can't take it in; even now, it's difficult to believe that it's true.'

'It's real enough, Mr McKnight; otherwise we wouldn't be sitting here. Now, I'd like to begin by asking you if you ever visited Mr Dashwood at his home, or if you saw him, perhaps somewhere in the village, between Sunday lunchtime and Friday evening?'

'I would never have visited that old curmudgeon, not even if my life depended on it. He was an extremely tactless and ill-mannered man whom one would cross the street to avoid.'

'So, that's a 'no' then, is it?' Falconer asked, just wanting to make sure he'd been given a straight answer, and not been fobbed off with a personal opinion that confirmed or denied nothing.

'No, I never visited him; and no, I didn't see him anywhere in the village – or anywhere else, come to that. I thought he was a bit like a musical vampire, never leaving his coffin in bright sunlight if he could help it.'

'Well, of course, he *is* in his coffin now, isn't he, Mr McKnight?'

'Sorry! That was in rather bad taste. But I don't think he could've been anybody's bosom buddy; no one's best friend.'

'I get the picture, and you're not the first one who's painted it today. I think I can guess the answer to this question, but could you tell me how you got on with Mr Dashwood, and perhaps about any altercations the two of you may have had: any differences of opinion or disagreements?'

Falconer took a glance over at Carmichael, to ensure he was engaged in taking notes, and had to put his hand over his mouth at the sight which greeted him. Lanky Carmichael looked like nothing more than a giant grasshopper, the small chair defeating his long legs, the knees of which hovered at about the height of his head, and somewhere in between these hairy lengths he somehow contrived to fit in his head and arms, to achieve his goal.

McKnight must have had the same idea, as following the inspector's glance, he made a reference to a very old television series, by saying. 'Ah, Glasshopper!'

To which Carmichael came right back with the information: 'American, Kung Fu, early seventies, David Carradine,' without ceasing his scribbling, or lifting his head. His reply was the only acknowledgement that McKnight had said something that he thought would embarrass the young man, and the sergeant had paid him back by not turning a hair (*very short though that hair may be, after his shaven-headed phase the previous month*).

In fact, it was Cameron McKnight who blushed, because Carmichael's refusal to be embarrassed had made him realise how crass and superior he must have sounded, and he took a few moments to apologise.

'If we can get back to the matter in hand, please, Mr McKnight – differences of opinion and disagreements, to refresh your memory,' Falconer reminded the man, in a somewhat icy voice. No one made fun of Carmichael! That was *his* job, and he was jealous of his position of privilege.

'To be perfectly frank with you, the man was appallingly rude to me about my playing. I've been playing the violin since I was a child, and with considerable style, I might add. Then along comes this bounder, and says I play out of tune. The bloody cheek of it! He even had the gall to remove me as 'first violin', and replace me with that old biddy, Gwendolyn Radcliffe, who has the style of a beginner, and absolutely no vibrato at all, or panache with her bow. I don't know how he had the bare-faced cheek to suggest such a thing!'

They were interrupted at that moment by the sound of someone entering the house, and a loud cry of, 'Coo-ee, my poppet!' A short, very fat man, in his mid-thirties, entered the room and, on seeing that Cameron was not alone, immediately exclaimed, 'Oops-a-daisy!' and covered his mouth with both hands. 'I didn't know we had company, ducky, sorry. I'm Oscar Littlechild, by the way.'

'And do you live here too?' Falconer leapt in with this question, thinking that the element of surprise might produce a more honest answer.

'Yes! No!'

'No! Yes!'

They both answered simultaneously, then swapped answers, and then Cameron took another shot at it, and said, 'Sometimes.'

Falconer introduced himself and Carmichael, who had to fight his way out of his pseudo-yoga position to shake hands. At the sight of this, Falconer nearly lost control of his dignity, for

148

the 'glasshopper'-inspired words, 'Herro, ritter Rotus Frower,' had just appeared in his head, and he had to cough to cover his amusement.

Littlechild hurled himself into one of the chairs, making it creak ominously, and McKnight scowled at this action in disapproval. Ignoring the silent admonishment completely, Oscar began to explain their situation, ignoring all the non-verbal signals from Cameron to the opposite.

'I actually do live here with Cam – that's pretty evident by the fact that my cats live here, too. By the way, where are my babies? Ooh, there you are, my pretty little darlings. Come to Mummy!' All this was said with a complete lack of embarrassment, and he briefly turned his attention to a blue Burmese cat and its companion, a red-point Siamese, that were just sauntering into the room with a very arrogant and superior manner.

'May I introduce you to Kelly Finn, and Petite Fleur: Kelly Finn's the blue,' he stated, smiling at the two detectives, adoration shining out of his eyes. 'They live here with Uncle Cam while I'm on tour. I'm away a lot of the time, you see, because I'm in a travelling opera company, and we perform all over the world. I sing tenor – so, obviously, I get all the best arias. Ha ha! And "yar boo and sucks" to all the silly old growly basses!

'Come here and let Mummy cuddle you. Of course, the Burmese, more often than not, gets referred to as Figaro, as befits an opera singer's pet, and my little flower is sometimes summoned by the name Madama Butterfly, aren't you, my precious? We don't often use your registered names, do we, because you're my little opera darlings, and I wouldn't have you any other way, would I?' he concluded, lifting both cats on to the enormous paunch that did duty as his lap, and stroking them both devotedly.

'So, what's been going on, to bring the police to the house? Have you been out streaking again, Cam?'

'Don't be so silly, Oscar, or so flippant. These gentlemen might just believe one of your stupid comments, and it could cause all sorts of trouble.'

'Oo, get you! What a bitch we are today!'

At that point, Falconer rose from his chair, asked McKnight if he'd be good enough to call into the police station in Market Darley to sign a statement, requesting that Mr Littlechild come along too, just to confirm where he had been for the last few days.

'Oh, that's an easy one, dear heart. I got back a week ago, but I had some stuff to sort out with my agent up in town, so I put up there until we had everything signed and sealed, and pootled on down here today.'

Falconer said that they'd let themselves out and, as they walked through the house to the front door, they could hear the sound of a hissed argument going on, Cameron making deep growling comments, Oscar's squeaky tenor, throwing back teasing and facetious replies, refusing to take anything seriously.

When they were out in the open once more, Falconer commented, 'Talk about the odd couple!'

'Laurel and Hardy, if you ask me,' was Carmichael's reply. 'I bet they keep that one quiet.'

'Me too,' agreed the inspector. I expect, to everyone else in the village, Oscar is just a musical chum, who pops in now and again for a bit of a holiday, and McKnight probably passes those cats off as his own.'

'Durn right, sir!'

Next, it was back down Chopping Knife Lane and into the High Street where The Parsonage could be found. The vicar may not have been a member of the band, but he'd had quite a lot to do with Dashwood, and ought to be included in the questioning. As far as the other residents of Swinbury Abbot were concerned, Dashwood may never have existed, so reclusive was he, except for his musical obligations.

PCs Green and Starr had been sent to make house-to-house enquiries along Honeysuckle Terrace and Columbine Cottages, as these had been his nearest neighbours, but Falconer doubted they would turn up anything of interest.

The door of The Parsonage was opened by the vicar himself who, fortunately for him, had no wedding services to officiate at today, and they found him dressed in a similar vein to Carmichael. 'Hello!' he greeted them, took one look at the sergeant, and cried, 'Snap!' in a joyous voice. 'We could be the Caribbean twins,' he chuckled, inviting them into the substantial old building.

'I'm afraid I was a bit wary about giving my full name last night, simply because it sounds so silly. I'm very sorry to have to tell you that the full monty is Reverend Christian Church – it wasn't sense of humour on the part of my parents; more that my father, who was also in clerical orders, was determined that his son should follow in his footsteps, and I must admit, his plan worked. What else could I have done with a daft moniker like Christian Church? It makes me sound like a church in a non-Christian country as in, 'Where's the Christian church? 'Down there on the left; you can't miss it.''

'I see what you mean, Vicar,' Falconer agreed, but I'm sure you serve your calling very dutifully. You realise why we've called here, don't you?'

'About that unfortunate business with Campbell Dashwood?'

'Correct. Is there somewhere we can sit and talk?'

'I'm sorry; my manners seem to have gone astray. Come into my study where we'll be both cool and private.'

The vicar automatically placed himself behind his desk, and left the two detectives to settle themselves in the chairs that were placed on the other side of the desk, for the convenience of visitors there on parish matters.

His wife, Olivia, popped her head round the door, and asked, 'Can I get you a cold drink? I heard someone arrive, so I just thought I'd check. Am I right in assuming that you're the two policemen that Chris met last night?'

'You are, my love,' answered her husband, looking at her with adoring eyes.

'Three shandies, then, is it?' she said, checking that this was

OK.

'Only if they're not too strong, Mrs Church. We do have to be very careful in our profession,' Falconer advised her.

'Oh, they're mostly lemonade. There's just a wee bit of beer in them, to give them a bit of taste,' the vicar explained. 'In my position, I have to be very careful as well. I can hardly turn up for a service reeking of booze and swaying around, now can I?'

'Point taken! Now, we know that you weren't a member of the village band, but we realise that you were probably the only other person in this village who had any conversation with Dashwood. I wonder if you can recall your meetings, and what they were about?' the inspector asked him.

'That's a tough one. I speak to so many people in my job. Hmm; let me see. He came to see me shortly after he moved in, which wasn't really very long ago, now I come to think about it. It just seems longer because of the amount of acrimony he caused.

'Of course, he was all sweetness and light, when I met him. I had intended to call on him later that day, to welcome him to the parish, but he beat me to it. Anyway, we ended up talking about the band, and how it had no Musical Director, and that's when he became really animated.

'He gave me his life history in music, said he could back it all up with references and testimonials, and almost begged to be able to have a shot at the position. At that time, he seemed the answer to a prayer – but enough of that! I had no idea what sort of man he really was, and I, in all my innocence, arranged for him to go to the next band practice.

'Myles made no demur, and I think the members were really looking forward to having someone in charge again – someone who could arrange music for them, who could write parts for instruments that lacked them, and to having a proper conductor for the first time in ages. And didn't I prove to be the naive innocent? He went in like a lamb that evening, the only 'bum note' being that he was tee-total, and the members of the band are certainly not.

'The next time he came to me … oh, excuse me a minute.'

Olivia had managed to open the door, and was now entering with three pint mugs on an old wooden tray, their outsides glistening with pearls of icy condensation which ran down their sides and made little puddles on the wood, and the vicar rose to relieve her of this heavy burden.

As he did so, a large red setter trotted in on her heels, and made straight for Falconer, jumping up with his front legs, to plant them on the inspector's shoulders.

'Hey, don't try to get on the inspector's lap, you silly dog. Here, I'll take the tray, and you get him out of the room, Liv. Sorry about that! That was, or is, our very spoilt and over-indulged dog, Chalice. He's just so friendly, and he doesn't seem to realise that not everyone is a dog-lover.'

'I think it must be the other way round with me,' Falconer remarked, brushing his front down. 'They seem to love me, and aren't backward in coming forward to demonstrate it.'

'Liv will toss him out into the back garden now, so we shouldn't be troubled again. Now, where was I? Cameron's second visit: he came to see me again, concerned about Edmund holding the position of church organist. He seemed very distressed that the playing was inaccurate, and appeared to be anxious that the music should not be detrimental to the services.

'That was when he offered himself as organist. I explained that it wasn't a paid position, and that there would be weddings and funerals, which would be paid, but that the fee was derisory, but he was undeterred in his attempts to usurp Edward. I, again very naively, fell for his concern and pious attitude. In the light of what I heard later of his character, I have bitterly regretted both decisions, and intend to put things right as soon as possible, with, of course, the most abject of apologies to all concerned.

'That's about it, really. I've had various phone calls since then, from some very distressed and angry members of the band, but it took me a long time to see through the man. He must have taken me for an innocent abroad – I realise that doesn't sound right, but you get my meaning.'

'You mentioned going to visit Mr Dashwood, to welcome

him to the parish,' Falconer reminded him. 'I know you didn't go that time, but did you, at any other time, have occasion to visit his house?'

'I've never seen the inside of it. The previous owners were Roman Catholic, so I wasn't exactly on calling terms with them, and the owners before that left the parish before I came here. I'm sorry I can't be of more help to you.'

'Well then, that's about it for today. I'd be grateful if you'd allow us to use your bathroom before we go. A pint of shandy can make matters a bit pressing, if you know what I mean,' requested Falconer, aware of the pressure in his bladder, and sure that Carmichael must be beginning to feel a similar discomfort.

'Be my guest. It's right across the hall, by the kitchen door, and don't worry about Chalice. He's still banished to the garden.'

Chapter Fourteen

A right turn, out of the other end of the High Street and into the Stoney Stile Road brought them straight to The Limes, which was situated just behind The Leathern Bottle. This afternoon, Gwendolyn Radcliffe was dealing with the weeds in her front borders, and eased herself slowly to her feet at the car's approach.

'Hello, there,' she called, waving a mud-encrusted hand fork at them as they got out of the car. 'We meet again! I was just thinking of taking a little break, so why don't we go into the house, and I'll put the kettle on,' then, noticing Carmichael for the first time, asked, 'And what have you come as today, young man?'

Without waiting to see his reaction to this rather cheeky question, she preceded them into the house, pointed them in the direction of the living room, and disappeared into the kitchen to fulfil the task of preparing refreshments for them all.

The room proved to be furnished with solid, good quality, old-fashioned pieces, and had the spick and span appearance of a room in a house that boasted only a single occupant. There was a large over-mantel mirror above the fireplace, and the walls were hung with pretty watercolours. It may have been very clean and tidy, but it was a homely room, and they felt welcomed by it.

When they heard the sound of crockery tinkling, Carmichael got up, without a word, and left the room, appearing an instant later bearing a laden tray, saying over his shoulder, 'Of course I couldn't leave you to carry in such a heavy tray. My ma brought

155

me up to have good manners, and I've never forgotten them.'

'What a very nice young man,' were Gwendolyn's first words, when she let herself fall gratefully into a well upholstered, sturdy armchair. 'So many young men these days have the most appalling manners – and foul mouths, too. I don't know what the world's coming to, I really don't. So nice to meet someone that reminds one of the old school!!'

'Thank you, ma'am,' chirped Carmichael, now her best friend, and Falconer was surprised not to see him attempt to tug a forelock, but he wouldn't have had much luck there, as his hair had only been re-growing for a few weeks, and was only about half an inch long all over.

There was a plate with slices of home-made cake on the tray, along with another of jam tarts; both very welcome, as it seemed a long time since they had sat in The Leathern Bottle.

'I'll be mother,' Gwendolyn announced, 'and you two help yourselves. I know how hungry young people get when they're working.' She certainly knew all the right things to say, after that original *faux pas* about Carmichael's appearance. Now, she was a sweet old lady, pleased of the company, and to have someone with whom to share her afternoon tea.

'I suppose you've come about what happened to that Dashwood chap?' she enquired, putting down the teapot and helping herself to a jam tart. 'I always think the strawberry ones are the best,' she commented, lifting the confection towards her mouth, 'but I always make other flavours, just the same. Not everyone likes strawberries, and if they don't, that makes all the more for greedy old me,' and she smiled as she made these remarks. 'Do tuck in, or it'll only go to waste.'

Falconer had already tucked in, having no one to cook for him, and relishing the opportunity to consume home-baked goodies. Carmichael now made haste to catch up with the inspector for, although he did have someone to bake for him, in the shape of his wife, Kerry, he was starving again, despite his enormous lunch. Feeding a Carmichael was an onerous task, which needed to be carried out several times a day.

No mention of why they were here was made as they

consumed their tea, as dictated by manners, and would have been terribly bad form. Falconer knew this from his upbringing, Carmichael from an innate instinct as to what was right, and what was unacceptable.

When cups had been tidily put back on their saucers, having been drained for the second time, and tea plates were stacked next to them, Carmichael carried the tray back out to the kitchen before they began their questioning, but it was Gwendolyn who started it.

'Isn't it all too ghastly for words?' she began. 'I know he was an absolute pill, but nobody deserves to die like that; and in his own home, too. Have you nicked anybody for it yet?' she concluded, suddenly slipping into modern-day slang, and looking embarrassed about doing it. 'I believe that is the modern term for it, isn't it – 'nicked'?'

'Yes, it is, and, no, we haven't, to answer both of your questions succinctly,' replied Falconer, keeping an eye on Carmichael, to check he wasn't falling asleep after food, the way snakes and babies do. 'The reason we called on you today was to ask you if you had ever visited Mr Dashwood's property, or seen anything of him, between Sunday lunchtime and Friday evening.'

This really was getting repetitive now, but as he always told Carmichael when the latter said he was bored, being a detective wasn't about car chases and summoning armed response teams. It was about routine – asking the same questions over and over again, and writing up the reports, hoping that something jumped out at you. Sometimes you got a lucky break, but the greater part of the job was shoe leather (or tyre rubber) and paper and ink, and he shouldn't let anyone persuade him any differently. He gave himself his own well-rehearsed little lecture now, and leaned forward politely to hear Mrs Radcliffe's response.

'Mr Dashwood said some very cutting things about my performance on the violin, but he did also give me the opportunity to play 'first violin'; something I've coveted for years, so I can't say I bore him any particular personal grudge. He was awfully rude to the others, of course, and about the band in general, and some members were getting quite worked up about all the changes.

'Edmund Alexander behaved in a very civilised and nonchalant way when he was suspended as practice pianist, and with great dignity, when he was replaced as church organist. I think underneath, though, he was devastated. Apart from looking after his beloved garden, and caring for his parents, music is the love of his life, and he'd had it torn from his grasp, by an ill-mannered, arrogant in-comer.

'He must have been harbouring such resentment towards the man, that I'm surprised he didn't have a minor celebration when he was murdered. Oh dear, I mustn't say things like that to you, must I? It's only speculation, after all, and only my personal opinion. Strike that from the record! Sorry, m'Lud! I must get back to what I actually know.

'He had a terrific go at Gayle Potten about the way she dressed for rehearsals; more or less said she dressed like a slut, or a prostitute, and told her to get her body covered up in a more seemly manner before the next practice. That'll have hurt her pride. Harold Grimes, of course, worships the ground she walks on, and feeds her all this guff about how beautiful her body is, and things like that which have given her an inflated idea of her own attractiveness.

'What was that, young man?' Her question was addressed to Carmichael who had spoken, but very quietly, unable to help himself, but hoping not to be heard. 'She ought to what?'

'I'm sorry. I said she ought to be made to wear a burkha. I shouldn't have said it, but when she answered the door to us, she was practically naked, and she's so fat and saggy. It made me feel quite ill, having to look at her, with almost nothing on.'

'That's quite all right, Sergeant. In many ways, I agree with you, but I wouldn't dare say anything in front of Harold. He adores her, and wouldn't have her any other way. Now, who else has he been particularly rude to? Oh, just about everybody had their hackles raised when he was around. Why, I even had a visit from Cameron McKnight – you know, the one who used to be,' (she relished these last three words) '*first violin*. Pleading with me, he was, to go back to how things were, but I was having none of that. I'd been offered a chance, and there was no way I was going to turn it down, not after wanting it, and waiting for it for so long.

'But to answer your question in full, I would say, with a certain amount of confidence, that every member of our band hated him, and he won't be missed by any of them. There, will that do?'

'Admirably, Mrs Radcliffe. Your information has been most interesting, and we'd like to thank you, not only for your time, but for the delicious afternoon tea, too. It was most appreciated. And now, we'll let you get back to your gardening in peace.'

Their next, and penultimate, call was only next door at Thistle Cottage, and Mrs Radcliffe begged them not to bother moving their car, as it wasn't in the way in her drive, and it hardly seemed worth starting the engine for such a short trip. So they left it there.

The door of Thistle Cottage was opened by what at first sight looked like a child, and an adult who seemed to be rising from a crouched position by its side. Before he knew what was happening, the rising form resolved itself into a fully-grown deerhound, and had jumped up to rest its vast paws on Falconer's shoulders, and was proceeding to lick his face with evident enjoyment. If there had been any spots of jam on his chin from his recent repast, there were certainly none, now.

'Get down, Maurice! This minute, I say! Bad boy! Leave the poor man alone!' The child was suddenly a woman, if a very petite one. She was only just over five feet in height, and must surely have taken a dress size 8 and had thick, highlighted hair that had bleached slightly in the recent sunshine.

'I'm so sorry,' she apologised. 'It's just that he's so friendly, and I bought him for a bit of protection, out here in the country, all on my own. If anyone ever broke in, he'd probably lick them to death rather than act like a guard dog.' Casting her gaze down to the dog, she said, 'You're a soppy old Maurice, aren't you?' and patted his head, making him whine for more attention. 'You're going out in the garden while I deal with these gentlemen. Come on, and I'll throw your stick for you. That always works,' she called over her shoulder to her two visitors.

She had addressed this final remark to them, as she left the doorstep. 'He never seems to realise that I'm only throwing it once, so I can close the door on him and get a bit of peace. He really is a silly old Maurice. You go on into the sitting room – it's on the right – and I'll be back in just a minute.'

In her absence, Falconer, after drying his face with his handkerchief, and grimacing in disgust, asked, 'Why does just about every other household in these damned villages own a pooch?'

'Company; protection; exercise; something to love …'

'All right, Carmichael, I get the picture, but I'll tell you something.'

'What's that sir?' asked his sergeant.

'I'm just bloody glad I'm not a postman. My lower legs would have been bitten to ragged, bloody bones by now.'

They learnt nothing new from Wendy Burnett, who professed not to have liked Dashwood, but only because he had suggested that she have an egg cup of water on the floor by her feet in which to rest her reed when she wasn't playing, so that she didn't have to keep it in her mouth to keep it moist. 'I quite hated him, though,' she concluded, 'because of what he did to the others, and to the band. He ruined it, and after a whole decade. I think that's evil!'

Falconer's ring at the doorbell of The Grange was answered by a call from inside. 'Just hang on a minute, while I get Acker corralled in the dining room.' The voice was Myrtle's, and she must have known it was them.

'All clear!' she informed them, opening the door just a few moments later, and ushering them inside. 'We've made a decision about the band,' she informed them as they sat down, thinking they might be interested, after all that had happened. 'We've decided to practise on the second and fourth Fridays of the month, but to have the meal after we've played, and put in a bit more practice in between.

'We may have hated that man, but it looks like he taught us something before he got his comeuppance, but I'll never forget all those insulting remarks he hurled at me, about my skill as a musician. They were unforgiveable! But at least something good may have come out of it, although that's almost impossible to believe. I think that if he'd lived to stay on as Musical Director, we'd just have closed down the whole thing, which would have been a pity. I still hate the vicious old bastard, though, even with him being dead.

'No, I think that things are only looking up, band-wise, because he *is* dead, and I suppose, in some perverse sort of way, we ought to thank the person who did away with him, because they did us all a favour. Now, what can I do for you, gents? Something to drink – a little cocktail, perhaps, as we're approaching the cocktail hour, or at least we are, in the world I live in.'

'No thank you, Mrs Midwynter. We just wanted a quick word with you and your husband, to confirm what you told us last night, and to ask you to pop into the station in Market Darley sometime soon, so that you can sign your statements, which will be ready and waiting for you,' Falconer explained.

Myles was summoned, and Carmichael was again horrified when, wearing only an apron, as he had been outside lighting the barbecue for another al fresco meal, he strolled to the far side of the room and straightened a picture that was hanging crookedly on the wall. Carmichael had had his fill of buttocks for the day, and was beginning to see Swinbury Abbot as a den of iniquity.

First there had been Gayle Potten, wearing two tiny items that could not be dignified with the name garments, then Lester Westlake, wearing only a towel, having been sitting stark naked in his Jacuzzi, and now this, a man whom he considered quite elderly, wearing only an apron, and with guests present, showing off his saggy old buttocks to all and sundry. It really was too much!

161

Nevertheless, he got out his notes from the previous evening, and diligently went through them at speed, but there didn't seem to be anything they could add to what they had already said, so the visit was a very short one, and they stood ready to take their leave after only about ten minutes, and very relieved indeed was Carmichael.

'I'll show you out,' offered Myles, conscious of his duty as host. He went on ahead of them, and the sergeant kept his eyes firmly fixed floorwards, opining that the flooring was a much better aspect than what lay ahead of him at just below waist height. He could have been more on guard, though, for when Myles opened the door, and Falconer stepped out into the hall, a furry bundle, which had obviously smelled him, and must have been lying in wait, made a bee-line for the inspector, and gave him a sharp nip on the left buttock, before tearing off towards the kitchen. Falconer could almost hear the dog's laughter, as it retreated to a safe distance.

'Myles! Did you let him out of the dining room on your way through?'

'Well, he was whining, and I thought he'd been shut in by accident, didn't I?'

'You fool! I'm so sorry, Inspector. Would you like me to take a look at it?' she asked, with a wicked twinkle in her eye.

'No thank you, Mrs Midwynter. I shall have the police doctor look at it, in case I need a tetanus jab, or something. Good evening to you both!'

When they were out of sight-line, Falconer turned and tried to look over his shoulder. 'Are my trousers torn?'

'Yes, sir,' Carmichael confirmed, 'but at least they're your 'old Harrys', and not a good pair.'

'Is there any blood?' the inspector asked, anxiously.

Folding himself in half, Carmichael applied his eyes to the offended area, and confirmed that there was no sign of bleeding. Yet!

'Thank God you got me to change into these old trousers for this afternoon. If there's no blood, I won't have to show my bottom to Christmas, which is just as well, as he'd never let me hear the end of it. We've still got to go back to the office, to take an overview of what we've got, but I'll tell you one thing, Carmichael.'

'What's that, sir?'

'The first thing I'm going to do, when I get in, is have a nice, long, hot shower. My whole body seems to have been covered in dog lick, and my rear end seems to have suffered an extremely undignified experience at, if you'll excuse the mixed metaphor, the hands of a dog's teeth.'

'Good idea, sir. And it might be a good idea to repair the hole in your trousers, because we're sure to need to speak to some of these people again and, with your luck, it'll only be the ones with dogs,' were Carmichael's final words on the matter.

It was early evening before they got back to the station, and Falconer removed the trousers he had donned that morning from the boot of his car, and took them upstairs to the office, to change into them His 'old Harrys', he'd have to take home with him that evening to repair them and run them through the washing machine. They were too soiled with memories of today for him to be able to face putting them on again without them being surrendered to a good hot wash.

'Right, Carmichael!' he said, safely back in unsullied strides, 'Let's look at them all – means, motive, and opportunity, and list the inter-band tensions as well, to see what bearing they might have on the case, if any. Still, at least we've had a deal of 'Grass Thy Neighbour', and we've only just finished round one.' Here, he gave a tiny smile of satisfaction.

'Motive first, I think. Did they all have a motive to murder Dashwood?'

'Yes, sir,' answered Carmichael.

'Did they all have the means?'

'Yes, sir, after what Mr Grimes told us about forgetting to lock up the church on Sunday.'

'Did they all have opportunity?'

'Yes, sir. I say, this isn't getting us very far, is it?'

'Not really. Do you want to call it a night, and sleep on it?

163

We'll be fresher in the morning, and we can look through those inter-band tensions then.'

'But it's Sunday tomorrow, sir.' Carmichael looked concerned.

There's no such thing as a Sunday off when we're in the middle of a murder enquiry. We've been working together long enough for you to know that.'

'Sorry, sir.'

'Just get yourself off home, and let Kerry do the feeding of the five thousand,' Falconer concluded, dropping a sly wink in his sergeant's direction, so that he'd know he was only joking.

'Good idea, sir. What with the heat and everything, I'm fair cream-crackered.'

'Me, too. And I'm infected with dog-lick. Ugh! Let's get out of here, and start again in the morning. Will your car be running by then?

'I should think so. The new bloke at the garage said he didn't think it was anything serious, and he should have it ready for me to collect tonight.'

'In that case, I'll see you at the office.'

'Yes, sir.'

Chapter Fifteen

Sunday 18th July

Carmichael's car was, indeed, back on the road for Sunday morning, and both men arrived at the police station within ten minutes of each other, just after nine o'clock. They had agreed a slightly later start to the working day, as it was, for a great many others, a traditional day of rest.

As Carmichael entered the office, Falconer glanced up at him briefly, then looked back up, to make sure that he could believe his own eyes. Instead of yesterday's colourful Caribbean glory, today, Carmichael was dressed exclusively in black. His tee-shirt was short-sleeved and black; his trousers, a pair of jeans that Kerry had cut off at the knee and frayed, were black; his baseball cap was black, and so were his sunglasses.

'Good God man, are you trying to scare the life out of me?'

'What do you mean, sir?' asked the sergeant, bewildered.

'Well, yesterday, you looked like an escapee from the Notting Hill Carnival, today, you look like the Angel of Death just about to leave for his summer holidays.'

'It's not on purpose, sir. Kerry just thought I was a bit too colourful yesterday, and so she left these togs out for me, to give me a more sober appearance, given the gravity of our work, like.'

'Well, tell her, in future, that a variety of muted colours would do the job better.'

'Will do, sir.'

'OK! Let's get going, then.'

Preferring to work in the old-fashioned style he was used to, Falconer scorned the new see-through boards they had been allotted in this new station, and used instead good old pen and paper until he was ready to transfer anything of importance on to what he referred to as 'the graffiti window'.

From the old supplies, he had discovered an elderly roll of flip-chart paper, and spread out a length of this on his desk, which was always so tidy that there was room for this sort of caper.

'Now, come over here, Carmichael, so that we can put Dashwood in the middle and spread all those who could've done it round him. I usually do this sort of thing at home with index cards, but this seems more the thing to do with this particular case. Then we'll start making connections, and sort out what else was going on between these people. You know how it is, if you've got a lot going on in your life that isn't so good? One tiny thing can trigger off a huge temper, or even violence – 'the straw that broke the camel's back' sort of thing.

'We'll include the vicar in this, and Grace Alexander. Who can tell what a mother may be capable of, when her son has been treated really badly?'

Quickly noting the names down with a marker pen – quickly, but neatly – they were soon at a stage where lines could be drawn, linking the players together in other ways, that did not involve Dashwood.

'Let's not bother linking them all to the victim. We know that none of them was at all fond of him. Let's just draw the lines between other members. If you get out your notes from yesterday, Carmichael, we can go through them, one by one, and see what we come up with.'

Carmichael moved his chair round to the front left corner of Falconer's desk, took out his notebook, and started flipping through it, to find his notes from the previous day. 'We went to Tile Cottage first, sir, to see that Caroline Warwick.'

'She was a strange, colourless character if ever I've met one. You leave her cottage, and it's so characterless and bland, that the memories are almost in black and white,' Falconer mused, remembering the drab interior, that spoke more about an empty house, than an inhabited one.

'She said her husband had an affair with Gayle Potten, and then, when he was found out, high-tailed it off, and left the both of them,' Carmichael offered, deciphering his own idiosyncratic form of shorthand, never dreaming that Isaac Pitman would be spinning in his grave if he could see it.

'Peter!' Falconer exclaimed. 'His name was Peter!'

'So?'

'So, nothing! I was just seeing if I could remember, after that whole raft of interviews we carried out yesterday. So Ms Warwick isn't very fond of Ms Potten, then. Draw a line to connect those two.'

'Next, it was Gayle Potten's, sir.'

'She poses for dirty pictures for Myles Midwynter.'

'I think you'll find that Midwynter will refer to them as artistic, rather than dirty, but we'd better put a line between her and Myrtle Midwynter, who may resent it bitterly. Oh, and Harold Grimes as well. A man so besotted, would naturally resent his beloved shedding her clothes for another man, no matter how artistic it was claimed to be,' Falconer gave as his considered opinion. 'Now, who's next?'

'Harold Grimes – I say, sir; is your name Harry short for Harold?'

'It most certainly is not!' retorted the other, glaring at him as if he had been gravely insulted. 'It's short for Henry.'

'Like that vacuum cleaner with a face?'

'If you must, Carmichael,' Falconer admitted, with a heavy sigh. 'But don't go spreading that about. I like being called Harry. I've been called Harry since I was in the nursery, and I'll not put up with being addressed as Henry because you can't keep your gob shut. Understand? Not a word! Not even to Kerry!'

'Completely understood, sir! You should know better than expect me to blab. I told you what my real name was on our first case, and you've been discreet enough never to mention it since.' [see: Death of an Old Git]

'Right! Let's get back to work, and no more said on either name. Agreed?'

'Agreed, sir!'

'We've already got Grimes linked to Myles Midwynter. Apart from Dashwood, can you think of anyone else he wasn't getting along with?' asked Falconer, furrowing his brow in thought.

'Not really. He seems a fairly laid-back old man – I mean, he's not ancient, or anything like that, he's just not young, and he looks as if he said 'goodbye' to middle-age quite a while ago.'

'Well put, Sergeant. So, who's next on our list of dastardly murder suspects?'

'Fern Bailey. I can't really see her getting in a tizzy with any of the others. We've heard nothing about any fallings out, and she appears to be a fairly mild woman.'

'Excellent evaluation, Carmichael. It's that double bass player next, isn't it? Remind me of her name, if you would be so kind?' Sunday was really bringing out the gentleman in Harry Falconer.

'Vanessa Palfreyman, sir.'

'Oh, yes. Not only did she hate Dashwood, but for some reason she didn't go to the church service before they did that sound test. I wonder why that was? We'll have to ask her next week. You never know, it might have some bearing on the murder, though I can't imagine what.

'However, the devil's in the detail, Carmichael, the devil's in the detail, and we must never forget that. And she said that she thought Myrtle Midwynter was really out for Dashwood's blood. Perhaps you ought to draw a line between the Palfreyman woman and the vicar. It's possible they had a falling out over something. Whatever it was, we need to know.'

'Then it was Lester Westlake.' Carmichael nearly spat the man's name.

'Now, now, little green-eyed monster, Carmichael,' Falconer soothed.

'I'm not jealous. I just don't approve of how he earns his money. As far as I'm concerned, it's dirty money, and he's a dirty blighter.'

'I tend to agree with your sentiments, but not quite so strongly. I don't think there's anything there to interest us. He doesn't seem to socialise with the village, apart from band practices; keeps himself to himself, guarding the nature of his wicked job. I'm sure that that's how he feels many of those in the village would judge it to be, and so he chooses to live anonymously.'

'Did you see that flash car he had in his drive?' Carmichael asked, resentfully.

'Don't let it get to you, Carmichael. A car is only an extension of the penis, isn't it?' Carmichael's face flushed bright crimson at such an explicit biological term being bandied round the office, especially on a Sunday, but the inspector ignored his reaction. 'And that is the particular organ – not the car,' continued Falconer, unfazed, 'that gets him all those nice juicy tips – I said *tips*. Stop laughing! So, his job and the car go together, in his mind. It's the respectable representation of his organ, and promises of things to come, to his clients, if you like.'

'You've got a flash car, sir!' stated Carmichael, still giggling like a girl.

'That's completely different, and don't you ever forget that, Sergeant!'

'No, sir. Sorry, sir!'

It took a moment or two for Falconer's temper to simmer down a bit, and for Carmichael to recover from corpsing (if such a thing is possible without a stage), for Falconer had, finally, been so affected by the giggling, that he had been moved to join in, simply because the sound was so infectious; but they got straight back down to business, when the mood was slightly more sober – or rather, they didn't.

'That was when we took a break for lunch, and had a bite in The Leathern Bottle, giving you an opportunity to change into your old trousers – I still can't believe you haven't got any jeans!'

'Well, I haven't, but what say we take a break now, and go along to the canteen. They may still have some doughnuts left,

169

and, I don't know about you, but I'm a bit peckish.'

'Lead on, sir. I'm starving! As per usual!'

In the canteen they found Bob Bryant, tucking into an apple Danish, a huge cup of tea sitting on the table in front of him, and Falconer went over while Carmichael got their coffee and doughnuts – one of the latter for Falconer, and three for himself!

'Not on the desk, Bob?' Falconer greeted him.

'No, Merv Green came in for something, and said he'd hold the fort for a while so that I could have a break. There's not much action down there, anyway. Dead as a dodo, on a lovely Sunday like this.'

Carmichael approached with a loaded tray, and the other two noted that he had put two bananas and a chocolate bar on the tray, as well as what he had been dispatched to fetch.

'Got to keep my strength up,' was his only comment, when he saw the direction of their gaze.

'Seen anything of old 'Jelly' recently?' asked Bob Bryant innocently. This was a reference to Detective Superintendent Chivers, whom Bob knew was the bane of Falconer's life, always hauling the inspector over the coals for something he had done, or had neglected to do.

'No, thank God,' Falconer replied, unable to help himself take a quick peek over his shoulder, as if naming the man might summon him as well.

'Did you know he and I sometimes used to work together, in the old days?' asked Bob, whose fish had just taken the bait he had so subtly cast upon the conversational waters.

'Did you? That's news to me,' said Falconer, looking interested.

'Oh, I could tell you some tales about that one, so I could. There wasn't a trick he wouldn't pull or a corner he wouldn't cut to get the result he wanted, and he was a dab hand at getting other people to do his dirty work for him, I can tell you. He was also as rough as a badger's bum in his habits as well, and absolutely shameless.'

'Do go on. This doesn't sound like the Chivers we all know and fear,' Falconer encouraged him.

'Well, I'll tell you the sort of 'don't give a shit' character he used to be, and the story that's just come to mind is totally apt, given what I've just said. Back in those days, he was a DS and I was just a uniformed PC. Anyway, he was sent out one night on surveillance, with strict instructions to stay alert – he said that would be OK, because he'd always been a 'lert'. There was to be no listening to music, or reading the newspaper, and *definitely* no having a little doze to pass the time. It was imperative that he was attentive on that job.

'Anyway, the time gets round to eleven-thirty, everything black as pitch, out there in the sticks, where he was watching this place, and the station radioed him to say that the surveillance had been aborted, as there'd been a leak.

'Well, there was no answer from his radio, and none of us had anything like a mobile phone in those days, so they just kept on trying his radio. Ten minutes go past, and still no response, and the old chief started to get worried. Ten minutes was a long time not to answer your radio, even if you'd stopped for a jimmy riddle in the hedgerow, so I was allotted a car, and told to drive out to where he was supposed to be, and see if everything was all right.

'I was only young then, and quite worried about what I'd find when I got there. I had all sorts of gruesome thoughts in my head, and then I saw the car. It was parked half on the road and half on the grass verge. The interior light was on, because the driver's door was wide open, and when I got out and approached it – carefully, mind – I could hear the radio squawking away, for anyone in the vicinity to hear.

'But there was no one in the car. It was completely deserted. That's when I really got worried. What if he'd been rumbled, and then been kidnapped? Even worse, what if he'd been rumbled, and they'd done him in, and just dumped the body somewhere nearby? I was nearly peeing my pants, when I got round to having a bit of a scout, calling out 'Guv! Guv!' as loud as I dared, and scouring both sides of the road for him.

'I was just about to give up, and report him missing, when there's this really loud noise, of what sounded like someone trying to get through the hedge, and they were doing it just about where I was standing. God, was I frightened! I thought they'd done for him, and were coming back for me, too.

'So, I move away from the hedge, locating where all the noise is coming from, and I have my torch in my hand, ready to dazzle the bugger with, when out steps Chivers, looking exactly like he'd been pulled through a hedge backwards. "Where the hell have you been?" I asked him, furious at the worry he'd caused me, and not giving a fig, that he was my superior in rank.

'"I've been for a 'tom-tit'," he replies, cool as you like. "Can't I even take a dump in peace these days? So, what the hell do you want?"

'"You've been where?" I asked, thoroughly confused by now.

'"Into that field. If you take a look through that gap where I squeezed through, you'll find it's full of cabbages."

"What do cabbages have to do with it? I don't understand."

"Well, You've got to think of the nature of cabbage leaves, if you know what I mean."

"I don't", I replied, still none the wiser.

"They're nice and crinkly, aren't they?"

"Yes, sir," I replied, calm enough to remember my place by now.

"And there ain't no toilet paper in a field full of cabbages, is there, son? But a nice crinkly outer leaf does a lovely job when there's nothing else to hand. All those wrinkly bits clean your rim off a fair treat."

'And that was that. He just got into his car, called in, and was told it was all off, and then drove away, without even a goodbye, or a backward glance.'

'I don't believe it!' exclaimed Falconer, laughing nonetheless.

'He can't have done!' Carmichael stated, shocked at how coarse the superintendent's behaviour was being related as

172

having been when he was younger.

'I swear, on my mother's life, that every single word of that story is the gospel truth; cross my heart and hope to die. Anyway, lads, got to let poor old Merv get back on patrol. And if you like, when we three meet again, I'll tell you another. Promise! Ta-ra!'

'When shall we three meet again ...' muttered Falconer.

'Don't know, sir,' answered Carmichael, taking the statement, of course, literally. 'But I bet you didn't know that Bob Bryant's first name is really Trevor.'

'Never! Oh, that rhymes!' declared Falconer. 'But, how the dickens do you know that?'

'I have my sources, sir,' said Carmichael, dropping a slow wink to the inspector.

'So why does he call himself Bob?'

'For the same reason that you and I don't use our given names: it's simply a matter of taste!' For a moment, the sergeant sounded very nearly upper-crust.

'Come on, you – Mr Master-Spy – back to the office. We've wasted enough time in here, listening to fairy tales.'

Back at Falconer's desk and the large sheet of paper, they set to, once more, to try to map the tensions between the various members of the band.

'Who's next?' Falconer asked, as Carmichael picked up his notebook and attempted to find his place in it, but they were interrupted by the ringing of the telephone, and Falconer reached for it, while Carmichael froze, his finger firmly between two pages of his notes.

'Market Darley CID, Detective Inspector Falconer speaking. How may I help you?'

'It's me, Harry; Philip Christmas. I tried your home number, but you weren't answering, so I just thought I'd try the office first, knowing what a workaholic you are. Then it would've been your mobile, but I've got you now, so that doesn't matter anymore.'

'Anything to report?' asked Falconer, hopefully, and

automatically turning the phone on to speaker so that he would not have to waste time explaining everything to Carmichael afterwards.

'Indeed I have. Firstly, the victim seems to have received a blow to the throat, right about where the Adam's apple is located, and secondly, it would have taken a considerable amount of effort to shove that thing in. It went right through his heart, you know. Oh, and I estimate that he died nearer to Monday than Friday. Definitely the early part of the week, but that's about as close as I can get, given the condition the body was in and the action of the hot weather.'

'That's all very interesting.'

'And get this! I've examined that spike. It's not a skinny little thing, nor is it anything like a sharp knife. Granted, it is a spike, but it was never an arrow, and it's old, so the end was blunt – hence the amount of force needed to get it into his body. You're either looking for a very strong person here, or a maniac, and I don't know which.'

'Thanks a lot for that, Philip. We'll bear it in mind when we're looking for someone to frame for this one.'

'Pull the other one, Harry. You're one of the most honest men I know. Now, away and do your job, so that you can get home, and put your feet up for just a couple of hours on a Sunday evening. Bye.'

'Goodbye, Philip.' Falconer ended the call and gave a low whistle. 'So, there was an injury we didn't know about – hence no signs of a fight or even a scuffle – and we're looking for someone who's strong enough to have pushed that spike right through his ribs and into his heart. Very interesting!'

'I wonder if it was a lucky blow, or whether we're looking for someone who knew exactly what they were doing?' asked Carmichael.

'Don't know yet, but we can get back to everyone we interviewed, and try to find out if any of them have ever taken classes in self-defence or the martial arts. If it was someone adept at one or the other, we don't even need to be looking for a man – it could just as well be a woman. And as for the spike, if you've got your victim out spark-o, you haven't got him struggling against you as you try to push the spike through his flesh, so again, it could have taken time and effort, rather than sheer brute strength.

'Now, let's have a look at these people again, and consider the inter-band tensions, then try to see if we've got someone here who didn't need much to push them over the edge; and a nudge from Dashwood did the trick, and homed all their anger in on him. I'm almost beginning to feel sorry for him. He was, after all, only trying to improve their playing: it was just that he took it all so seriously, and they were just, if you'll excuse the pun, playing at it. So, what've we got?'

'That first lady we went to see seems to have a lot of axes to grind within the band,' offered Carmichael.

'The one next door to Dashwood, in Tile Cottage? Played the piccolo and 'miscellaneous percussion'? Makes you think of saucepans and biscuit tins, doesn't it, that expression?'

'I'm sure she would be mortified if she could hear you, sir,' the sergeant gave as his opinion on this comment, and then continued, 'Geraldine Warwick's her name. If you remember, she really got her knickers in a twist about Myles's trolling around naked, then about Gayle Potten going round to The Grange and being photographed in the buff.'

'Yes, and she really took offence at the Potten woman and Harold Grimes' canoodling. Not surprising really, considering that her husband had an affair with the woman, then ran out on both of them. That really is a big bundle of axes, but she's so tiny, if I remember correctly. Do you think she'd have had the strength to do what was done to the man?'

'People can find extraordinary strength if they are angry or passionate enough about something. You hear stories of women lifting cars because their child is trapped, and then having no idea how they managed to do it,' replied Carmichael, giving an example of this phenomenon.

'True. So what else have we got? That 'first' and 'second' violin' seem to have been at loggerheads since the band started.'

175

'That's Gwendolyn Radcliffe and Cameron McKnight, and she certainly seems to be the winner in this situation. I can't really see her murdering the very chap who gave her a chance to play the part she's coveted for years, can you, sir?'

'No, but Cameron McKnight's a completely different proposition. He's got that opera singer 'sort of' living with him – Oscar Littlechild, that's his name – and he didn't seem very happy about us finding out about him. You can bet your boots, that his presence is a deadly secret, known by no one else in the village.'

'Closet queer?'

'Carmichael! Live and let live!'

'Sorry, sir. Only using it as a verbal shorthand description.'

'In that case you're forgiven, but if you want to use it at any time in the future, I'd be happier if you used the initials, CQ. I know you haven't got a prejudiced bone in your body, but if anyone else heard you say something like that they might see it as homophobia.'

'Got it, sir! What about that Edmund Alexander? He's absolutely against change of any kind. He seems to want everything to stay exactly as he remembers it as a child. I know his only beef seems to be Dashwood, and he gave the impression that he had taken it in his stride.'

'Bravado! Sheer bravado! I think you might have something there. It must have been a devastating blow to him to be suspended as the band pianist, then to have the same little weasel worm his way round the vicar and steal his job as church organist. That was his role in the village, and he's had the rug whipped right out from under his feet. You could see it in his eyes when he was telling us about it yesterday. Scrub what I said earlier. I haven't an ounce of sympathy for our not-friend, Dashwood.'

'You could be onto something there. I mean, Alexander's not exactly normal, is he?'

'In what way, Carmichael?'

'He's not what you could call anywhere near young, anymore. He's not married, and there doesn't seem to be any sign of a girlfriend – I'm sure it would have been mentioned, if such a person had existed, if not by him, then by one of the others. He lives at home with Mums and Pops, and I'd put money on him being an only child.'

'You mean he's never had to grow up?'

'That's it in a nutshell. I don't know if he works, or has ever worked, but his world seems very small to me – just his music and the garden, and his parents, of course.'

'That's longhand for 'could be a nutter', isn't it Carmichael?'

'Yes, sir, but I think he has to stay in the frame, don't you?'

'I agree. That Westlake guy who plays the sax, has also got a guilty secret, that he wants to keep from his fellow band members, hasn't he?'

'What, the fact that he's a gigolo?'

'Spot on! What would he do to keep that quiet, I wonder? He's got a big house, a flash car, and, I suppose, a certain amount of respect for his material success, but how would people feel if they knew he was a male escort?'

'That's just another name for a prostitute, sir. Just because he's a man with money, what he does is no different to what hard-up women do in alleyways or in the back of cars.'

'Oh, you *have* got a bee in your bonnet about him, haven't you, Carmichael?'

'I think what he does is despicable, seedy, and immoral.'

'Actually, I tend to agree with you, but that doesn't get us any further forward, does it? Who's left?'

'The Midwynters; Fern Bailey – viola; and Harold Grimes, the bloke with the trumpet.'

'I don't think there's anything to be held against the Bailey woman. She's just a great big overgrown schoolgirl, still mad about her dog, and although what Dashwood said to her must have been hurtful, in the end, it was probably like water off a duck's back. She didn't seem the sort of person to hold a grudge, to me.'

'Me, neither, sir. What about Gayle Potten's boyfriend?'

'He seemed a perfectly likeable fellow. He knew he had

shortcomings, musically, but he's happy to work at it, he's happy with his girlfriend. No, I can't see anyone falling out with him. The only black mark against him is that he did lie to them about locking up the church, but I think that's just a bit of everyday life that would never have seen the light of day, if Dashwood hadn't been murdered, and that being the only period when the cello spike could have been taken.'

'That's not quite true, sir. There was another opportunity.'

'When?' asked Falconer, perplexed.

'When it was back at The Grange, sir. Who's to say that one of the Midwynters didn't remove it? It could've been Myles, and after all, it seems to have been those two who were instrumental – sorry, sir – in forming the band. I know they've had other Musical Directors, but I bet they were more compliant than Dashwood.'

'You're right! He could've been eaten up with jealousy. I mean, the band rehearsal pattern was completely exploded and everything they'd been doing for the last ten years was just wiped out, almost instantly. He probably loved having the practices at his place, hence no problem with having to pay for the food and wine for them all, and then it was just snatched away from him by this in-comer.'

'He was probably absolutely furious about the way things were going, and the man had a real go at him, about his standard of playing.'

'And that goes for Myrtle, too, Carmichael. She has played lady bountiful for a decade, and now she's just another member of the band. Add to that the fact that he aimed rather a lot of his criticism at her, and she could easily have taken the spike herself, and then acted absolutely horrified, when she 'found' it gone,' concluded Falconer.

'Or they could even have been in it together, sir. What about that?' suggested Carmichael, really getting excited now.

'We certainly can't rule that out. It seems highly plausible to me. Well done, Carmichael. Have six house-points, and go to the top of the class.'

'Thank you very much, sir. Do I get a gold star, too?'

'You certainly do! No – make that two! Well, that's everybody covered. I think we should call it a day, and start looking at the case from the points of view which we've just discussed, on the morrow.'

Very late – conversation

'I didn't expect to see you, and why so late?'

'Oh, you know, couldn't sleep and what not.'

'Come on in, and I'll get us something to drink.'

'Nothing alcoholic for me, thanks. In fact, I've brought some herbal stuff with me, for you to try as well. It's a little something from my garden that I found the recipe for in an old book. I find it very energising, and I thought it might give you a bit more fizz in this hot weather.'

'Thanks. I've got a bit of a summer cold, and I can't taste anything at the moment, but if it'll perks me up, I'm game. Did you really mean what you said the other day?'

'Oh, let's not talk about that. I'll slip into the kitchen and get this made, and I'll bring it through, shall I?'

'Lovely. I'll go and sit and wait then, shall I?'

'Yes. You just relax. It won't take a minute.'

Chapter Sixteen

Monday 19th July

The morrow started a little earlier than either of them had suspected, with a call to Falconer at home at a little after half-past seven. The caller was Dr Christmas, and he sounded very grave. 'Harry, I think we've got another murder on our hands in Swinbury Abbot. I'm at The Old Manor in Dark Lane; family by the name of Palfreyman: mother, father, and grown-up daughter.'

'Yes, I know who you mean. What's happened?'

'Well, apparently the daughter always brings her parents a cup of tea in bed at half-past seven every morning. This morning she failed to show, so Mrs Palfreyman went to her daughter's bedroom and found that her bed hadn't been slept in. She went on downstairs to see if she could find Vanessa, and she did – but not up and about.'

'She found her in an armchair in the sitting room, dead – been dead for hours, in my opinion. But in front of her was a cup and saucer, with some liquid dregs left in the cup. I don't think this is suicide: there's no trace of a note, but I am very suspicious of what's in the bottom of that cup. I'd like you over here as soon as possible, if you can manage it.'

'I'll ring Carmichael, and alert a SOCO team, and I'll be there in about ten or fifteen minutes. Don't let anyone touch anything in that room. That applies to the kitchen too, if it's not already too late for that, but whatever you do, don't let them touch the kettle. And it was only the one cup and saucer, was it?' asked Falconer.

'Yes, but that doesn't mean that there hadn't been another

181

one that had been rinsed out and put away.'

'I'm on my way. *You* ring Carmichael, and get him to summon a SOCO team; that'll save me a minute or two. See you very shortly.'

Falconer and Carmichael's cars arrived virtually simultaneously in Dark Lane, but nothing was said about the speed at which Carmichael must have driven to complete a longer journey than Falconer's in such a short time, and they approached the house together, pointedly not saying anything about speeding, or reckless driving. 'Well, this is a bit of a turn up for the books, isn't it, sir?' asked Carmichael.

'It certainly is. I've been cudgelling my brains all the way here, and I can't think who might have a grudge against Miss Palfreyman. She seemed to get on with everyone in the band, and she doesn't seem to have much of a social life, outside its members. Why would anyone want to kill *her*?

'I mean, if it had been Gayle Potten, I might have been able to justify it. She had Caroline Warwick on her case, both about breaking up her marriage, and the mucky photographs with Myles, and I'd have had a list of suspects to back that up; but Vanessa Palfreyman? It just doesn't make sense.'

'There must be something we've missed, sir. Nobody would commit murder for nothing!' stated Carmichael, logically and emphatically.

'But what is it we've missed?' asked Falconer, similarly bewildered at the identity of the victim. 'We're going to have to re-interview everyone involved, but this time from a different angle. Which of them wanted both Dashwood and the bass player dead? Still, best get inside first, and see what's what.'

They found Philip Christmas sitting on a dining chair, keeping well clear of both the sitting room and the kitchen. The deceased's elderly parents he had escorted round to The Parsonage for tea and sympathy, allowing them only time to fetch their dressing gowns before they left.

'I thought it was best that way,' he explained. 'That way, the vicar and his wife can see to cups of tea, and any breakfast, if they can face it, and do the old pastoral care bit, leaving us a free rein here. I've phoned the station as well, to let them know what's going on, and they've confirmed that there is a SOCO team on the way. *She's* in there, if you want to see her,' he said, rising from his uncomfortable perch, and leading the way.

Vanessa Palfreyman was slumped down in an armchair, on one side of a coffee table, a nearly empty cup on the table, just in front of her. A small trickle of vomit had made its way down her chin from the left hand corner of her mouth, and made a small pool on her pyjamas, implying that she had got ready for bed before ingesting whatever it was in the cup. There were also other visible signs of the body having finally let go of life. These were unpleasant, but quite normal, and need not be gone into in the interests of this narrative.

'Why on earth would she get ready for bed if she intended to take her own life?' asked Falconer.

'And if she wanted to die in bed, why did she drink whatever was in that cup down here, and not take it to bed with her?' This question was added by Dr Christmas, to be followed by a comment from Carmichael.

'If she was intending to do away with herself, wouldn't she at least have left a note? You said you didn't find anything, Dr Christmas?'

'I didn't, but that's not to say that there isn't one, lying about somewhere else in the house. I haven't conducted a search because I didn't want to contaminate any of the other rooms, but there certainly isn't one downstairs.'

'And I don't think anyone will find one,' Falconer opined. If she meant to die in bed, she'd have taken her potion upstairs, and left a note by her bed. If she wanted to die downstairs, she'd have left the note down here – probably on that coffee table. No, I think this is definitely a suspicious death, and I suggest we treat it as such from the word go. Philip, get the post mortem results to us as soon as you can, and we need some of that liquid for analysis.'

Looking out of the window, Carmichael announced, 'SOCO's just arrived, and so has the mortuary van.'

'Right, we'd better let them get on with their jobs, and make ourselves scarce for a while. I wonder if it's possible for Mr and Mrs Palfreyman to stay at The Parsonage until tomorrow. They certainly can't come back today with it being a crime scene.'

'I'll go round there when I've finished here,' Christmas offered.

'No, you're all right. I've got to speak to her parents anyway, and there's no 'good' time to do it, so it might as well be now. I'll ask while we're round there questioning them,' said Falconer, fielding this kind offer for the sake of procedure.

'Well, as far as I can see,' concluded the doctor, 'she suffocated on her own vomit, but I'd say it was poisoning for definite. I don't know what with, but the toxicology chaps will be able to give us an answer as soon as they've analysed what's in these dregs, which I hope will match up with the contents of the stomach. I'll get back to you as soon as I've got any news.'

They found Vanessa's parents in the drawing room of The Parsonage, the vicar sitting with them, comforting them in low tones, his wife in the kitchen making a fresh pot of tea.

'They're awfully shocked, poor things,' Olivia informed them. 'Chris is trying to convince them that their daughter is 'safe in the arms of Jesus', and all that stuff, but I don't think they're taking in a word.'

'I won't take up any more of their time than is absolutely necessary, at this point,' Falconer assured her, and the two detectives made their presence known.

The Palfreymans looked up with blank expressions, their eyes shocked and red with weeping. It was Mrs Palfreyman who broke the awkward silence. 'I know who you are, and I know we've got to speak to you now. All we want to know is who could do such a terrible thing to our little girl?

'We looked everywhere, you know, when we'd summoned help and realised there was nothing we could do. There's absolutely no sign of a note anywhere. Someone did this to our daughter, and I realise, now, that I'm furious that they abolished hanging. Whoever did this should be hanged by the neck until

184

they're dead: prison's too good for them. An eye for an eye, it says in the Bible, doesn't it, Vicar?'

Before the vicar could chip in with the difference between the Old Testament and the New Testament, Falconer made his bid for control. 'We're all so sorry for what has happened, and DS Carmichael and I are as anxious as you are to apprehend the person responsible for this appalling destruction of life.

'I need to ask you if your daughter had any enemies. I know that sounds a bit dramatic, but perhaps you could just have a think, and tell me if your daughter had fallen out with anyone recently? Nothing is too trivial to consider at this point of the investigation.'

'The only person she had any words with was that Dashwood individual, and he's already dead,' stated Mrs Palfreyman, picking at the threads on her old-fashioned candlewick dressing gown, unaware of her hands' independent activity, in her distress.

'That damned old bully of a Musical Director had got right up her nose,' Mr Palfreyman said, but it was all a bit of a muddle, as they spoke simultaneously.

Falconer cocked an eyebrow at the vicar, and he nodded, to confirm that this was a habit of theirs. 'Jolly good luck to Carmichael,' thought Falconer, wondering how he would manage to take note of two simultaneous answers to every question.

'Did she have any friends outside the band, in the village or elsewhere?' he asked.

'None that we're aware of. She always was a bit of a loner.' (Mrs Palfreyman)

'A shy little thing, she used to be, and didn't make friends easily.' (Mr Palfreyman)

'That's a 'no' then, I take it?' asked Falconer, just to confirm that he had un-jumbled the two answers correctly. 'And did she have any particular friends in the band?'

'She got on well with Myrtle Midwynter. They used to go on walking holidays once a year.' (Mrs Palfreyman)

'She wasn't much of a one for mixing, but she hit it off with that woman who plays the cello.' (Mr Palfreyman)

'Anyone else?' Falconer was finding this 'talking at the same time' very hard work.

'That chap up at The Hurst, who played the violin.' (Mrs Palfreyman)

'Mr McKnight, up on Chopping Knife Lane.' (Mr Palfreyman)

'I think we'll leave it there, for today. Thank you very much for your time, Mr and Mrs Palfreyman,' said Falconer, beginning to feel his head spin.

'There wasn't anyone would want to hurt our little girl. She was as nice a person as you could wish to meet.' (Mr Palfreyman)

'No one would want to harm our Vanessa. She was such a sweet natured girl, if a bit solitary.' (Mrs Palfreyman)

A final couple of questions occurred to Falconer, and he asked it, as he rose from his seat. 'On the night before you found your daughter in such tragic circumstances, did either of you hear the sound of someone arriving for a late visit – the doorbell, for instance, or a knock on the door?' he asked, hoping that they might have heard something, old people being notoriously bad sleepers.

'Nothing, Inspector. We don't sleep well in this hot weather, so we usually take a tablet before we turn the light off, then we don't know another thing until our Vanessa wakes – used to wake …' Mrs Palfreyman's voice cracked here, and she couldn't go one, sinking her head into her hands, and beginning to sob again.

'We always take a sleeping tablet when the weather gets hot. Nothing short of the Crack of Doom would wake us after we've taken one of those things,' stated Mr Palfreyman, simultaneously with this wife's reply, then clammed up, his face white and drawn, his eyes staring into the middle distance, blank and uncomprehending.

'I'm sorry to have to question you so soon after this terrible thing, but I only have one other question, and this one is for Mrs Palfreyman only. I'm sure you didn't give this a thought earlier, but when you get back home, I wonder if you would be so good as to look in your crockery cupboards for us, to see if anything is slightly out of place.

'I ask this because we are convinced that someone visited your daughter, very late last night, and brought whatever was used to poison her with them. It's very likely that, to avert any suspicion, they had a drink themselves. That vessel would probably have been rinsed out and put away, to infer that whatever your daughter drank, she drank on her own, and had made the decision to taken her own life.

'Have a good look, and give me a ring afterwards, whether anything's been moved or not. We need to know one way or the other, and a woman knows the contents of her own cupboards best.'

For once, Mr Palfreyman said nothing, maintaining his faraway look, apparently unaware of his surroundings or anything that was going on in them.

'If I haven't heard anything, I'll get in touch with you when we know more, and we'll speak again,' Falconer assured them.

'You just get whoever done this, and lock them away forever.' (Mrs Palfreyman)

'You'd better find who's responsible before I do, or I'll do for them myself.' (Mr Palfreyman)

Once out of the drawing room, Falconer gave the vicar an old-fashioned look, and he held up his hands in surrender. 'Sorry, Inspector: there was no way I could warn you, but that's how they always speak. No wonder Vanessa was a quiet child. I should think it was impossible for her to get a word in edgeways. I should have told Olivia to warn you if she got to you first.'

'Well, at least we know now. I shall have to have two note-takers with me if I have to speak to them again. It was like having two radios tuned to different channels, but both on at the same time. What do you think, Carmichael?'

'I think I'm getting a bit of a headache, sir.'

'I'm not surprised!'

187

'What say you, we go to The Leathern Bottle, have a morning coffee, and see where we're going next?' suggested Falconer.

'Good idea, sir, but I think I'll probably just have an orange juice. I've gone right off tea and coffee.'

'Since when? You've never said no, when we've been interviewing people in their own homes.'

'Since I got home last night. I expect it's just a temporary thing, but the very thought of them makes me feel sick.'

They entered The Leathern Bottle together, and Falconer went to the bar to order a latte and an orange juice, the barman asking him if he wanted ice in the juice, but when he turned round, he found himself alone. Of Carmichael, there was no sign. 'You'd better put a couple of cubes in, then if he doesn't want ice, he can always hoik them out with his fingers,' decided Falconer, on his partner's behalf.

Having paid for the drinks, he put them on a tray and went outside to see where his sergeant had got to, and found him seated at one of the outside tables, looking mournful.

'Whatever's the matter with you? You look as miserable as a bloodhound that has lost its sense of smell,' Falconer declared, putting the tray down on the table.

'I wish I could lose my sense of smell, sir. As soon as we walked through the door, and I smelled the stale beer, my stomach turned a somersault. I knew, right away, that if I didn't get away from it, I was going to be as sick as a dog,' answered Carmichael, still looking woebegone.

'Look, I've got you an orange juice with ice. If you don't fancy the ice, you can just pull it out with your fingers, and throw it away.'

'I don't even feel like an orange juice, now. The thought of all that acid – ugh!'

'I know you've got a dicky tummy, but I can't say that we've seen anything to set it off today. Maybe you've got a bug, or something,' offered Falconer, examining his sergeant's face, and finding it pale, pasty, and beaded with sweat. 'Look, why don't you get along home and spend the afternoon in bed:

see if you can't sweat it out, or starve it, or whatever it is you need to do.

'I've got plenty of paperwork, back at the office, which I can be getting on with, and we'll see how you are tomorrow, and if you're not better then, you'll have to go to the quack, and I'll have to see about getting in a replacement, but I'd rather not do that if I don't have to.'

'Thanks, sir,' muttered Carmichael and, covering his mouth with his hand, just to be on the safe side, made his way to his car and shot straight off as if all the hounds of hell were after him.

'Well, I wonder what's up with him?' asked Falconer of no one. 'Maybe it was just that trickle of vomit from the victim's mouth. He's not very good with vomit, so that must be it,' and then he shut up as a couple approached the door of the pub, and he realised he was doing a grand job of appearing like some nutter, who was sitting talking to an invisible friend.

Chapter Seventeen

Tuesday 20th July

Carmichael was back in the office, and only slightly late the next morning, claiming to have found a sickness remedy at home, and stopped off at a pharmacy on the way to get some more. He declared himself to feel much better, and, in fact, he certainly looked healthier than he had the day before when he had fled the car park of The Leathern Bottle.

'Any idea what it was?' Falconer asked him, assessing his appearance and finding it improved.

'Not a clue, sir, but if I take this jollop, and it's no better in a couple of days, I'll take your advice, and go and see the quack,' he replied.

'Good thinking. It may just blow over, but if it doesn't, it's best to be on the safe side,' counselled Falconer, who was never ill himself, but liked people on whom he relied to look after themselves, with regard to their health. That way, he was never inconvenienced.

When they took a break for coffee – bottled water in Carmichael's case – Falconer raised the subject of the identity of yesterday's victim, again. 'Why her? Why do you think she of all the band members was killed, Carmichael?'

'I really can't think of a motive, sir. It would seem that she kept herself to herself and, basically, wouldn't say 'boo' to a goose.'

'And can you blame her?' Falconer asked with a smile. 'My God, those parents of hers! They really took the biscuit, didn't they? However did you manage with your notes?'

'Don't ask. I did my best to catch up with what they'd said

when you were asking questions, but I think it's all a bit muddly. I wasn't feeling particularly chipper, either, but I don't think they said anything we didn't already know from our other interviews, did they?'

At that moment, the telephone shrieked its urgent summons, and Falconer answered it, to find Philip Christmas on the line, and the doctor rushed straight into the information he had to impart, as if he was so excited, he didn't have time to waste, on any of the usual social niceties.

'There was a right old minestrone of ingredients in the dregs we found in that cup, yesterday. You wouldn't believe the mixture of things – all plant extracts – that went to make up that concoction, whatever it was supposed to be.

'I've already opened her up, and there's a direct match with the stomach contents, apart from the odd biscuit or two, and the remains of a light meal, about six hours before she died.'

Falconer was glad that he was taking the call and not Carmichael. This would be likely to send him off once more, to his sick bed. 'What have you got, then?' he asked, pen at the ready. This was one call that certainly wasn't going on speaker, to be shared with his sergeant.

'Everything which could be picked up in a country garden, or in the nearby countryside – and one exotic extra, but I'll tell you about that in a minute. For now, whoever made up that witch's brew, needed access to valerian, foxgloves, deadly nightshade, and laburnum.

'Those are the easy bits to get hold of, although I expect you'd have to know what you were doing.'

'So what's the wild card, then, Doc?'

'Ricin! Very deadly, and there's no known antidote. I think that girl was lucky, really. The valerian knocked her out, and her stomach obviously rebelled against what had just been introduced to it, and tried to get rid of it. It was a much more peaceful death, choking on her own vomit, than what that lot could have done to her. Merciful, in its way.'

'And what about the ricin? What plant does that come from, and why is it the exotic ingredient?' asked Falconer, starting to doodle on his pad, as he waited for an answer.

'It's extracted from the seeds of the castor oil plant, but it's not something that is grown in this country as a rule. It requires more tropical climes than ours. Mind you, I'm not discounting someone being able to grow one, if they used a greenhouse, or a very favourable spot. They're normally kept as houseplants in this country, if they're kept at all, and don't usually produce seeds, if kept indoors.'

'Wasn't that what was used on some agent, or spy, a few years ago? He was pricked with the end of an umbrella containing it, I seem to remember.'

'That's right, and it was curtains for him. There's absolutely nothing that could be done for him, even in this day and age, and that still stands today.'

'What! No antidote at all?'

'None, whatsoever!'

'Very nasty,' commented Falconer, turning his pen to the sketching of a skull and crossbones. 'Well, if we're talking gardens here, I think I've got someone in line for that, although I can't perceive a motive, at the moment. He had a humdinger, though, for murdering that other chap. Thanks, Philip. I owe you one, for getting the information to me so swiftly.'

'I'll be in touch if anything else turns up. Good luck!' and the doctor was gone, back to his grisly task.

Having explained the nature of the poison to Carmichael, he put forward the suggestion that they ought to have a word with Edmund Alexander. Not only had he been severely treated by Dashwood and, with his nature of not embracing change, had adequate motive for his murder, he also had a garden full of lovely old cottage flowers, and a wild garden – the perfect place to gather the ingredients for such a deadly brew as the doc had just described.

'But what about the ricin, sir?' asked Carmichael. 'And a motive for killing Vanessa Palfreyman?'

'Mere details at the moment. He'll probably have a greenhouse or something, somewhere, in a part of the garden that we haven't seen yet. But there's something we don't understand, yet, about this case. There's something we don't know, that will make all the difference to the way we investigate it. I'm willing to bet that we'll get that 'unknown something' from Edmund Alexander, and I'm going to arrest him on suspicion, and bring him in for a recorded interview.'

'As you like, sir. I know there's a vital piece missing from the jigsaw, *too,* but I don't know if Alexander is the right-shaped piece. We still don't have anyone with a viable motive for getting rid of Miss Palfreyman, do we?'

'The answer is out there, Carmichael, and we might just be about to find it. Come on! Let's not waste time jawing about it: let's get it done.'

When they arrived at Dunspendin, Grace Alexander greeted them with the news that Edmund had just popped into the village for some shopping for her, but would be back in ten or fifteen minutes.

Falconer took this opportunity to ask if she would be good enough to give them a tour of the garden, and educate them a little about what they were growing. Edmund's absence was a piece of serendipitous luck, and they might have already located the suspect plants before his return; something that would give them even more reason for asking him to come in for formal questioning.

Grace was a little more mobile today, and escorted them, at rather more than a tottering snail's pace, around her and Edmund's pride and joy. She pointed out plants as she went, and indeed, there were the offending items, all growing on their patch of ground – all except the castor oil plant.

'Do you also love your house-plants, Mrs Alexander?' asked Falconer, guilelessly, an expression of complete innocence on his face.

'Not at all, Inspector. In fact, I loathe them. I feel about them, rather as I do about caged birds. Plants should be outside, in their natural environment, not cooped up in pots, inside people's homes, no matter how decorative they are.' She was adamant. Not one houseplant had ever crossed her threshold.

194

Any plants she had been given, over the years, had been decently planted outside, to live a natural life, and if they hadn't thrived, that was what nature had intended.

'Unlike her son,' thought Falconer, calling to mind the cage she seemed to have kept him in since childhood. 'Do you have any other children, other than Edmund?' he asked, again with a perfectly innocent face.

'It just wasn't God's will,' was her answer. 'Edmund is our only blessing, and he has been such a blessing, since old age caught up with me and my husband. I don't know how we should be able to manage without him.'

God, that made Falconer feel like a genuine, twenty-four carat rat: here he was, in this garden, under false pretence, just waiting to take their carer in for questioning as a suspected murderer. Being a detective could be a right bummer, at times.

Edmund returned, as they reached the front of the property again, and greeted them politely, asking if they'd made any progress with Dashwood's murder, and saying how awful it was, that Vanessa Palfreyman had seen fit to take her own life.

'We're not treating it as suicide, Mr Alexander. As far as the authorities are concerned, it is a suspicious death, and must be investigated as such,' explained Falconer, wondering what it could be, that he might learn from this man, that had, so far, eluded him.

'You mean it's another murder? No!' Alexander exclaimed, scandalised. 'Not in Swinbury Abbot: it can't be! This is such a quiet village. We never have any problems here, except when The Clocky Hen gets a bit rowdy, and a patrol car usually sorts that out and clears the bars without any trouble.'

'Knowing how much you know about life in this village, I wonder if you would mind accompanying us to the police station in Market Darley, so that we can pick your brains?' requested the inspector and, totally unsuspecting, Edmund accepted, perhaps even a little proud, that he had been chosen as an expert on the village he loved so much.

There was no way Falconer could tell him he was being taken in as a murder suspect; not with his mother present. That would be too cruel to even contemplate. If he was guilty, she'd have to face up to it sooner or later, but on the outside chance that he was wrong about her son, he needed to handle this situation with dignity and diplomacy. There was no point upsetting the old lady, either unnecessarily or prematurely.

'I'm just going off to help the police with their enquiries,' he chirruped to his mother, with a grin, 'but only as an expert witness. Ha ha!'

Back at the station, they escorted Edmund into an interview room, and explained the real reason they had brought him in. As they went through the caution and the official arrest procedure, on suspicion of the murder of Campbell Dashwood, his face drained of colour, and he swayed on his feet, as if he were about to faint. 'I don't understand why you picked on me,' he stated, looking both confused and frightened.

'We shall, of course, obtain a warrant to search the property, and you will be held here, pending the outcome of this interview, and the subsequent search,' Falconer informed him.

'But I wouldn't hurt a fly, let alone a fellow human being,' Edmund blustered, devastated by what was happening to him. It was a nightmare scenario for him, and his first thoughts were for his parents, but Falconer assured him that, in the event of him being detained overnight, he would get in touch with Rev. Church, and ask him to go round to the house to make sure they had everything they needed. 'Beyond that, I cannot comment at the moment, Mr Alexander,' the inspector concluded.

The recording of the interview was underway, and Falconer began to explain the chain of logic that had come up with him, Edmund Alexander, in the frame. 'We realised how much Dashwood's high-handed snatching of your positions – both as band accompanist, and as church organist – really meant to you. You did a good job of covering it up, but it was just possible to see the seething anger, bubbling just below the surface. It was your eyes that gave you away.

'It must have been a devastating double-blow to you, considering how long you have held these positions. On top of that, the way you talked about village events from your childhood, convinced us that you were very resistant to change, wanting things to stay as you had always known them, and resenting anything that interfered with what you considered the right and proper life of the village.

'I know that everyone in the village band had some bone to pick with Mr Dashwood, but yours seemed particularly important to you, and must have left an enormous hole in your life, and a seething mass of resentment and hatred.

'With regard to the death of Miss Palfreyman, she was poisoned with a cocktail of natural ingredients, the majority of which I discovered this morning could easily have been gathered from your garden. There was only one ingredient missing, but I'm sure you could have laid your hands on some, if you had asked around.'

'This is all complete and utter rubbish. You've got no proof of anything. Everything you've said is circumstantial, and means nothing. And what about this mystery ingredient that you think I pursued and acquired, before murdering a very shy and quiet girl, who never did me any wrong?'

'Ricin, Mr Alexander,' Falconer informed him.

'What? I've never even heard of the stuff, let alone hunted it down to kill someone with. What on earth is it?'

'It's from the castor oil plant, sir.'

'But they don't grow in this country – at least, not outside. I know some people have them as houseplants, but that's as far as my knowledge goes. And, no, I don't know anyone who has such a plant in their home, if that was going to be your next question.

'As for Dashwood, he would have worn out his welcome sooner or later. He was slowly killing the enthusiasm of the band, and his pompous, know-it-all manner would soon have led to conflict between him and the vicar.

'Angry and resentful I might have been, but, when I examined the situation logically, I realised that it would only be a matter of time before everyone tired of his bullying and pedantic manner, he would find himself out on his ear, and things could just go back to how they were before he turned up in Swinbury Abbot.'

Try as he might, Falconer couldn't get anything incriminating out of the man, and after an hour of intense questioning, decided that, should nothing be turned up during the search of the house and garden, he would have to let him go. He could find no holes in what Alexander had said, and he had detected no obvious signs of lying. Of course, it could be that he was just a superb actor, and had fooled him big-time, but he doubted it. It would seem that he, Falconer, had just picked on the wrong man, for the parts of both first, and second murderer.

Having left Edmund to sweat it out in a holding cell, both detectives retired to the office for what, in a sporting event, would have been referred to as a half-time team talk.

'Who on earth could have killed them both?' asked Falconer, taking his place behind his desk. 'We've got an embarrassment of suspects for Dashwood's murder, but not a soul in place for that of Vanessa Palfreyman. Can you think of anything, Carmichael? Anything at all?'

'Not off-hand, sir. Mrs Palfreyman did say she was friendly with that violinist, Cameron McKnight, and with Mrs Midwynter. Perhaps we'd better go back to the village, and speak to both of them. She might have confided something to them, that no one else knows, not even her parents.'

'That's a good idea, Carmichael.'

'And here's another, sir. I'd bet my shirt on the Palfreyman woman definitely having had a late visitor on the night of her death. We're sure it's not suicide, and if it's murder, how on earth would you persuade someone to drink something that toxic?'

'You're definitely cooking with gas today. That dose of collywobbles must have done your brain good, Sergeant. Let's get going. We won't phone to warn them in advance: we'll just turn up out of the blue, and see how they react to that.

'But before we go, I want to send out a couple of officers, to go through Dunspendin with a fine-tooth comb. The warrant for the search is signed, and waiting to be picked up from the desk. Can you ring round and see if Green and Starr are available?'

They were, and less than five minutes later, the face of PC Merv Green poked itself round the office door, smiling like the cat that had got the cream. 'What can I do for you, sirs?' he asked.

'There's a search warrant, currently in the care of Bob Bryant. It's for a property in Swinbury Abbot with the unappealing name of Dunspendin. I'd like you and Starr to go out there ...' Here, he gave them an idea of what they were to look for and, when he had finished, noted that Green was still grinning like the Cheshire Cat.

'What's got into you, Green? You've got a definite twinkle in your eye today.'

'I've got my eye *on* a Twinkle, you mean. I've only gone and asked PC Starr out for a drink tonight, and she's agreed!' he informed them, with glee.

'You want to watch yourself with that one, Green. To my knowledge, she's done at least two self-defence courses,' advised Falconer, mirroring the man's infectious grin.

'I wouldn't try anything on with *her,* sir. Not only would that be disrespectful to the lady, but I've got the feeling she might be something special.'

'You'd better not try it on. She's special to me, too, as the most reliable PC I've got, so behave yourself!'

'Yes, sir.' And he was gone, the door closed with unusual gentleness.

Heading first for The Hurst in Falconer's car, they decided to cut through the Wild Flowers Estate, just to get a feel for how different life was amongst the smaller and more modern dwellings of Swinbury Abbot. Nearly everyone they had spoken to, so far, had lived fairly comfortable and moneyed lives, in large houses with sizeable gardens. Those that were cottage-dwellers still seemed to live well, and have no money worries, and they were interested to see if there was a contrast, not just in size of property, but in the way that the houses and gardens were kept.

The answer to that one was rather like the curate's opinion of his egg – excellent in parts. Some houses had owners who obviously prized their homes, and the exteriors were well-kept, the gardens a riot of colour, at this time of year, some with a decorative pond, or the addition of garden gnomes, and other garden ornaments.

Others were less well-appreciated. There were small clusters of houses with blistering and peeling paintwork, cracked windows, and unkempt gardens, some with a variety of furniture and discarded domestic appliances in them.

Taking in this contrast, Falconer said, 'It's a funny old world, isn't it?' just for the sake of something to say. Carmichael, however, spoke with a more direct subject in mind.

'Did you see that ice-cream van, just a few houses back, sir?'

'No. Why?'

'Just see if you can turn round in one of the side-roads. Look as if you're lost, or something. Anyone would believe that, with the sort of car you're driving, on this estate.'

Falconer did as he had been requested, and executed what, in the old days, used to be called 'a three-point-turn', but is graced with the description of 'a turn in the road' now.

Driving very slowly, as if looking for a road name, or a house number, he eyed the ice-cream van surreptitiously, as did Carmichael. 'There are so many adults in the queue. Not parents or anything – more adolescents,' was Falconer's first comment. 'Where are the kids?'

'I've taken down the registration number, sir. I think he's selling something other than ice-cream, and that's why the kids aren't there. I heard a whisper from Merv Green that there's an ice-cream van operating locally, who's known as 'Mr Spliffy', and it's nothing to do with the frozen products that he peddles. Of course, he keeps a few lollies and ice-creams in the freezer compartment, just in case he gets some innocent customers, but that's not his intention at all.'

'Can you make a call to the station, and get someone out

here? Maybe there's a patrol in the area that can pick up his trail. We might as well do what we can, while we can actually see him, but you've got the registration number, and we can't really leave our own investigation, to go chasing after some suspected drug peddler,' said Falconer, of the opinion that a murder investigation beats a drug dealer, hands down.

'Will do, sir. If there's no one to pick up his trail, his number can always be traced through the computer, and then we'll have him.'

Speeding up, as if he'd found his way at last, Falconer drove straight to The Hurst and parked in the drive.

There was a terrible noise coming from the house. Its origin might have been musical, but there was so much wavering of tone, and so many out of tune notes, that it sounded more like a cat in pain than a tune. A front window had been left ajar, unleashing this dreadful cacophony, out, into an unsuspecting world, and Falconer was pleased to think that their surprise visit would be the means of making it cease.

Cameron McKnight answered the door still clutching his instrument and bow, the two objects expertly held in one hand. 'Oh, good morning, Inspector, Sergeant. What a surprise! I'm sorry I can't shake hands, as I still seem to be carrying my instrument. Do come in and tell me how I can help you,' McKnight welcomed them, not seeming an iota put out by their appearance.

They spent the best part of half an hour asking him about his acquaintanceship with Vanessa Palfreyman, but, apart from the fact that they both played a stringed instrument and had a shared love of crime novels, he said there was nothing else they had in common, and that he really couldn't help them.

One of the cats strolled in at that moment so that the shifty look in his eyes, when he had given this last answer, was masked, as he turned away his face, to call to her. 'Come along, my pretty little Butterfly, and let Uncle Cam give you a lovely stroke,' he cooed, still keeping his face averted, until he could recover control of his expression.

'No Mr Littlechild today?' Falconer asked, the entrance of

the cat reminding him of McKnight's secret lodger.

'No, I'm afraid not. He's off on another tour. Won't be back for a few weeks yet. Ah, the trials of a musical life, but one must not let one's public down, must one?' he asked, a wistful look in his eye, now. Oscar was evidently living the sort of life that Cameron would have liked to live, but lacked the talent to break into.

'Before we go, sir, I've got one final question to ask you. Did you by any chance, make a very late visit to Miss Palfreyman, either on Sunday night, or in the early hours of Monday morning?'

'What an extraordinary question,' exclaimed McKnight, lifting the cat on to his lap. 'Of course I didn't. I mean, what for? What reason could I possibly have, for doing something like that?'

'Because she was going to spill the beans about darling Oscar and your sexuality,' thought Falconer as they were leaving, but that would mean that Vanessa Palfreyman had killed Dashwood, and it just didn't seem to add up.

It was Myrtle Midwynter herself who answered the door of The Grange to them, and bade them go into the back garden, and take a seat. 'Don't worry, Inspector, I'll make sure that you're not ambushed by Acker. As far as I know, he's asleep under the old apple tree, making the most of the shade.'

Myles was out on some sort of errand, but this didn't matter, as it was his wife to whom they wanted to speak.

'We're making enquiries about the death of Vanessa Palfreyman, and her mother has suggested to us, that you and her daughter were particular friends: that you'd even holidayed together, in the past. Is that correct?'

'As far as it goes, Inspector. I suppose I could be referred to as a 'particular' friend, because Vanessa didn't really have any friends, as such.'

'How do you mean, didn't have any friends "as such"?' asked Falconer, somewhat confused by the way she had worded her answer to his question.

'Apart from the band, Vanessa was a loner. She's – sorry, wrong tense – she was always shy, and didn't seem to know how to get on with other people. She had no social skills, if you know what I mean.'

'And yet you went on holiday with her? Now, why would you do a thing like that?'

'Pity, more than anything else, if you want the absolute truth. We only went three times – walking in Austria and Switzerland – and only ever for a week at a time. I wouldn't exactly call us bosom buddies, but I like walking, and I felt sorry for her, cooped up in that house with those parents of hers who always talk at the same time so that you can't possibly have a sensible conversation with them.'

'I've met them. Say no more,' Falconer sympathised.

As Carmichael made notes, he also took the opportunity to look at the garden, admiring the jewel-like colours of the flowers in the sunlight, and taking pleasure from the sight of the dog, asleep under the tree, occasionally twitching in his sleep, as he dreamt of chasing rabbits, or some other doggy activity that excited him.

'Is there anyone you can think of, that Miss Palfreyman may have fallen out with, recently?' he asked, hoping for a positive response, but she disappointed him in just a few words.

'I don't think Vanessa would have the guts to say 'boo' to a goose.'

'But she definitely had a grudge against Mr Dashwood?'

At this point, Myrtle burst into peals of disbelieving laughter. 'She didn't like him, of course, because he criticised her playing. But as for doing anything about it, and then topping herself, forget it, Inspector. She just wasn't that sort of gal.'

'That's what I'm trying to get at, Mrs Midwynter. What sort of 'gal' was she?'

'She was a non-entity. I think that's the kindest way of putting it. And that's it!'

'One more question before we go, Mrs Midwynter. Did you have occasion to pay a call on Miss Palfreyman, either very late on Sunday night, or in the early hours of Monday morning?'

'What a weird question, Inspector, but no, I didn't. I don't go visiting in the middle of the night, and I'm sure no one else round here does, either.'

'Excuse me for saying this, but you seem rather cheerful, for one who has just lost a "sort of" friend and musical colleague. Is there any particular reason for that, if you don't mind me asking?'

'Of course not, Inspector, and, as it happens, there is a particular reason for it. I'll explain as briefly as I can, because I don't want to take up any more of your valuable time than I have to.

'Myles and I decided, when we got married, that we didn't want any children. He was much older than I, and already had grown-up children from a previous marriage. Well, I'm getting on a bit now, and my biological clock has turned itself into a veritable Big Ben.

'We spent months discussing it – sometimes into the early hours of the morning, and we've finally come to the decision that we'd like to try for a family, which now seems to be the most important thing in the world to me.

'Of course, there's a bit of plumbing work that Myles has had to have sorted out first, having had a vasectomy before he and his first wife separated, but that's all done and dusted, now, and the doctor doesn't think we should have much of a problem. I'm so excited, I'm sure I could fly, if I only tried!'

'Well, congratulations in advance, Mrs Midwynter, and thank you for your time. We'll leave you now, to enjoy the day. Don't worry about seeing us out. We can cope on our own. Goodbye.'

Falconer entered the house via the French windows, and had a good look around, then went into the other downstairs rooms swiftly, raking each one with his eyes, in search of houseplants, but he found none, and they left The Grange, no further forward than they had been, when they arrived.

The rest of the working day was spent doing a round of all the other band members, to see if any of them would admit to making a late call on Vanessa, but it was a lost cause. The person who had actually paid an unexpectedly late visit would be the murderer, and they were hardly likely to spill the beans, now were they?

Invitations

'Hello, Geraldine, Myles here. Look, I won't keep you, but there's to be a band rehearsal at ours on Friday. Usual time, usual timetable.'

'Don't you think that's a tad disrespectful, to have it so soon after all that's happened?'

'Not at all, Geraldine. Life must go on, you know. See you on Friday, if not before.'

'Hello Lester, Myles here. Band at ours, on Friday. Back to normal, at last.'

'Sorry, Myles. I've got to work, so I can't make it.'

'Can't you rearrange work, for our first proper meeting since we were invaded by that ghastly little man?'

''Fraid not, old chap. I'll just have to leave it till the next one. Sorry'

'That you, Cameron? Myles Midwynter here. Shoulders to the wheel again, on Friday – band, round at our place. That OK with you?'

'Only if you can sort out this distressful business of me being demoted to 'second violin'.'

'I'll see what I can do. See you Friday.'

'Hello Wendy. Myles here. Are you up for band on Friday evening? At our place?'

'So soon, Myles? We've just lost our Musical Director, and our double bass player. Shouldn't we wait just a little longer?'

'And what good would that do us, with the concert still to prepare for? We've got to take care of the living. The dead can take care of themselves.'

'Well, it seems very cold-hearted to me, but if everyone else is in agreement, I'll be there.'

'Thank you Wendy, my little poppet. I knew you wouldn't let Uncle Myles down.'

Myles continued with his telephone marathon, contacting all the remaining members of the band, with the exception of Edmund Alexander, who was still in custody. To Grace, he had assured her, 'He'll be home very soon. You say they've searched the house? Did they take anything away with them? No? Well, there you are then. He'll probably be home within the hour. Just pass the message on when he gets back, and we'll expect him as normal. Chin up, Grace, and just keep faith.'

After his final call he turned to Myrtle, who had been hovering in the background. 'That's the lot, except for Edmund, but he's sure to be home tonight or tomorrow.'

'What makes you so sure?' asked his wife.

'Well, you can't honestly think that that milksop had the guts to drive a cello spike into old Dashwood's chest, can you?'

'I suppose not. But you never can tell what someone will do if they're desperate,' and with this final pronouncement, she left the room.

Chapter Eighteen

Wednesday 21st July – morning

'How are you feeling today?' asked Falconer, as Carmichael entered the office.

'Could be better. It seems to be worst in the mornings, and whatever it is, Kerry seems to be going down with it too.'

'Well, you'd better keep it to yourself. I don't want it.'

'No kissing then, until I'm better?' asked Carmichael, with a smirk.

Immediately catching the joke that had been so subtly thrown, Falconer replied, 'Well, no tongues, at any rate,' and grinned back at his sergeant. 'Let's get straight down to a proper evaluation of the situation. We need to decide who had a motive to kill both Dashwood and Palfreyman.'

'I've been thinking about that, sir ...'

'Don't strain yourself. I don't want you walking round with me with your head in a bandage because you've sprained your brain.'

'Stop messing about, sir. I'm serious. What if nobody had a motive to kill them both?'

'That seems highly unlikely to me, Carmichael.'

'I know, but what if the murders aren't connected in any way?'

'They must be! It's too unlikely, that two people would be murdered within such a small group, and for that group to contain two people with murderous intentions.'

'Unlikely, but possible, sir. If we can establish a solid motive for Vanessa Palfreyman's murder, it might indicate a totally different person from the one we think responsible for

Dashwood's murder. And the methods had nothing in common. What links being stabbed with a cello spike and being poisoned? Nothing that I can see.'

'Go on,' urged Falconer.

'I know we've got an embarrassment of suspects for the first death, but maybe we can whittle that down, and take a really close look at the deceased young lady's life. There must be a clue there.'

'I'll tell you who we haven't talked to properly yet, Carmichael.'

'Who's that, sir?'

'The vicar – Rev. Church. We've been told that Vanessa didn't attend church, and, if my memory serves me correctly, that she was of the opinion that the vicar didn't approve of her. Now, why was that, I wonder? And why did whatever the vicar thought about Vanessa, not affect her parents? They were taken straight round to The Rectory after they found their daughter dead, and they seemed perfectly at ease there – or as at ease as you could expect anyone to be, after finding their only child dead.'

'Brainwave, sir! Vicars know a lot more than they let on,' Carmichael agreed.

They both stood to leave and collect their jackets from the coat stand, for the weather, this being England in July, had turned in the night, thick cloud rolling in from the west, and the rain had begun to fall in great gobbets, immediately soaking anyone who had the misfortune to be outside.

This morning, the sky was sullen, with iron-grey clouds drooping pregnantly towards the land, their bellies swollen with unshed water. The temperature had also dropped like the proverbial stone, and the wind was beginning to rise, promising a squall in the very near future. Oh, to be not in England, now that's summer's here! The British summer could easily borrow its description from that of St Petersburg's – nine months of anticipation, followed by three months of disappointment.

Before they could leave the office, the phone rang, and Falconer sighed, and returned to his desk to answer it. 'Good morning. Detective Inspector Falconer speaking. How may I help you? Oh, hello Mrs Palfreyman.' He had automatically put out his hand, to put the phone on to speaker, so that Carmichael could share in any triumph or defeat.

'I did what you said, Inspector, and took a look in my crockery cupboard.'

'Yes, Mrs Palfreyman?' Falconer found that he was holding his breath with the suspense.

'And you were right! A cup and saucer were slightly out of place, and when I looked in the cup, there was the tiniest bit of water in it, as if it had only been briefly rinsed out and replaced, because whoever had done that, hadn't wanted to spend any more time in our house than was necessary.' Mr Palfreyman could be heard muttering away in the background, adding his own two-penn'orth to the conversation.

The old bird was more astute than Falconer had thought, and this definitely proved it was murder. 'Thank you very much indeed Mrs Palfreyman, for your sharp eyes and good memory. We shall now be able to bring the person responsible for your daughter's death to justice,' he assured her, but with his fingers crossed behind his back, because at the moment, the possibility of that ever happening seemed very slim indeed.

The journey to Swinbury Abbot was through driving rain, visibility greatly reduced due to spray from the road, and a mist rising from the previously sun-warmed ground. Two consecutive days could not have had more contrasting weather, in the absence of a blizzard.

In the sun's absence, The Rectory appeared a bleak pile of a building, with its shroud of ancient trees, a leftover from when the ground that it was built on was part of the old churchyard.

They were greeted at the door by Olivia Church, who was enough of a vicar's wife to let no dismay or surprise show on her face as she led them to her husband's study, quickly confining Chalice to the dining room by the simple action of kicking the door shut as she passed, having seen him in there, asleep under the table.

'Chris, you have visitors,' she announced, opening the study door, after a discreet knock, to announce their presence. 'It's Inspector … Falconer, and Sergeant Cartwright.'

'Carmichael,' Falconer corrected her in an undertone.

'Oh yes, sorry. Sergeant Carmichael.'

'Good day to you, gentlemen. How may I be of assistance? Are you any further forward with those two dreadful cases of murder yet?' asked Rev. Church, rising from the seat behind his desk, and coming over to shake hands.

'Nothing definite so far, Vicar, but we would like to ask you a couple of questions that may provide us with useful information,' replied Falconer, accepting the man's firm handshake.

'Well, I don't know what I could possibly tell you that would be of any use, but take a seat and fire away,' invited Rev. Church, re-taking his own seat behind the desk, the room not being large enough to accommodate any more seating than it already had.

'What we would like to know, Vicar, concerns Vanessa Palfreyman. We understand that she did not attend church services, although her parents did. Is that something that has been so for some time?'

'I suppose you could call it long term. Vanessa used to attend, but she stopped about three years ago, if my memory serves me correctly.'

'She was also of the opinion that you disapproved of her. Are these two things connected in any way, do you think?'

'I don't think …' replied the vicar, his brow furrowing with sorrow and concern.

'Can you tell us how they were connected?' Falconer pushed on, ignoring the man's expression of distress.

'I don't know if I should,' he answered finally, letting a silence settle around the three of them.

'Yours is not a Catholic church, so I presume there is no complication of the confidentiality of confession?' asked Falconer, hoping against hope that St Back-to-Front's wasn't a High Anglican jobby, where confessions *were* heard, if requested.

'Not as such, but I believe it was told to me in confidence, in an appeal for advice.'

'Look, Vicar, whatever it is, if it plays no part in the outcome of our investigations, it will not be made public, but we really need to know everything we can about the deceased young lady to bring her murderer to justice. I'm sure you can appreciate how we feel.' Falconer pleaded his case with as much emotion as he could muster.

'I do see your point, and I am willing to tell you what I know, provided that I have your firm assurance that this will go no further than it absolutely has to,' Rev. Church countered.

'You have it! We have no more interest in spreading spurious gossip than you do, Vicar.'

'Well, here goes, for what it's worth. Vanessa came to see me about three years ago, now. It was just after her first walking holiday with Myrtle Midwynter, and she seemed very distressed about something.

'I asked her what was troubling her, and she said it was something concerning whether or not she ought to take Communion, or if she even ought to carry on attending church. I, of course, was very concerned about this, and told her to explain her problem to me, and we'd see what we could do to make things better.'

Falconer was leaning forward in his chair, listening intently. Carmichael, slightly to the rear of the inspector, was busily scribbling notes, his tongue sticking out of the side of his mouth, as he concentrated on speed and accuracy.

'I told her there was little that she could have done that would necessitate taking such drastic action, and reminded her that Jesus died for our sins, and that God could forgive anything, if there was true repentance.

'It was at this point, that she burst into tears, and began to sob uncontrollably. Not feeling capable of offering sufficient consolation myself, I called for Olivia, and between us, we calmed her down, and coaxed her story out of her.

'The poor girl had never had such a thing as a boyfriend in

her life, but I think everyone, her parents included, thought that this was because she was shy and socially gauche. The truth could not have been further from this assumption.

'She had, over a number of years, come to realise that she was not attracted to the opposite sex, and, in fact, preferred members of her own sex, and had fought hard not to act on her instincts, and 'give the game away', to put it bluntly. Then Myrtle Midwynter sussed out her little secret, probably by sheer instinct. It wasn't until then that I realised that Myrtle 'batted for both sides', if you get my meaning, and that their holiday together had been a sort of lovers' tryst.

'Of course, I told her it had to stop. Not only was homosexuality forbidden in the Bible, but Myrtle was a married woman, and was, therefore, committing adultery, thus breaking one of the Ten Commandments. This, as you can no doubt imagine, brought on a fresh fit of weeping, during which she said she'd never felt like this about anyone else in her whole life, and that now she had discovered love, she couldn't give it up.

'At that point, I relented, and repeated that God could forgive anything, because, to be honest, I didn't know what else I could do for her. Myrtle would probably tire of her eventually, and maybe the whole thing was just a phase she was going through. Vanessa was very immature emotionally, and I wondered if this may not be just the sort of schoolgirl crushes that girls get on their teachers, or a senior pupil.

'I admit to the weakness of leaving it to her own conscience, to decide whether she should continue to take Communion, or even attend church services. I felt totally inadequate to make a judgement, on such a matter.

'She showed up for church twice more, but stayed away from the altar rail when Communion was being dispensed, not even coming to it for a blessing, and then stopped coming altogether. I don't know what her parents thought, but she must have fobbed them off with some excuse or another. I certainly didn't disapprove of her, or ask her to discontinue attending worship. That was her own decision, and nothing to do with me.

'I also said nothing to Myrtle. I felt that what Vanessa had told me was in the strictest confidence, and there was the Midwynters' marriage to consider as well, but, I must say, I felt relieved when Mrs Palfreyman told me recently that her daughter wouldn't be going on holiday anymore with Mrs Midwynter.

'I felt that my reticence had been justified, and that Vanessa would return to the fold, in due course, and then I heard that she was dead. At first, of course, when it was considered to be suicide, I felt the most tremendous sense of guilt, thinking that she had taken my advice after so much time, and couldn't live with what she'd done. I prayed hard that day, not only for her soul, but for my own forgiveness, for advising her in the first place.'

'Don't worry, Vicar,' soothed Falconer, the change of voice from the vicar's long monologue sending a little frisson through the atmosphere of the room. 'It had nothing to do with you. We know, now, that she was murdered, and your advice can have had nothing whatsoever to do with it.'

'Thank God!' exclaimed the cleric, in genuine relief. 'May her soul rest in peace!'

It would have been very ill-mannered just to get up and leave at this point, so Falconer decided on a bit of brisk improvisation, to tide them over to the point where they could end their visit.

'A word of advice in your ear, if you don't mind, Vicar. On the day of that fateful gathering of the band in the church, you left the church key with Harold Grimes. Is that right?' Falconer knew it was, but gave the vicar the opportunity to join in with the change of subject, and maybe lighten his mood.

'That's right. They all wanted to go over to The Leathern Bottle for a drink, but had a problem because of their instruments, because the pub is invariably very crowded on Sunday lunchtimes. I said they could leave them in the church, and collect them when they had finished, and I gave the key to Harold, to lock up in the meantime, as he was staying behind to do something or other with his trumpet.'

213

'Well, it might not be such a good idea to do that again, in the future. Mr Grimes has admitted to us that he actually forgot to lock up the church, and only discovered his lapse of memory when they all went back for their instruments, covering up for himself by fiddling around with the key in the lock.'

Rev. Church looked at first, perplexed, and then angry. 'He certainly did *not* forget to lock up. I wonder why he told you that. I sent Olivia round to the church to collect my travelling Communion box, so that I could spend the rest of the morning going round administering the Sacrament to the sick and the very elderly, forgetting that I'd asked Harold to lock up, and that the key would be in the pub.

'When she got there the door was definitely locked. It wasn't stuck, or anything like that; it was genuinely locked. Of course, when she came back empty-handed, I remembered what I'd done, and thought better of going to get the key from him, because that would leave me insufficient time to complete my visits, without coming back home for lunch, then going out a second time, so I decided just to wait until he dropped it through the letterbox, when they'd all finished their business in the pub, and gone home.'

'But, why would he lie to us?' Falconer asked, now with a face that bore the mark of confusion.

'I have no idea, my dear Inspector. You must ask him that yourself. I must say, it's very unlike him to tell lies. Are you sure it wasn't just a misunderstanding?'

'Perfectly!' exclaimed Falconer, and rustling Carmichael out of his seat, they thanked the vicar for all his help, and left The Parsonage.

Falconer's mind had been racing all the way back to the office. Now he had discovered a possible motive for Vanessa Palfreyman's murder, and an inconsistency in the information gathered through initial interviews.

Throwing himself into his office chair, he stared with such vehemence at Carmichael, that the younger man actually looked over his shoulder, then back at the inspector, and said, 'What?'

I think we've got the information that we were missing before, and the 'something' that we simply didn't understand.'

'Is that right, sir?'

'Of course it is. Don't you see it?'

'You'll have to help me on this one. I'm still feeling a little peculiar.'

'You've always been a little peculiar, but you're beginning to turn into a hypochondriac, in my opinion, Carmichael,' stated Falconer, with a distinct lack of sympathy. 'Look, the vicar handed everything to us on a plate. All we've got to do is sort out exactly what the implications are.

'First, he told us that Vanessa Palfreyman was batting for the other side, and was having a relationship with Myrtle Midwynter.'

'I told you that village was a den of vice, sir.'

'Look, Carmichael, you're entitled to your own opinion, but this isn't about your moral principles, it's about murder. At least we now have a suspect for the poisoning.'

'How do you mean, sir?'

'Well, Myrtle told us herself that she and Myles wanted to start a family. She wouldn't want the lesbian or bisexual tag hung round her neck if she wanted to become a respectable mother, would she? She'd probably do anything to prevent that happening.'

'I'll give you that, sir, but what about Dashwood, now that we know Harold really did lock the church door?'

'That's simple! She, and possibly with Myles as an accomplice, all for the sake of respectability, did the dreadful deed. When you think about it, it makes absolute sense, for she had constant access, whenever she wanted, to her own cello case.'

'Fair enough,' agreed Carmichael, 'but I don't understand, then, why Mr Grimes said he'd left the church door unlocked, when he'd done no such thing.'

'He's getting on a bit; probably just forgot. No, that's not our concern at the moment. It's Mrs Midwynter we want to nail.'

215

'Just what exactly does a castor oil plant look like, sir? I can't say that I've ever actually seen one,' Carmichael asked, feeling that he should at least know this, before the case was over.

Falconer ran his hands expertly over the keys of his computer, then called Carmichael to the other side of his desk, to look at what he had brought up on the screen. 'There, Carmichael! That's a castor oil plant.'

'But I've seen one of those, recently!' Carmichael exclaimed, jerking up from his bent position, and scratching at the short hairs on his head, in an effort to recall where.

'Was it inside or outside?' asked Falconer, urgently.

'Definitely outside.' There was a silence of, maybe, three seconds, and then Carmichael whooped with triumph. 'Got it, sir! It was when we were sitting in the garden at The Grange. When I was able to, I looked round at their garden, and they've got one little bit in the far right-hand corner, which looks like it was lifted straight from a scene from a Tarzan film.'

'No! Never!' declared Falconer. 'I didn't see it.'

'You had your back to it, sir. And I saw leaves, just like that, sticking through the foliage. It had these sort of heads, with sort of beads on it, shaped like a ball.'

'Those must be the seeds. That's it, Carmichael! Time to apply for a warrant.'

'But we've no proof as yet, sir,' Carmichael tempered with caution.

'Proof be damned! We've got a bloody great castor oil plant, right there in her garden, and we've got her with access to the murder weapon in the case of Dashwood. We've solved it, Carmichael. Let's go get her!'

Chapter Nineteen

Wednesday 21st July – lunchtime

Without waiting to have any lunch, Falconer arranged for a patrol car to follow them to Swinbury Abbot, and requested that the car contained PC Green and PC Starr, because they intended to arrest a woman. He didn't want to waste a minute, and they reached The Grange at four minutes past one, leaving the patrol car to be parked at a slight distance, outside the old meeting hall, so that its presence would not be observed from The Grange, but could be easily summoned at the moment it was needed.

Their arrival interrupted the Midwynters' luncheon, but Falconer made no apologies, and asked straight away if he could have a look round their garden. Puzzled, but not alarmed, Myles gave them permission, then returned to his interrupted meal.

They headed straight out to the back garden, where they found the dog asleep under the apple tree again. Walking softly, so as not to wake it, Falconer asked Carmichael to show him where he'd seen the plant, and they walked right to the very perimeter of the south-west corner, where two walls joined, to enclose the back garden.

'There it is, sir, between those two, and slightly behind it.' Carmichael pointed in the direction he had indicated, and waited for confirmation of whether his identification of the specimen had been correct.

'That's it, Carmichael. Well done! We'll just have another little search for the other plants used, but I think this one's the clincher, and then, I think, we're going to have to go in and

217

make a nuisance of ourselves,' announced Falconer, a severe expression on his face. This should have been one of the most satisfying parts of his job, but he found that he loathed it. Telling someone that you were going to lock them away for a very long time was never a pleasant task, even though he knew they deserved it.

All the necessary ingredients for the brew that had done for Vanessa Palfreyman proved to be present and correct, with the exception of the valerian – they would have to ask her where she had obtained that – and they took themselves back into the house to do what had to be done.

Myrtle came quietly, in the end, realising that there was little chance of her escaping justice. She knew that Myles was aware of her infidelity with Vanessa, and would have stood by her, but the fact that she was a murderess was beyond the pale.

He'd pleaded with her to explain why she'd gone to such lengths, as he'd known about it anyway, and wouldn't have cared who found out, but he couldn't stand by her after this. There was no place in his heart for someone who had taken a human life, for no other reason, than that there may have been gossip about her.

It was Myles's reaction that reduced Myrtle to an acquiescent state, where she offered no resistance to be taken away to be questioned.

They left the house, Myles sitting stunned on a dining chair, unaware of anything in his state of shock and disbelief.

Afternoon

Under questioning, Myrtle was co-operative, and informed them that she had collected the valerian growing wild when she had taken Acker for his walks in the nearby woodland. She said that all she had wanted to do was to end their 'pointless' relationship by ceasing their holidays together, but Vanessa had taken it badly, and in the end, had threatened to expose their once-a-year relationship.

'I couldn't have borne that,' she confessed, 'Not now that we were hoping to start a family. And Myles has a position in this village, and I didn't want to tarnish it. You don't know how stuffy small communities can be. If you don't toe the line with your behaviour, they can destroy you socially, and in your domestic happiness.'

'So Myles didn't know what had been going on between you and Vanessa?' asked Falconer.

'The same way as I didn't know he was taking photographs of Gayle Potten naked! It had been that sort of marriage, up to now. What didn't really matter had a blind eye turned to it, and was never discussed. But the thought of being parents – again, for Myles, and for the first time for me – put a totally different light on the situation, and we decided, tacitly, and without any actual discussion, to clean up our respective acts, and start living the lives of respectable people, with no sexual secrets or quirks.

'Myles was even going to give up wandering around the house and garden naked when we had a child – that was what broke up his first marriage, you know. His wife didn't think it was a suitable thing for him to be doing when the children got older, and he couldn't understand what she found unacceptable in the naked human body. I think he realised that children eventually learn to talk, and ask questions about why their daddy is different, or tell their friends about how different things are at home.

'Well, I've blown it now, good and proper. I'll no doubt spend the rest of my reproductive years in prison, and will never be a mother; never hold a child of my own in my arms. Oh God, I feel sick … now!' But it was too late. A fountain of vomit projected from her mouth, and just missed Falconer on the other side of the table.

'Oh, God! I'm so sorry! It was too quick to do anything about it.'

'It's all right, Mrs Midwynter, I'll get someone to clean it up, and we can move to another interview room. Interview suspended at …' Falconer stopped the recording and summoned help, suggesting that a doctor should be summoned to examine Myrtle. He didn't think there was anything really wrong with her, but he didn't want to take the chance that she had managed to ingest one of her own poisonous garden products while she was getting ready to leave The Grange.

Once settled in the room next door, the tape-recorder running once again, he began to introduce the subject of Dashwood's death, and how offended she and Myles must have been, to have had their pet project whisked from under their feet without a by-your-leave, but Myrtle immediately began to protest vehemently.

'Neither of us had anything to do with that man's murder. We may have felt like killing him, but, I can assure you, we did nothing – nothing at all. That church door was left unlocked by Harold – silly, forgetful old man – and anyone had the chance to nip in there and help themselves to my cello spike.'

'I'm afraid that's just not true, Mrs Midwynter. The vicar has told us that he sent his wife to fetch something from the church while the band members were in The Leathern Bottle, and it was locked up, tight as a drum. Harold *did* lock it, when he went over to join you, so that leaves just you and Myles in the frame, I'm afraid.'

'No it doesn't, you stupid man. Can't you see what's right under your nose?' she screeched at him, making him sit back in his chair, apprehensive that she might just reach across the table, and grab him by his lapels, in her vehemence.

'Harold could easily have waited until he got home to oil his valves, and there's hardly ever a hymn book or service book out of place after a service in that church. The vicar's got his congregation too well trained for things not to be returned to their proper places, after services. If Harold stayed behind, you can bet your boots that he had an ulterior motive.'

'Are you suggesting that Mr Grimes was the one who killed Mr Dashwood, Mrs Midwynter?' asked Falconer, the penny finally dropping.

'Yes I bloody well am!' she shrieked back at him, rising slightly in her seat.

'Now, calm down, and tell me what's on your mind. You've obviously got some theory or other, and I'd like you to outline it to me, quietly and calmly,' he requested.

Myrtle dropped back into her chair, took several deep, shuddering breaths, and looked him straight in the eye. 'Harold Grimes put himself in the position of being the only person left in that church, with the express objective of stealing my cello spike.'

'You can't know that, Mrs Midwynter,' said Falconer, surprised at her certainty.

'He was one of the band members most at risk of being dropped because he couldn't really read music. Let's start with the trivial reasons, shall we, Inspector?' she asked. 'He only came along to band, and started to learn that blasted instrument, because he was so besotted with his girlfriend Gayle Potten – God knows why, because she looks like a hippo on the game to me.

'He adored her, and would have done anything for her. Let me finish,' she instructed, holding up a hand to Falconer, who had opened his mouth to speak. 'I know much more about them than you do. Harold was irate, whenever Dashwood criticised her. He could probably have coped, if it was only criticism of her playing, but when the man ridiculed the way she dressed, deeming it inappropriate in the extreme, and asked her to moderate her dress for future rehearsals, I saw Harold's face, and it was murderous.

'I don't know if anyone has told you, but he spent his life in the army before he retired. Oh, he never reached a respectable rank, because every time he got promoted, he did something that got him busted back down again. In fact, he told us, that on one application for promotion, the commanding officer simply wrote, 'This man is a rogue!' across it, and that was i for Harold as far as internal promotion was concerned.

'He'd served in Northern Ireland, and was well trained in unarmed combat. It would have been no trouble for him to subdue Dashwood, and then stab him with the spike. He may be getting on a bit, but he has a tremendous amount of wiry

221

strength – he still runs and exercises to keep fit. I suggest that you'll find the murderer of Cameron Dashwood at number two, Honeysuckle Terrace.

'You're not pinning that one on me, because I had absolutely nothing to do with it. Harold only lied about leaving the church unlocked because he knew that that would provide the police with a wider field of suspects, and give him a chance to blend into the background, given how we all felt about that dreadful man.'

'Thank you very much for what you've told me, and I'll certainly look into it. Now, let's get you somewhere a bit more comfortable, and see if that doctor's arrived yet.'

Chapter Twenty

When Myrtle Midwynter had been seen safely off to be examined by Dr Christmas, Falconer and Carmichael waited in the office, digesting what had been suggested to them, and working out a plan of action.

'Well, I'll be blowed!' exclaimed Falconer. 'He nearly had one over on us, there – that Grimes. If the vicar had thought that the church being locked as it was supposed to be, meant nothing, we'd have been stuffed. Thank God I told him that Harold had confessed (*ha ha!*) to lying.'

'It would've come out in the end, sir,' Carmichael assured him. 'I guess it's just lucky that you brought up the subject when we were at The Parsonage.'

'But we didn't see the significance of it, until it was pointed out to us. I feel such a fool!'

'Well, you shouldn't, sir. We're going to clear up two murders, and have two murderers in custody by the end of the day. That's pretty good going, in my opinion.'

'Thank you, Carmichael. That does make me feel a bit better. It really is '*Midwynter Murders*' out there at the moment – at least, it would be if the body count was a bit higher!'

There was a rapid, light knock at the office door, and Falconer called out, 'Enter!' and Philip Christmas came into the room looking very chipper. 'Hi there, Philip. Got any news for us? She's not suffering from any fatal condition, is she?'

'Not quite. She's pregnant – not very far gone, but I've done a test, and it's positive.'

'Good grief!' exclaimed Falconer.

'That means she will get her baby after all,' stated Carmichael, looking slightly pleased.

'Yes, but it means it'll be a prison baby: not exactly what she'd planned for her little game of happy families.'

Falconer and Carmichael set off for the village of Swinbury Abbot in Falconer's car for what they hoped was the last time, with PC Merv Green following behind them in a patrol car. When they had made their arrest, Carmichael would travel in the rear of the patrol car with Harold Grimes on the drive back to the station.

Harold, too, was rather matter-of-fact about being found out, and was almost unnaturally calm, as he explained to them exactly how things had happened.

'I did it on the Sunday night. I just couldn't come to terms with the things he'd said about my Gayle. Not only was it very un-gentlemanly, but it was extremely spiteful, cruel, and hurtful, and my little lady cried herself to sleep when we finally got back to her place that Friday night.

'Well, I wasn't having that. Criticise her playing, he might, and he might even have been musically experienced enough to justify what he said, but what she wore, and how she wore it, had nothing whatsoever to do with him. I was in a blind rage about it, and it didn't go away either.

'So, on Sunday evening, I got out a metal clarinet that I'd bought on the internet, and decided to go round to show it to him; ask his opinion, like, make him feel important and clever. I even wore a pair of the white gloves that you use when you're cleaning a silver or brass instrument, so you don't leave dirty great greasy fingerprints all over it.

'He asked me in, when I told him why I'd come round, he took the instrument from me, in the kitchen. He never invited me any further into his house, and I'd used the back door, because there would be less chance of me being seen by anybody.

'He held it up in the light, to examine it, and started telling me all the reasons why I should never have bought such a battered old instrument, but me – I never waited for him to finish his diatribe. I chopped him one on the throat, when he had the instrument in the air and was looking up at it, criticising the hell out of it for the sheer pleasure of making me look like a fool.

'He fell back into the chair he'd been sitting on, while I was listening to him spouting forth his opinion, and I had the cello spike ready in my pocket, already wiped clean of fingerprints. It didn't take long to push it into him. I was aiming for the heart, by the way, just in case he had one. Then I just left him there to fester.

'I thought someone would have found him sooner, but he obviously had no friends to speak of, so it had to be us, and I had to keep the ladies away, what with all the hot weather we'd had in the meantime, and I made sure to put my fingerprints on the door, so that if any more were found, I'd have the explanation of having gone into his cottage to see what was wrong. I even used a double negative when I spoke to you, saying that 'I hadn't done nuffink', and you didn't pick me up on it.' (*Chapter eleven, section II, if you're like me, and would now drive yourself to distraction by looking for the line*) 'I honestly thought I'd got away with it. What gave me away?'

'Lying about having forgotten to lock the church door. That narrowed the field considerably,' explained Falconer.

'Dammit! I knew that lying was a risk, but how did you find out about the lie? I thought I'd covered my tracks pretty well,' Harold asked, eager to learn where he had gone wrong, in his plan for the perfect murder.

'The vicar sent his wife round to collect his travelling Communion set from the church, and the church was locked. He'd forgotten to tell her he'd given the key to you, so she didn't know, to come over to the pub, to collect it.'

'Bloody bad luck!' Harold exclaimed. 'If it hadn't been for that, I'd probably have got clean away with it, and I was going to ask Gayle to marry me, when all this had blown over. But, I suppose I spent so much time in the glasshouse when I was in

the army, that I won't find prison much different.'
Thursday 22nd July

Myles Midwynter was never one to brood about anything, and he wasn't even going to let the arrest of his wife make any difference to his plans. He was a less sentimental man than many may have thought, and he telephoned all the band members, reminding them that it was band practice round at The Grange on the following evening.

They all thought that this was a little premature, in the light of all that had happened since Friday of the previous week, but he assured them that all would be well.

To Cameron McKnight, he explained, as he had to all the other band members, 'I know we've lost Vanessa and Myrtle, but we've still got three others playing strings, and without Harold, Lester will have to make that deep, rich, brass sound on his own. Gayle Potten has offered to come round to do the cooking – I'm more than happy for her to do that – and we can get things back to normal, at last.'

'Cold-hearted bastard!' was Cameron's opinion, as he ended the call, but knew he couldn't resist going, just to see what would happen, and what the current gossip was, and he fancied that the others would feel exactly the same as he did.

Having got everything arranged, Myles sat, lost in contemplation. He'd watched Gayle Potten eat on several previous occasions, and been an enthusiastic onlooker. She didn't eat so much as devour. She used her fingers, licking, both them, and her lips frequently, and she never stopped eating until her inner-piggy squealed for mercy. Then she looked soft and contented, but with just a hint of a twinkle in her eye, as if she had other appetites to satisfy as well, and wouldn't mind doing so, when she had digested a bit. Watching her eat was an absolute pleasure, and he had, if he was honest with himself, found it an almost sexual experience.

Gayle was a fine figure of a woman – 'a real handful', would be a particularly apt description, and if her cooking proved to be up to snuff, he wouldn't mind comforting her, while she mourned Harold's arrest. They could comfort each other, and – well, who knows what might become of it?

He smiled, as his thoughts progressed, and decided that he was really looking forward to tomorrow evening. It was time his 'inner lecher' came out to play.

He hadn't really wanted to start a new family, at his age. There would have been too much disruption, too many broken nights, too much mess, and far too much expense, and by the time any child he and Myrtle had produced had grown up, he'd be an old man, trying to fund a university education on pensions, at a time when he would possibly need to pay for extra care for himself. No, he was well out of that!

In number three Columbine Cottages, Gayle Potten was rubbing her hands together with glee. The thought that Myles had asked her to cook for the band rehearsal was enough to start her trembling with anticipation.

She had been reasonably happy with Harold, but he was getting on a bit, even though he was generous enough when it came to unexpected gifts and the like, but Myles was just that little bit younger, and he had that fabulous house, which she'd always coveted.

She'd seen him look at her on many an occasion, when they had been having their pre-practice meal, and he had looked as hungry for her, as she was for the food. He wasn't a bad-looking chap, and, not being one who dwelled on the past, or on the negative things in life, she could already see a rosy future ahead.

Oh, she wouldn't push her luck, or try to make a move on him, because she had a fair idea that it wouldn't be too long before he made a move on her. And then she'd be the mistress of The Grange, and wouldn't have to watch every penny, always buying stuff in sales, and when it was on special offer. If she could satisfy his appetites, she may see a sizeable increase in her purse, as well as a much better lifestyle.

Yes, things were looking up for the future! She must make sure that she went 'commando style' to The Grange on Friday, then ensure that she engineered the opportunity to slip on to his lap, so that he could work out the secret message she was sending him through her outer garments.

Merv Green had caught them on the way back to the office, and commented that the arrests, particularly of Harold Grimes, had gone very smoothly, with no attempt at resisting arrest on the part of the man. Falconer took one look at him, and asked, 'Have you ever seen yourself, when you're wearing your expression of grim determination?'

'No, sir. What are you getting at?'

'You make quite a forbidding figure. I certainly wouldn't like to cross you, when you look like that, and I know you.'

'Thank you very much, sir,' answered Green. 'By the way, I think it can be said that Twinkle – Linda – and I may be considered 'an item'.'

'Well done. You'll make an excellent team, same as you do at work.'

'I'll tell her what you said. Thanks again!'

As he and Carmichael finally reached the office, Falconer finally remembered to ask his sergeant if there was any news on that ice-cream van they had spotted on the Wild Flowers Estate; the one that was apparently referred to as 'Mr Spliffy'.

'Not a sniff, sir. I got the licence number run through the PNC, and it apparently belongs to a Fiat Panda, registered to a Mrs Gladys Fairchild, somewhere in Rochdale. I got the local force to check it out, and it is her number plate, and it is affixed to a Fiat Panda.

'There must be a garage, or a workshop involved, somewhere along the line, then. I bet it never goes out twice with the same number plate.'

'We'll just have to keep our eyes open, then, and get the patrol cars to look out for it, too. By the way, how are you feeling? Still got that dicky tummy?'

'Only when I wake up, in the morning. I don't know what's causing it, but I feel fine for the rest of the day.'

'You really ought to see a doctor about it. It's not natural for something like that to go on for so long, especially if you've been taking some sort of jollop for it,' Falconer advised him. As he finished his sentence, Carmichael's mobile phone rang, and he apologised to his boss briefly before he answered it.

'It's Kerry, sir. I've told her not to call unless it's an absolute emergency, so I'd better answer it.'

He moved his chair round slightly, so that he was not speaking in Falconer's direction, and lowered his voice, as he asked what was wrong.

Falconer could see from the man's ear and profile, though, that his colour was rising. From normal through to pink it went, then to bright red, and then, it was as if someone had switched off a light, and the whole side of his face was suddenly a dead white, as he ended the call.

'Whatever is it, Carmichael. Is there anything I can do to help? Tell me!' urged Falconer urgently. Carmichael turned round to face the inspector again, and seemed momentarily incapable of speech.

'What is it man. Spit it out!' Falconer was now almost frantic with worry, imaging one of the boys dead or injured, or one of the dogs killed on the road. He had to know, before his head exploded, with all the ghastly images forming in it.

Carmichael finally gathered his thoughts together, and said, in the most shocked of voices, 'All that sickness – it was just sympathetic morning-sickness. I'm going to have a baby, sir,' before slumping back, in a dead faint, in his chair.

Falconer then had the unique experience of shaking the hand of an unconscious man, in congratulations, which he did, very happily, and completely un-self-consciously.

Toxic Gossip

A Falconer Files Brief Case #4

Andrea Frazer

Chapter One

Miriam Darling stood in her new sitting room, missing suddenly the hurly-burly of the removal men and their cheery banter as they had transferred all her worldly goods into her new home.

Since yesterday afternoon, her world had been filled with these energetic and talkative men. First, as they packed her precious breakables, and loaded most of her furniture into their large van, leaving her only a bed and the means of making them all a cup of tea in the morning, and again today, as they moved her two hundred miles to her new address.

At first, she had found their inconsequential chatter a nuisance, and had taken herself off to the garden to sit on an old stool on the patio, but, as the afternoon wore on, she had found herself going indoors more frequently, coming, little by little, to enjoy the sound of life in the home that she would be leaving the next day, for ever.

By mid-afternoon, she found herself in the kitchen, brewing a pot of tea, and scrabbling round in her almost bare cupboards for a packet of biscuits. Sugar for energy, she thought, as her searching hand fell upon a packet of chocolate digestives she didn't realise she still had.

A tea-break meant a sit-down, and they settled themselves happily on the sitting room floor, now bare of its furniture and all its decorative trappings and pictures. She was just about to leave them to enjoy their tea and biscuits in peace when one of them called to her to join them if she wanted to, and, quite unexpectedly, she found that she did want to sit down with them, and engage in a normal conversation, for the first time in months.

They really were a jolly crew, who clearly enjoyed their work and their travels, and got on well with each other. As she sipped at her hot drink and nibbled on a biscuit, they regaled her with tales from their various trips together, exaggerating the mishaps and disasters to such an extent that she found herself laughing, and was grateful for their happy banter.

When they finished for the evening and took a taxi to a local public house to eat their evening meal, she threw the last of her left-over food together for a make-shift meal and contemplated the fact that, after today, this house would no longer be her home. That a new start was a good idea, she had no doubt, but she had lived at the same address for so long that not having the address any more would feel like an amputation – a new telephone number in her head, like a betrayal of who she was and how she had got to be this woman called Miriam Darling.

A new area would allow her to become someone new – someone whom nobody pitied and no one sought to comfort, or pointed out in the street, whispering to their companion about her history. Somewhere else, she would just be 'that woman who'd just moved into the house on the corner'. She could be anonymous, and start life afresh, with a clean sheet, provided she could banish the memories and, somehow, suppress the nightmares.

Today had started in a whirl of activity, making sure that the old house was in a fit and presentable state to greet its new owners, and that nothing had been forgotten. At the last minute, she had grabbed the old kitchen clock from the wall, where it had been abandoned for no good reason, and carried it out to her car, to put it safely on the back seat where it would not be jostled around too much.

And then they were off, at six o'clock on a Friday morning, heading for pastures new; leaving everything familiar and previously comforting behind. Following the removal van, she let her mind wander as she kept the vehicle in easy sight, due to its sheer bulk. She tried to remember all she could of the town and street she had chosen for the next phase of her life, and the few people she had met so far in her visits to the new address.

These, given the distance between the two places and the infrequency of her visits, consisted only of the estate agent and his assistant, and the two next-door neighbours, one beside her new home, the other round the corner, on the rear perimeter of the garden. They had seemed nice enough, and she supposed that people were the same just about everywhere. It was one's attitude to them, and theirs to you that really decided whether you sank or swam in a community. Then she nearly bit off her tongue at the inappropriateness of the wording of her last thought.

Silently chiding herself for being over-sensitive, she focused on the rear doors of the van, once more, and made her mind a blank for the next fifty miles. It was suddenly catapulted back to the present as she saw the van indicate to turn left. It pulled off up a slip-road towards a gathering of establishments that comprised a service stop with wide swathes of parking spaces, and a variety of eating places.

The removal men had had only a cup of tea from her this morning, and she presumed they were hungry and in need of a proper breakfast. She didn't feel in the least like eating, herself, but knew it would make good sense to put something in her belly, to give her some energy for dealing with the unloading and directing at the other end. Thus decided, she joined them in the queue for the till with a tray loaded with a full English breakfast, a pot of yoghurt, and a mug for tea.

She initially seated herself at a separate table, but was urged, before she had even sat down properly, to come and join the merry gang at a larger table at the rear of the dining area. Since their arrival the previous day, this small group of strangers had offered her a re-entry into human affairs, and she realised how much she appreciated it, when, on joining them, the 'head honcho' and owner of the van said that he had a bottle of champagne in his cab, to be cracked when all her possessions were in the new house.

He was of the opinion that all house moves should be celebrated as a moving on in life, and did this on a regular basis, unless he suspected that the couple were breaking up, or moving down-market due to financial problems. This gave her another reason to be glad that she had chosen this one-man-band to move her, and not one of the faceless large companies.

The last half of the journey passed without mishap, and it was only eleven o'clock when they pulled up outside number 45 Essex Road, in Market Darley. She had realised, about forty or fifty miles ago, how beautiful the countryside was becoming, and reached the town, from which she would commute to her job the three days of the week that she worked, with thoughts of appreciation of its architecture and surroundings.

It was an old market town, with a market cross and square, and many of its shops, if one raised one's eyes above display window level, clearly advertised their age. It looked like a place she could learn to forget and start life anew, and this made her smile, as the two vehicles in the tiny convoy pulled up outside her new home.

The rest of the day had been a whirlwind of activity for, although she was not involved in the unloading or transfer of her furniture and the boxes containing her smaller possessions, she was the one 'directing traffic', as it were. Yesterday afternoon, she had tried to keep abreast of the efficient and swift packing, to mark each box before it was loaded on to the van, but she had not managed to label them all, and she also wanted the furniture to go into the correct rooms while she had sufficient muscle to put it in place. Once they had gone, and she was on her own again, anything heavy in a wrong room would have to stay there until she had got to know someone with enough muscle-power to help her shift it to its correct position.

At lunchtime – about one-thirty, by choice of the removal men – she drove off to the local parade of shops which she had discovered on a previous visit, and bought enough fish and chips to feed them all, no matter how big their appetites proved to be. It was the least she could do, after all their friendly overtures to her, and she was saddened to think that she would never see those same faces again. They would just retreat into her past, after today, for they were not local, and would become just another memory, but a happy one this time.

Even her reception in the chip shop had been positive, with the man behind the counter, who turned out to be the owner, spotting a new face and asking her if she was just visiting – then wishing her the best of luck when she explained that she was only that day moving to the town.

When she arrived back with the food, the removal men had set up the dining table, attaching the top to the legs after its journey, had rooted out the dining chairs, and escorted her to what they had assumed (correctly) would be the dining room. They received their parcels of greasily steaming sustenance with suitable gestures of appreciation and gratitude, and set to, to make short work of her offerings.

As she scrunched up the empty papers to put in a black plastic bag from a roll she had, with forethought, brought with her in the car, she called out to see who wanted tea, and, after receiving a volley of affirmatives, entered the kitchen to find the kettle in pride of place, together with the box packed last, with mugs, tea, coffee, and sugar in it, waiting for her on the work surface. The milk, they had thoughtfully removed from the box in which it had been packed, and put into the newly brought-in and connected fridge.

After a flurry of, 'Left hand down a bit,' 'No, lift, not push,' 'Twist it so that we can get it through,' and 'Mind the doorframe, you donkey,' while the tea brewed, they came to collect their steaming mugs with gratitude, and not a little horse-play, more for her entertainment, she thought, than their own.

She had wondered if cold drinks would be more appropriate on an afternoon in August, but the British weather was behaving true to form, and a thick blanket of clouds hid the sky and smothered the heat of the sun, so it was quite a cool day, a good prod to her to check out the central heating system before autumn arrived, as it was likely to do, well before its traditional date, in this country.

The men had finally left at seven-thirty, wishing her good luck to a man, and waving frantically out of the cab window as the van drove away, an almost intimate part of her life for a day and a half, and she hadn't even known their names. And suddenly she was alone again, in a strange town where she had no friends or relatives, and just herself to bother about.

Chapter Two

Friday 6th August, 2010 – evening and onwards

Shaking herself back to the present, she began, slowly, to move from room to room, inspecting her new home with a critical eye. All in all, it was a good house, although just a bit too big for her on her own, but it was in good decorative order, if not to her taste, and it had been well maintained by its previous owners.

It had also been left immaculately clean and for this she was grateful. Her energy levels had been sapped and she no longer had the enthusiasm for the mundane jobs previously undertaken without thought. She considered that it was possible that she would be happy here, and looked forward to the time when this would be so, and she could feel like an ordinary person again.

Maybe she should get a dog or a cat, she wondered, just so that there was an extra heartbeat in the house, and something to talk to, so that she didn't feel as if she were going mad any more, when she talked to herself. A cat would be best, she decided, with her having to go to work three days a week. Dogs needed to be exercised, but a cat, although it walked to the beat of its own drum, could come and go as it pleased, with the addition of a cat flap, and would be an additional comfort to her on cold evenings, sitting on her lap and purring.

Oh! There was already a cat flap in the kitchen door, something she had not noted on any of her trips to view and measure up. Well, that was that decision made, then, and she determined to look in the Yellow Pages to try to locate a rescue centre from where she could choose a homeless animal to take in, and give the love and care it needed. Two waifs and strays together. What a team they would make!

Having ended her tour in the kitchen, having ascertained that all the bulky items of furniture were where they should be, she remembered that there had been a portion of chips, a saveloy, and a battered burger left at lunchtime, and she was glad she had not thrown them away. It was too late to look for shops open, and she was physically and emotionally exhausted from the rigours of the day. A few minutes on a plate in the microwave, and she could eat good old English comfort food, and go up to make up her bed for the night.

As she finished eating, however, there was a sharp rap at the front door, and she opened it to find the woman she had met previously, from the house next door, on her step. Introducing herself as Carole Winter, she extended an invitation to come round to her house for a glass of sherry.

Miriam was taking her first step into what was to be a period of whirling activity, as she was rapidly introduced by Mrs Winter, to the Women's Institute, where a young-for-her-years lady called Mabel Monaghan showed her their programme of events for the following autumn, and urged her to attend the special summer-break meetings. These were all talks by local people, about their particular interests, including local history, and the decline, rise and decline again, of agriculture in the surrounding area.

This sounded a good way to learn about where she was to make her new life, and she agreed, with alacrity, to attend the meetings, and join as soon as she was given the opportunity.

A meeting of the local book club, which this month was held at the home of a woman in her mid-thirties called Justine Cooper, introduced her to women a little closer to her own age, and she was fascinated that their list of books for the coming months included some quite racy titles.

She sat with them for two hours while they discussed the current volume under scrutiny, and found their impressions and insights intelligent and informative. Invited to the next meeting, she accepted immediately, and made a note of the book they were discussing earlier, so that she could get a copy, and add her own impressions to the general pot of opinions.

The ladies of the library, Liz and Becky, bade her a similar welcome to their world of literature, and provided her with a temporary ticket on the spot, informing her that she would receive her permanent ticket through the post, and telling her that they looked forward to seeing her again in the near future

In that first week, Carole was very dedicated, taking her to many other organisations, introducing her each time to the individual who ran it, and making her head spin with the plethora of new names she felt she needed to commit to memory. Mrs Winter seemed to know everyone in Market Darley, and so she should have done, having moved there from the north thirty-five years ago, on her marriage. She had lost almost all the accent that had identified her origins up until her move south.

Carole had also insisted on taking her to the local church on Sunday to meet the congregation, even introducing her to the members of the choir. The vicar welcomed her warmly to his parish, expressed the hope that she would become one of his flock, and join in with all the parish activities, which didn't seem impossible to Miriam, once she had met everyone that morning. His congregation was young, and the notice board in the entrance filled with notices of meetings, groups and social events. Maybe life would be kind to here, in this, her new start.

So busy and pleasant had her first days become in this new setting that she found herself, one evening, arranging a couple of vases of fresh flowers, one each to brighten up the dining and sitting rooms, and humming a tune as she cocked her head to one side to consider the balance of her arrangements. Without her realising it, she had moved from feeling numb to a sense of happiness and contentment, so long missing from her existence that she hardly recognised it.

Her commute to work was about the same as it had been from her old address, the transfer to another branch going without a hitch, and it seemed that life now held some promise for her. Her telephone started to ring with invitations from new friends, and her social life became almost as busy as it had been many years ago, when she had been young and carefree, and had no idea of the blow that life would one day deal her.

Carole Winter was an avid gardener, and began to help Miriam plan her own little piece of land. At the moment it was all laid to lawn, without a bed to break the runs of grass at front and back, and they began to go out to garden centres to see what was available for autumn planting, and what bulbs would go in in the autumn for the next spring.

Books from the library accelerated Miriam's interest in this hitherto unconsidered pastime, and she began to watch gardening programmes on the television, becoming hooked on the subject within a very short time. This, she considered, was because she had lived her life in limbo for so long. She could feel herself waking up, as if from a long hibernation, and it felt good to be part of everyday life again.

She also began to make friends at work, and sometimes spurned her usual home-coming train in favour of going out for a few drinks with colleagues from the office, returning home much later than usual, and feeling quite young again. Locally, she joined the reading group and attended a couple of meetings of the WI, as time-fillers, and found to her surprise that she enjoyed them, adding them to her list of regular outings. It seemed that, at last, she would be left in peace to lead as normal a life as she could, without all the hassle she had left behind when she had moved away.

She and Carole next door, who seemed to be relieved to spend a little time away from her husband, who was now retired, and whom she said got under her feet all the time, were happy to go into Market Darley on a Saturday afternoon to window shop and have a coffee and cake in the local coffee shop.

On Sunday mornings they walked to church together, even though Miriam had never been a regular church-goer in her life before. She even said her very first sincere prayer – one of thanks and gratitude that her nightmare seemed to be over, and that she was starting life anew.

On Sunday afternoons, Miriam drove while Carole sat in the passenger seat, and they toured round the various garden centres that seemed to surround the town, all of them hard to get to without a car. Carole had almost convinced her to dig a little vegetable patch, or even grow vegetables in pots, as there was nothing like food straight from garden to plate, she said.

It was on one such afternoon, just over a month since she had moved in, when they were discussing whether to go to all the trouble of turning over a patch of ground, or whether to use troughs, pots and planters for tomatoes, courgettes, strawberries and the like, and even maybe a plastic dustbin for new potatoes, that Miriam realised that she was doing most of the talking, and that Carole was uncharacteristically quiet.

'Are you OK?' she asked, wondering if maybe Carole and her husband had had a disagreement between the church service and now, or whether she just had a headache, or something similar, that was making her feel under par.

'I'm fine,' was the curt answer, and she lapsed back into a silence that soon became awkward for both of them.

'What is it?' Miriam risked another question, wondering if something she'd done had unintentionally upset her new friend.

'Nothing. You carry on with your plans,' her passenger replied, but there was the very slightest of chills in her voice, and the rest of the journey to the garden centre passed in silence.

Carole was equally distant as they walked around the area where packets of vegetable seeds were sold. She indicated, with a pointing finger, the varieties she recommended for container growing, hardly communicating at all, and leaving Miriam upset and mystified at what could have caused this sudden change in her previously very friendly neighbour.

Asking her brought forth nothing more than denial that there was anything wrong, and, in the end, Miriam suggested that they go back home early, without going on to a second establishment, because she had a headache – which wasn't a lie. The replacement of her normally irrepressible and ebullient friend by this uncommunicative and distant stranger had affected her considerably, and her temples were beginning to throb with pain.

Back home, Carole bade her a less than enthusiastic goodbye, with no comment that she would see her soon, and disappeared through her own front door without turning to wave, or thanking Miriam for the lift. Miriam entered her own house in considerable puzzlement. Her neighbour had seemed fine that morning at church, but by the afternoon, she had appeared not to be comfortable in her company any more. What on earth had she done?

Chapter Three

Monday 13th September

Miriam had not spoken to her neighbour again the day before, and left for work on Monday morning as confused as she had been the previous day. Her work and colleagues proved sufficient distraction during working hours, and she gladly forgot about this little glitch in her friendship with her neighbour. She agreed to go for a drink after work, partly because she knew she'd enjoy it, and partly because she was delaying going home; shelving the coolness that had so unexpectedly arisen between her and Carole.

Six of them went to the Jack of Three Sides, an old pub just off the town centre, situated on a small triangular island of land where the roads were unusually convoluted. It was an old building that had stayed in character, and to which she had never gone before.

The inside looked less contemporary than many of the public houses in the town where she now worked, and more like the establishment as it had existed many years ago. Every piece of wall was covered with pictures, framed sepia photographs and newspaper cuttings relating to the tiny area in which the pub stood. Pewter tankards hung from the beams, just below the very darkly nicotine-stained ceiling, and even this surface was not neglected, as some inventive soul had found a way to fasten pictures and paintings to the ceiling, so that even looking up was a delight.

The chairs and tables were, similarly, a mishmash of styles, but none of them new or out of place, and she stood at the bar just looking round in admiration at the fact that there was no dust. In a bar crammed with memories, there was nowhere one could see a plain surface, and yet everything was wonderfully clean.

Living near the station in Market Darley as she did, there was nothing to stop her having three glasses of wine, as she would not have to drive when she de-trained, and she thoroughly enjoyed herself that evening, sipping her chilled drinks, and gossiping with the others with whom she now shared her working life.

When her train finally arrived at her destination, it was much later than she usually arrived home, even after staying on for a drink, but she was relaxed and happy after the little boost of alcohol, and the bonhomie she had shared. It fleetingly crossed her mind to just dump her bags and knock on Carole's door and confront her, asking her outright how she seemed to have alienated her friend, but given the lateness of the hour, and the lovely relaxed feeling she was enjoying, she slid her key into the door, and dismissed the idea from her mind. A long, relaxing bath and then to bed with a book would round off the day very nicely, and she didn't want to spoil how she felt now with any bad-feeling.

That feeling evaporated completely when, picking up her mail from the hall carpet, she noticed that the top envelope had a very badly hand-written name, and no address, implying that it had been delivered by hand: and it was to Mrs Miriam Stourton, not Ms Darling.

Her hands immediately began to shake, and she sank down on to the carpet as her legs threatened to betray how she felt. No! Not here! Not again! she thought. It can't have followed me here! Letting go of the envelopes she held in her unsteady hand, she put her hands to her face, and began to sob. Her recent euphoria had completely evaporated with this one small discovery.

Monday 20th September

A steady flow of letters began to arrive, some in the naive hand of the first one, others in letters cut from newspapers and magazines. Some came in the post, others were dropped through her letterbox at night, and Miriam's newly minted self-confidence and happiness disappeared, from the receipt of that first missive.

Her applications to join various organisations were suddenly turned down, with no explanation given, invitations were withdrawn and, eventually, stopped being issued at all. Even at church, the previous morning, Carole had pleaded an upset stomach, and Miriam had found herself blanked and shunned by members of the congregation who had previously appeared friendly towards her. Even the vicar shook her hand very limply after the service, and moved on to the next person quickly, to rid himself of her company, it seemed to Miriam.

After a month of contentment and comparative happiness, within a week she had been reduced to a social pariah, and she knew it had started all over again, but this time she'd have to do something about it. She'd lived with it in her old home, but this time she was going to involve the police. She couldn't live the rest of her life constantly running away. She had to find a platform from which to plead her case, this time with the help and support, maybe even the protection, if things escalated, of the forces of law and order.

Detective Inspector Harry Falconer of the Market Darley CID was just scanning his diary for the week and exchanging morning pleasantries with his detective sergeant, 'Davey' Carmichael, when the telephone shrilled on his desk and, with a sigh of 'here we go again', he answered the call, holding up his free hand to stem the flow of Carmichael's enthusiastic conversation.

The woman on the other end of the line was almost hysterical, and it was a few minutes before he could calm her enough to be able to comprehend anything she said. She was obviously in a highly emotional state and, given that he had little in his diary for the day – and the state she was in, he decided, in the circumstances, that the situation merited a trip to her home, to interview her in privacy without the necessity of her making a trip to the police station.

'Come on, sunshine,' he cajoled his sergeant, as he ended the call. 'We've got a damsel in distress to rescue. Get your armour on, and we'll ride over to her tower and see what we can do for her.'

'What armour, sir? What tower? Ride? I don't know what you're talking about,' was his sergeant's reply.

'I know you don't, Carmichael, but that's about par for the course.'

'Why are you talking about golf now?'

'Come on, you. We've got the beginnings of a nasty case here. Make sure you've got your notebook, and I'll explain in the car on the way over. It's not far.'

'But where are we going? I don't underst…'
Carmichael's questions echoed all the way down the
stairwell, as they made their way out of the station and
into the car park.

Once safely strapped into Falconer's ritzy little
Boxster, he began to relate what he had learned from the
hysterical woman on the phone.

'Something's evidently happened in her life, in the
past, that she's moved here to forget, but it seems that her
story has followed her and caught up with her, and now
she's receiving hate mail. I don't know any more details
than that at the moment, but it sounded like she wasn't in a
fit state to drive to the station, so I said we'd come to her.
Somehow, although I don't have the whole story, this one
doesn't feel like a storm in a teacup to me. It feels nasty.

'She says she's had abusive phone calls – numbers
withheld, of course – silent phone calls in the middle of
the night, and about seventy-odd letters, threatening her
with all sorts of things. I don't know what happened yet,
in her past, but it seems to have caused a furious reaction
amongst those she's met and become friendly with, since
she moved here.'

'She must be terrified, sir,' Carmichael commented, his
brow furrowed with the effort to imagine his own wife in a
similar situation.

'Well, she certainly sounded it on the phone.'

Chapter Four

When Falconer knocked smartly on the door of Miriam's house, there was a delay, during which they noticed the net curtains twitch, to establish who was calling, no doubt. Then there was the sound of bolts being drawn back and keys turned, before the front door opened just a crack, to the extent of its security chain, at which point they displayed their warrant cards to identify themselves.

The face that greeted them was blotchy and swollen, the eyes, as they surveyed their identification, red, and full of fear. In silence, the woman stood back and allowed the door to open just enough to admit them, before closing it again, and locking and bolting it behind them. Miriam Darling was still in her dressing gown, her hair tousled and wild, and she looked to be in the extremes of anxiety, as she preceded them into the living room.

The first thing that confronted them was a sofa completely covered in pieces of paper, some in scrawled childlike handwriting, others with cut-out letters to spell out their messages. There were dozens of the things, completely swamping the green leather surface, and Miriam simply looked at them, and then at her two visitors.

At that moment, the telephone rang, and, as she dragged herself across the room to answer it, Falconer looked at Carmichael, whose face was scrunched up in anger at this material evidence of hatred and spite.

She listened for a moment, then cried, 'Who are you? What do you want? Why don't you say something?' Her voice was shrill and harsh in the silence of the house. She slammed down the handset, pulling the plug from the wall in her impotent anger and frustration, then just wandered back to them, before collapsing into an armchair.

'What am I going to do?' she asked, in a voice hoarse with weeping. 'I can't keep on running. I've already gone back to my maiden name, but someone's found out. Am I never to be free of it? I haven't done anything wrong. It was just a tragic accident, and as if that wasn't enough, here I am being hounded again, like some sort of criminal.'

Falconer nodded at Carmichael and the letters. The sergeant, in complete silent understanding, donned a pair of latex gloves, and began collecting together the sheets of paper and putting them in evidence bags, to be checked later for fingerprints. The inspector took a seat in the armchair on the other side of the fireplace and gathered his reserves for interviewing this deeply distressed woman.

Miriam just sat in her chair, her hands in her lap, her head drooping, like a marionette that had had all its strings cut. She was evidently steeling herself, too, for the ordeal to come.

His task swiftly completed, Carmichael sank down on the now unencumbered sofa and removed his notepad from his pocket, ready to record what the woman had to say. He waited in silence for Falconer to commence his questioning.

'I'd like you to tell me what it is in your past that has 'followed' you here, and why the reaction is so extreme.

There's no need to rush. Just tell it in your own time, so that we can understand what has been happening to you recently,' he said, his voice quiet and almost tender.

'It was something that happened just over a year ago.' Miriam's voice was so low, they could hardly catch what she was saying, but after clearing her throat and shaking her head, she continued at a more easily discernible volume.

'One year, one month, and six days ago, to be precise – I can't seem to stop counting the time that has elapsed. I was married then, and we had a son. Mark, my husband's name was, and Ben was our son, only four years old, and full of life.' Here she had to break off, as her voice cracked, and tears began to track down her cheeks.

'My parents moved to Spain three years ago, when Dad took early retirement, so we went out to visit them in the summer, and at Christmas. Although it was rather expensive, it was cheaper than taking a break through a travel agent, and it meant that at least they saw their grandson twice a year. We used Skype, of course, but Mum wanted to cuddle Ben, and Dad wanted to take him to the beach and play football and all those sort of grandfatherly things.

'It was when we went out last summer that *it* happened, and my nightmare began, although I didn't realise people were so cruel, and it would go on for so long that I wouldn't have time to come to terms with it in peace, and mourn them in privacy.'

'What was *it*?' asked Falconer, feeling that they weren't really getting anywhere, and he needed to get to the nub of the matter, and discover the details of the mystery event.

'We had planned to go along the coast to a little cove that was very beautiful, but usually completely empty of holiday-makers. Ben was excited at the thought of getting a bit of beach to himself, so that he could make his sandcastles without a game of football being played through his efforts, and people's dogs arriving to dig in his turrets.

'I suggested that we walk along the cliffs to get to it, as there was a rudimentary set of steps there, although they were difficult to descend, having been cut out of the cliffs, but Mark had very different ideas. He'd been a bit scratchy that holiday, and I didn't want another argument – we'd already had quite a few blow-ups, and I knew he was fed up to the back teeth of always going to the same place, and having to stay with my parents.

'I was determined that we wouldn't fall out that day, and that maybe the deserted cove would work its magic on him, and put him in a good mood for once. How naive I was; and how little foresight I managed to display, when you consider the outcome.'

Carmichael was scribbling like fury, but found a second or two to look at the inspector, and roll his eyes at the prolonged explanation of what had happened; that event still seeming a long way away, buried in this miasma of memories, as it was. Falconer acknowledged his partner's rolling eyes by pulling a face in reply. Miriam Darling sat with her head down, twisting her fingers together in her lap, lost in the past.

'So, what actually happened when you got to the beach?'

'Oh, Mark insisted that we go to the main beach and hire a little boat. He said that would be a much more picturesque way of approaching the cove, and would mean we didn't have to risk the old steps down from the cliff top.

'I wasn't sure, not knowing what the water was like round the slight headland, and disagreed, saying that we could take the utmost care on the steps, and pointed out to him that unknown waters could be dangerous. That was when we had our little row – the one I'd been desperate to avoid – with hordes of witnesses. In the end, I said I didn't want to go, if Mark insisted on hiring a boat.

'That was like a red rag to a bull for him, and he took Ben's hand and stomped off towards the man who rented out the small craft. I just stood by, feeling helpless as usual, but supposing that everything would turn out all right in the end, and thinking Mark might even be in a good mood if he got his own way on this one. If only, just that once, I hadn't played the part of the compliant wife!

'And so we set off. It really was a small boat – a wooden one. Do they call those little things 'clinker-built'? – and Mark, of course, took charge of the oars, being the man of the family. It seemed a perfectly charming way to reach our destination at first, but, as we rounded the headland, the going got more difficult, and Mark started to struggle to keep control of the little boat.

'When I realised he was in difficulties, I offered to take a turn on one of the oars, so that we could row together, and double our power to fight the current, but he would have none of that. He was always stubborn, and hated to fail at anything. At that point, this was a test of his manhood, in his mind, and he struggled on, but the further we disappeared from sight of the busy beach, the more unruly the sea became.

'That was when I got really frightened, and told him he ought to turn back, as the sea was getting far too rough.

The wind had got up, too, and we were rolling all over the place, with the waves breaking over the boat and swamping us. Ben was crying and I was holding him, trying to comfort him, and telling him that Daddy would soon get us back to the nice beach where he always played.

'That was the last coherent thought I had. There was a gust of wind, and a particularly large wave engulfed our tiny boat, and it capsized, throwing the three of us, plunging, into the roughness of the sea.

'There were incredibly strong currents there, and all I could think of was to catch hold of the underside of the boat and scream for help, although I knew my cries would be blown away by the wind. By the time I had a firm hold of it, I looked round, and both Mark and Ben were gone. That's when I really started screaming. I hadn't realised how one's life could be turned upside down in just a couple of seconds, the status quo irretrievably lost, the future completely blank and needing to be rewritten.

'I was the lucky one. Someone on the top of the headland, looking at the seabirds swirling around the inshore waters, happened to catch sight of my precarious situation, he alerted the coastguard – and I was rescued.'

Miriam paused here, to gather her strength for the end of the tragic tale. 'Mark's and Ben's bodies were washed ashore further along the coastline two days later; and my life effectively ended. I might as well have drowned with them. I feel like I'm already dead and suffering in hell, with all that's happened since, and now it's happening all over again.'

'And all the sorts of things that have occurred here, happened where you used to live?'

'Live? Huh! Existed, more like. But, yes, I was held in custody in Spain by the police. People remembered, you see, how we'd argued on the beach. My mother's neighbours remembered how we'd argued at her house – those villas are jerry-built, and the sound-proofing is non-existent. They thought I'd pushed them out of the boat, and that was the reason it capsized. I was cast in the role of a murdering wife and mother.

'I can't speak Spanish, and neither can my parents beyond a few words of greeting and 'please' and 'thank you', and I was dazed with my loss, and bewildered as to what was going on around me. It was a complete nightmare. There I was, locked away from the only comfort available to me – my parents – and I didn't understand a word of what was being said to me.

'Of course, eventually they brought in an interpreter, but it was a resort mainly for the Spanish themselves, and the interpreter, although she could speak some English, could not understand what I was saying, and seemed to make up her own mind as to what I had told her.'

'So what set off this toxic gossip, then?' asked Falconer, still pursuing his fox, but feeling that the further he moved forward the further away he was from his quarry.

'It started with the Spanish press. It was quiet in the journalistic world, it being holiday time; they seized my tragedy as a terrier seizes a rat, and I made the front page, painted as black as night. Just to add to my misfortunes, there was an English journalist on holiday about fifty kilometres away. He saw the story and descended on my parents and their neighbours like a wolf on the fold.

'He couldn't get to see me, but he did trace several people who had been on the beach that day – isn't it ironic that he spoke the lingo? Of course, he phoned it in, and started the same hare running in the English press. By the time I got back, I was branded as a murderess, and nothing I could say would change that, even though the Spanish police had traced someone on a fishing boat who had actually seen us capsize.

'I was harassed in my home by journalists. I started receiving anonymous threatening letters and silent phone calls, just like now. My car had paint-stripper thrown over it, people I'd known all my life, shunned me in the street. Some of them even spat at me, and one joker poured weedkiller over my front lawn one night, to spell out 'murderer'. That's when I knew what it was to be in hell.

'I took all the precautions I could to get away from it all. I moved to a rented property fifty miles away, adopting my maiden name, dying my hair and having it cut really short. I changed the way I dressed, and started not wearing make-up – anything so that I was not connected to what had befallen my family on that dreadful holiday.

'Eventually I moved here, and I seemed to have made a really solid start on a new and normal life. Carole Winter next door befriended me and introduced me to a host of people and organisations where I was made to feel really welcome. I'd applied to join the WI, I'd been invited to join a book club, I'd met the ladies of the church, the choir and the library, and Carole, who is a keen gardener, was helping me plan my little plot out at the back. Sundays were fun. We used to go to the service together, then go off in my car and stroll round the garden centres, looking for bulbs, seeds and plants that would be suitable for what had become my new hobby: gardening.

'Then, one day, she just 'cut' me: 'blanked' me as if she had never met me before. I found I was *persona non grata* wherever I went, and then it just started all over again. I don't know who made the connection, or why they passed it on, but I'm right back to square one, and now there's nowhere else to go,' she concluded on a mournful note.

'You *have* been through the mill, haven't you? Let me think a while and see what I can come up with. Do you work outside the home at all?'

'Yes. I work for a bank – Mondays, Wednesdays, and Fridays.'

'And has there been any trouble there?'

'Not so far, but I commute, and mix with a totally different set of people there. It's the only part of my life with some sanity left in it, the only place where I get treated like a normal human being. I'm not giving that up,' she stated in a firmer voice.

'OK. For now,' Falconer replied, 'what I can do is have a patrol car pass your house when you're at home, to make sure there's no physical attack on you, and put one of the uniformed constables to patrol this area, giving us a man on the ground.

'In the meantime you're going to have to consider changing your identity completely, perhaps disappear into the anonymity of a large city. Market Darley's fairly small, and people are nosier about their neighbours than they are in the sprawling confusion of a city.'

'I see your point,' she agreed. 'I do exactly as I planned before, but become the needle in a much bigger haystack.'

'Spot on! Now, I'll give you my card, and I'll write my home number on the back, so that you can get hold of me anytime. I hate bullying, especially the cowardly, anonymous kind, and when it's completely unfounded, it really gets my goat,' the inspector growled with great sincerity. 'There it is. Any time, day or night! And I mean that! I don't live far away – in fact I'm closer to you than I am to the police station, and I can be here in a few minutes, and alert the boys in blue on my way.

'In the meantime, may I suggest that when you are here you keep away from the windows. I know you've got net curtains and I don't want to frighten you, but I also don't want you to make yourself an unwitting target for some nutter.'

'Thank you for taking me so seriously,' she murmured, as she saw them out of the front door, opening it only wide enough to allow them to squeeze through it, and they heard her lock and bolt it again, as she had when they arrived.

Chapter Five

Tuesday 21st September

Falconer's home phone rang shrilly at just after half-past six that morning, rousing him from a light doze in which he dreamt of a woman he had glimpsed, briefly but devastatingly, earlier that year. She had skin the colour of ebony and was, in his opinion, the most beautiful woman he had ever set eyes on.

Things were going well in the dream, and they were sipping cocktails at some function or other, when the trilling of the telephone began to break up the conviviality of the occasion. As if a herald of the bad news that was to come in his dream, his old Nanny Vogel approached the bar, stopped by his side, and gave him her cruel and knowing smile, while the attractive woman, Dr Dubois, turned into a pillar of smoke and began to disperse.

Arriving suddenly to full wakefulness, he felt both cheated and disturbed as he reached for the handset beside his bed, answering it with an uncharacteristically blunt 'Yes?'

'Is that you, Inspector Falconer,' a distressed and tearful voice enquired. 'Only things have got worse.'

Recognising Miriam Darling's voice immediately, he pulled himself together, to treat her with a more professional attitude, even if he was in his pyjamas and lying in bed. These things mattered! 'What's happened now?' he asked her gently, hoping she hadn't been injured.

'I got a brick through my front window yesterday – well, during the night, actually – but as the curtains were drawn, it didn't really do any damage, but when I opened the door to take in the milk this morning, someone had sprayed 'killer' on my front door in black paint. I simply don't know what to do. Please help me, Inspector. I'm at my wits' end.'

'I'll get an officer over to take samples of the paint, and he'll take away the brick as evidence, although there's little likelihood it will offer anything useful as to who threw it. I'll get that organised, and I'll be with you in less than an hour to take another statement. I'll also arrange for a female PC to be billeted with you, as I seem to remember that you don't work on a Tuesday.'

'That's very kind of you, Inspector. I shall feel a lot safer for seeing you again, and a PC in the house will be a great relief. At least I'll have a witness to anything else that happens, and an ally, if I need physical help.' She sounded calmer already, and Falconer was pleased with his idea of having a PC in residence. If the officer herself made her presence known, maybe it would act as a deterrent.

'I'll be with you as soon as I can, Ms Darling, and I'll get on the phone straight after this call and set the wheels in motion for a SOCO officer and a PC to be dispatched.'

As soon as he ended the call, he rang the station with a cheery, 'Hello, Bob. How's tricks?' only to find that Bob Bryant – *Bob Bryant* – had taken a *day's leave*, and he was talking to PC Barry Sugden, more usually to be found booking in 'guests' in the custody suite.

'Sorry about that,' he apologised, 'only it always *is* Bob Bryant, so I simply wasn't prepared to find someone else answering the phone.'

'Don't apologise, sir – everyone else has said the same thing. I've just told them that, as one of the Immortals, Bob sometimes has to report to the planet Zog on what he has discovered in his current role, and then he'll get his transfer to another location round about the year 2073. Nobody's questioned my answer yet, but for your personal information, he's going to have a tooth out, and wants to slink back home and suffer in peace, but don't tell anyone else. The new boys, in particular, will be devastated, if they find out the reason for his day away from the station is such a mundane affair.'

Falconer knew only too well the web of bantering fantasy that existed between the younger members of the uniformed branch about the ever-present desk sergeant who, it was rumoured by these junior members of the force, had been there from the beginning of time, and would remain there, as an Immortal, until the end of the universe.

'Look, Barry, I need someone to come out to scout for evidence at the site of what I can only describe as a 'hate crime', and I need a PC – get me Starr if you can – to join me here.' After a little more explanation and giving the address, he hung up and got ready as speedily as he could, to visit Miriam Darling again. He could only imagine her distress and fear, and wanted to do what he could to reassure her as quickly as possible.

He arrived there less than half an hour after her distress call. When the door was opened by an even smaller crack than it had been on his last visit, he looked straight at her face, and, on gaining admittance, saw that she was already petrified with the escalation of events. He sat with her, giving what comfort he could, until PC Starr arrived and distracted her by asking to show the policewoman where everything was in the kitchen, so that she should be familiar with everything she needed to make tea, coffee and sandwiches.

Falconer left the two of them in the kitchen, opening and closing cupboard doors. Miriam seemed distracted enough to carry out this simple task; evidently feeling more confident now she had someone with her for the day.

Back at the station, he found that no activity in the immediate vicinity of the address had been reported by either foot patrol or passing patrol cars, and cudgelled his brain at how to get at the root of this spiteful behaviour. The neighbours were an obvious starting point, but he felt that they would be better left until Miriam went to work tomorrow, so that they would have had time to cool off, after being questioned, before she returned home from work.

Falconer got another early reveille the next morning – this time at 6.10, and from the familiar but unusually muffled voice of Bob Bryant; he must still have cotton wool in his mouth after his extraction the day before. Without preamble, the sergeant went straight into his story. 'One of yours, I believe, Harry. A Ms Darling. Been receiving hate mail, nasty phone calls and a brick through the window.'

When Falconer confirmed that this was his baby, the sergeant continued, 'Well, she's had another faceless visitor. Apparently she came down this morning at half-past five because she couldn't sleep, and decided a cup of tea would be a good thing. She hadn't had any more phone calls and was feeling quite cheerful, she said, when she started off down the stairs.

'That was when she smelled it. Someone had inserted a substantial amount of dog-shit through her letterbox, and then thrown the accompanying note, to land it clear of the first offering.'

'Nasty!' was the inspector's only comment.

'Quite!' countered the desk sergeant. 'But the note was much worse. It informed her that the next time it would be petrol-soaked rags, and that the author of the note always carried a box of matches or a lighter, so that he was never short of a flame. He then ended it by referring to her as a murdering bitch who wasn't going to get away with it, even if the law couldn't touch her.'

'I'm on my way, Bob, see if I can catch her before she leaves for work. Have we got anywhere we could use as a safe house for her at short notice? It would only be until she can find something to rent well away from here.'

'I'll see what I can do,' Bob assured him, and ended the call.

Miriam Darling was getting ready to leave for work when Falconer arrived, no longer shaking and crying, but showing a cold, hard side to her character that he had not seen before.

Allowing him a brief fifteen minutes, the most she could, to keep herself on schedule for catching her usual train, she sat down with him in the living room and listened to his suggestion about her moving temporarily to a safe house. Once she had chosen somewhere else to live, if she so desired, he could inform the local police station of her background, and get them to keep a discreet eye on her.

'I don't think that will be necessary, Inspector, although I'm very grateful for what you've done for me, but I think it's time for me to plough my own furrow now, don't you?'

He left her home that day more puzzled than reassured, and feeling that she was being blasé about the escalating danger to her, but there was nothing he could do about it. He could only provide the help and protection that he thought she needed if she was willing to accept it, and she'd been unbelievably distant when she'd spoken to him; almost as if she'd been a different person.

He didn't bother going home again, as it simply wasn't worth the extra to-ing and fro-ing, and seven thirty saw him behind his desk sorting through the paperwork that had accumulated since he had last sat there, and mulling over what had been happening in Ms Darling's life over the past couple of weeks.

It was the telephone that disturbed his reverie, but what an interruption it proved to be. PC Merv Green had been on duty in and around the railway station that morning, keeping an eye on vehicles in the station car park, and walking round the station periodically to make sure that there wasn't a pickpocket at work. Cities didn't have a monopoly on petty crime like this. It happened in relatively small places too.

He had been making his way along one of the platforms where the usually jostling crowd of commuters was waiting for the arrival of their morning train, all trying to be in a position to get into a compartment first and bag the best – or maybe the only – seat. As the train approached the station, there had been a yell from the furthest end of the platform, and cries went up: 'Woman under the train!' 'Someone pushed her! I saw!' 'I never saw her jump!' 'Get an ambulance!' and from one anonymous wag: 'Get a bucket and shovel!'

Green ran, pushing people out of his way in his anxiety to confirm what he had heard shouted; and they weren't wrong. The train was not so long that it still covered what was left of whoever had gone under it, and Green came perilously close to losing the contents of his stomach, just avoiding an unexpected rebate on his breakfast.

When Green called it in, although he had no name for the victim, or even confirmation of the sex, Bob Bryant had a gut feeling that this one was for Falconer, and called it through to him.

The inspector's response was unusually coarse and unexpectedly heartfelt: 'No! No! No, no, no! Damn! Damn it! No! Oh, shit! Bugger!' he yelled, to himself, rather than to Bob Bryant on the other end of the line. 'I should have waited, and escorted her to the train this morning, after what happened during the night. Bugger! Arse! What a negligent fool I am!'

'If it's her, Harry, it's hardly your fault, is it?' asked Bob Bryant, trying to dispel Falconer's feelings of guilt and anguish.

'But the threat in that last letter was chilling, and we should – *I should* – have taken it more seriously. That wasn't just a case of name-calling; that was a threat to her life, and even *I* didn't take it seriously enough. I suppose I thought that her tormentor would only act on his evil impulses when she was in her own home. Why didn't I consider her safety in going to work, or rather the danger she was in when she was in transit? I'm an absolute fool!'

'I should get yourself down to the railway station, and make sure it's her first, before you start beating your breast and tearing out your hair,' was the calm advice of the desk sergeant. Falconer took it at its worth, and calmed himself with difficulty while preparing to go to see the remains.

When he arrived at the railway station and sought out the correct platform, he realised what a good job Green had done. The man had used his loaf, and requested that the train be moved as far as it could along the track, allowing a clear view of where the victim had landed, getting those who were alighting at Market Darley to use the far exit, so as not to contaminate what must now be considered a crime scene.

The passengers waiting to board had been crowded into the station's waiting room, and were now waiting to be interviewed, bleating like sheep at how late they would be for work, meetings and the like, while yelling into their respective mobile phones trying to 'big up' what they were now declaring to be a bloody nuisance. But perhaps secretly believing that the morning's experience would be something that they could dine out on for months.

The area of platform itself had been isolated with blue-and-white crime tape, which now fluttered in the slightly chilly September breeze. Thus was the situation when Falconer arrived, in the sure and certain knowledge that Carmichael was not far behind him. That was cold comfort, however, as he felt he should have been able to save this poor, persecuted woman from having to pay the ultimate price for what was, in fact, an accident, blown out of all proportion and sensationalised by the press.

After Carmichael arrived, his face a woeful mask, it took the two of them an hour and a half to gather all the names, addresses and telephone numbers of the daily commuters, leaving them to reassemble at the far end of the platform in anticipation of the next train, all chattering like starlings about this unexpected interruption to their usual boring daily schedule.

There were already white-suited officers at work where the commuter had gone under the train: Falconer was able to give an adequate identification from scraps of torn clothing that had matched what she was wearing when he had visited her before she left for the station, but there was nothing really for them to find. What evidence does a little push leave? What trace could there be of the little shove, that just tips a person's balance, and causes them to fall?

Although all the other would-be passengers on that train would need to be interviewed, to see if anyone owned up to standing close enough to Miriam Darling to have witnessed whether she propelled herself in front of that train, or whether she was given a helping hand, it was a job they would leave to the uniformed branch. They would try to uncover the network of rumour and lies that had made Miriam's life such a misery before today, hoping against hope that they would be able to trace it to its original source in the town, but it would be a thankless task, and one unlikely to be successfully concluded.

Falconer finally left feeling very downhearted, and Carmichael had a glum expression that clearly indicated his feeling that they were facing a hopeless task. 'I don't know who is responsible for what that poor woman went through,' commented Falconer as they arrived back at their cars, 'but they might as well have handed her a chalice of poison and bade her drink it, for the outcome would have been the same.'

Chapter Six

Wednesday 22nd September

Falconer and Carmichael had spent the previous afternoon clearing their desks as best as they could to give them a free run at the new case, and had decided to start their investigations with the neighbours. Rumour and gossip usually emanated from someone close to the 'target' and, as Miriam had not lived in the area long, they had decided to start with those who had been physically close to her.

Their first visit was to Carole Winter, whom Falconer knew had befriended her new neighbour. If not involved herself, maybe she could give them some leads as to whom she had introduced Miriam to.

Carole's face 'closed' when she saw who was at her door, and they were invited inside reluctantly, her face bearing an icy smile that did not touch her eyes.

After introducing themselves, Falconer explained why they were there, although he had little doubt that she had realised that as soon as they had displayed their warrant cards.

'I was good to that girl,' she spat at them, defensively. 'I toted her around everywhere with me, introducing her to everyone I know, and then I found out what she had done – and not even a whisper to me that she had a past.' Mrs Winter sat bolt upright in an armchair, her hands clasped in her lap, a look of defiance on her face.

'She'd lied to me by her silence, and I wasn't having that – not having found out what she'd done and got away with.'

'Who told you?' asked Falconer, keeping his question as brief as possible so as not to prompt the flow of indignation and self-righteousness often found in some church-goers who would happily 'cast the first stone', and considered that they themselves were incapable of sin.

'It was Liz from the library. If she's bored, when the library's not busy, she amuses herself by 'Googling' new ticket-holders. The poor girl got much more than she bargained for when she searched for Miriam Stourton, nee Darling. And, before you ask, the application form to join the library service has a lot of seemingly irrelevant questions on it, including maiden name, and she had inadvertently put her married name in that space.

'Well, that really set the cat among the pigeons, and we had a long talk about what to do. It was Liz's suggestion – that's Elizabeth Beckett – that we spread the word that the woman was a danger to society. She should've been locked away, and the key thrown over a cliff. What a wicked deed, to kill her husband and her own child like that! She deserved to burn in hell, and I hope she is doing just that, now.'

'Crikey!' Carmichael later exclaimed. They'd certainly stirred up a hornets' nest of resentment at this house.

'Can you give me the names of the other people to whom you introduced Ms Darling?' asked Falconer, thinking to get a head start, but he'd stirred up another spurt of contumely.

'Darling, my bum! She was no more *Ms Darling* than I am the Aga Khan! Darling, my big fat hairy arse! But I'll answer your question, and then I want you out of this house. This has been a shocking time for me, ending up with a murderer living next door, and I want to forget it as quickly as possible, and get back to my normal tranquil life. What a good actress that woman was! I'd never have guessed she had such evil in her heart!'

The rest of the interviews conducted, from the names Mrs Winter provided, were either full of the same contempt, or with a holier-than-thou attitude that made Falconer's stomach turn.

Elizabeth Beckett at the library merely displayed astonishment that she could have uncovered such duplicity, but her colleague, Becky Troughton, claimed that she had taken an instant dislike to the woman, and that she had felt from the first that there was something wrong with her. How some people strive to find something a little bit 'special' about themselves, some supernatural ability that sets them apart from others! Falconer felt that this was the case here. Had the information never become public knowledge, Ms Troughton would probably be saying that she had sensed a good soul in Miriam Darling, and had taken to her at their very first meeting. Feelings, schmeelings! he thought in disgust.

At the church, although he spoke to the incumbent, a selection of the ladies of the congregation and choir, it was the holier-than-thou, pious attitude he encountered, many offering to pray for her forgiveness, yet none who believed in her innocence, and absolutely no one who would admit to making silent phone calls or sending anonymous letters. What an upright slice of society all these people seemed to form, and yet he had counted at least seventy letters on Miriam Darling's sofa the first time he had gone to her house.

Mabel Monaghan, the head honcho at the WI, was highly indignant that such a woman should even have considered joining the organisation, and admitted that she had torn up Miriam's application as soon as she had heard about her murky past.

'And you believed it without question?' Falconer had asked her.

'There is no fire without some smoke,' she had replied, getting the quotation right where so many others mangled it.

The only positive response he got was from Justine Cooper, the nominal leader of the book club that met once a month. 'I'd thought of asking her to give us a talk about her ordeal, so that we could, maybe, find a few literary similarities with this sort of persecution, and choose our next book along those lines,' she had admitted, when questioned.

'I suppose it was a rather morbid thought, though, given what she was going through, and for the second time. And now she's dead! Still, every cloud has a silver lining. We could still discuss her situation at our next meeting, and go ahead with that as a theme without her actually being there.' Now there was a hard-faced young woman, Falconer thought, as they left her house. She should have been a journalist, the way she seized things and twisted them to her ultimate advantage.

'I don't like these people.' Carmichael, as usual, summed up his feeling succinctly. 'I don't think I've ever met such a bunch of two-faced, trouble-making people who aren't actually criminals.'

'I'm with you on that one, Carmichael,' agreed Falconer, and then noticed that his sergeant had his pen in his mouth again – a habit of which he thought he had broken him.

'Put out your tongue, Sergeant,' he ordered, at the kerbside, in public.

Looking a mite embarrassed, Carmichael removed the ballpoint pen from his mouth and complied.

'As I thought! The colour of an aubergine! When we get back to the station, go straight to the canteen and see if you can get them to serve you up a cup of coffee from the very dregs of the urn. That's the only thing we've found that seems to strip the ink.'

'Yes, sir,' agreed Carmichael, glumly.

Nothing was gleaned from the uniformed staff who had spent the hours after the return of the commuters trailing around the addresses given at the station that morning. Oh, yes, they'd come across a few who admitted to standing near, but not directly behind, Miriam Darling, but none that would admit to having pushed, or even accidentally nudged her, and no one had seen anything to which they were willing to admit.

With a heavy heart, Falconer knew that all the officers involved would just have to start all over again, and see if they couldn't coax a reluctant memory from someone, even if not an admission of guilt, but it was going to be a long and tedious job, and he still felt himself responsible for what had happened. What had possessed him, leaving her to make her own way to the railway station? He should have accompanied her. He had been negligent, and a sorely put-upon, innocent woman had paid for his lack of forethought with her life.

If only he had advised her not to go to work until she had been installed in a safe house. If! If! If only he had driven her to the station and waited with her. He would have kept her well away from the edge of the platform and, maybe, by the time she had returned to Market Darley that evening, he could have met her from the train with the address of a safe house into which she could move with immediate effect.

The week after Miriam Darling had been mangled by an incoming train was a week of reflection, regret and soul-searching for the inspector, and he was in an unusually glum mood when he picked up a white envelope from his post, one morning and slit it open, to find it was from Miriam Darling's bank manager, and had a smaller envelope enclosed with it, marked with his name.

'Well, I'll be blowed!' he exclaimed. 'What on earth can this be?'

'This' was a letter from her bank, explaining that the enclosed envelope had been handed to the manager by Miriam Darling herself, with the instructions that it was to be kept there in safe keeping, and only sent, in the event of her death, and even then not until a week had elapsed.

'Curiouser and curiouser,' quoted Falconer, as he slit open the second and smaller envelope. Inside, he found a letter, handwritten, explaining everything, and which saddened him even more than he would have thought it could. He read:

Dear Inspector Falconer,

I apologise for all the work I must have caused you and your colleagues over the last seven days, and now is the time for explanations. If, as I have planned, I have gone under a train at the local station, then my intentions will have gone as I hoped, and I shall be dead.

I knew I couldn't face starting yet another life, because I think my past will follow me to the ends of the earth, given the information technology available today, so I have decided to join my husband and son 'on the other side'.

I didn't want to leave this life without a little bit of revenge on those who had tormented me, so I will have made my death look as much like murder as I can, and have left it for you to suspect and question those who tormented me, and I hope they are made to feel hellishly uncomfortable.

My last hope is that, with the delivery of my letter to you, the truth will be made public, so that they can feel the guilt they share in my carrying out of this act of self-destruction. I don't wish to carry on as things are, and I hope that what I did will give them cause to think, next time they are in receipt of a juicy piece of gossip, and maybe hold back, when they are tempted to pass it on.

Many thanks for your help and support, and to your colleagues who did their best to keep me safe,

Miriam Stourton, nee Darling

Falconer's throat was almost closed with emotion as he finished reading and, putting the letter on Carmichael's desk, in full view, where he would find it as soon as he sat down, he left the office and went for a walk in the clean, clear air of a beautiful September morning.

THE END

The Falconer Files

by

Andrea Frazer

For more information about **Andrea Frazer**

and other **Accent Press** titles

please visit

www.accentpress.co.uk